SKYE
PAPERS

JAMIKA AJALON

THE FEMINIST PRESS
AT THE CITY UNIVERSITY OF NEW YORK
NEW YORK CITY

Published in 2021 by the Feminist Press
at the City University of New York
The Graduate Center
365 Fifth Avenue, Suite 5406
New York, NY 10016

feministpress.org

First Feminist Press edition 2021

NEW YORK | Council on
STATE OF | the Arts
OPPORTUNITY.

This book was made possible thanks to a grant from New York State Council
on the Arts with the support of Governor Andrew M. Cuomo and the New
York State Legislature.

▲ ▼▼
ART WORKS.

This book is supported in part by an award from the National Endowment
for the Arts.

First printing June 2021

Cover art by Elise Peterson
Cover and text design by Drew Stevens

Library of Congress Cataloging-in-Publication Data
Names: Ajalon, Jamika, author.
Title: Skye papers / Jamika Ajalon.
Description: New York City : The Feminist Press at the City University of
    New York, 2021.
Identifiers: LCCN 2021003737 (print) | LCCN 2021003738 (ebook) | ISBN
    9781952177965 (paperback) | ISBN 9781952177101 (ebook)
Classification: LCC PS3601.J35 S58 2021 (print) | LCC PS3601.J35 (ebook)
    | DDC 813/.6--dc23
LC record available at https://lccn.loc.gov/2021003737
LC ebook record available at https://lccn.loc.gov/2021003738

PRINTED IN THE UNITED STATES OF AMERICA

To all the Skyes past, present,
and yet unborn.

PART I

*An orb of light dissolved the mask from my face,
leaving it well, smooth, and unidentifiable.*

This city leaves a gritty taste under my tongue, dissolving into blood vessels. Playing surrealistic games with my mind. Jazz notes sit caught in my vocal cords. One too many. Whenever I speak it comes out in scat: that / that / would not / a be ba / be me. That, that would be me, remains as fluid as my essence. The lie scratches the back of my throat as I inhale the urban air.

I kick through the grunge on the sidewalk and walk past the eerie rise of smoky stench shooting from the guts of NYC. It smells of roasted rat. Testing the firmness of perception, I walk a path worn in my memory, looking for bottle caps, Lucky Strike butts, a bent fork, a sign. I can taste the texture, the returning.

Leaning back on the splintering wooden bench opposite the "stage" in Washington park squared, a.k.a. Washington Square Park, I close a tattered black notebook. Already the air is thick with heat as dawn settles in. A police car drives up opposite, completing one of its many circles around. I brace myself. So far they've left me alone even though, hood and baggy jeans hiding my gender, I could be mistaken for any "boy in da hood"—a cliché made flesh with this forty-ounce in tow. Doesn't help that I'm taller than most chicks. I sit up straight and cling to the bottle, paper bag a damp skin molding to my hand.

It just doesn't taste the same though. Here it is, the same brew, the same park bench. But nope. It's different. Even the thrill of illegally drinking in public has dulled. Gulping down the last of the warm beer, I kick the empty under the bench. It clangs hollow against a tequila bottle. Flipping back my hood, I let an Indian-summer breeze blow through uneven curls sprouting from my uncombed Afro. It's mid-September '92 and bloody hot. Sweat beads brown skin, creating a glistening frame around my insomnia-etched face. An older face. Sitting back on the bench it hits me that only just over a year has passed. One solitary year! This time last year, I was starting my first semester at the University of Chicago, away from home. By second semester, spring had moved me eastward, through New York and clear across the Atlantic to the UK. London seems like a dream now. I'd only been sent back home to Crickledown, Missouri, a few weeks ago. Seems like another lifetime: waking up shell-shocked in the private hospital bed somewhere in London. I guess part of me is still waking up again.

Back in my hometown, Crickledown, still reeling after the London incident, I went through the required hyperin-tensive so-called reassimilation sessions with ole Bug Eye, or Dr. Thomison, as most called him. I called him "Bug Eye" 'cause whenever he put on his glasses, his eyes through Coca Cola–bottle lenses extended into concave saucers. He was one of those well-mannered Negroes with a good education and a respectable job—what I had been destined to become and ran like mad from.

"So let's get started," he'd said at the start of our first session, full of well-meaning smiles. He had a whole stash of them. Those smiles. I wanted to punch them off his face. It wasn't my fault entirely that I was in this mess, that I had to come here. After all, I wasn't *really* any crazier than when I'd left Crickledown. And I was not exactly jumping for joy to be back. He'd said that what I'd gone through was very traumatic, and he wanted me to feel safe enough to speak about anything. *Anything.* The tag marking that imaginary bucket of grins Dr. Thomison kept on his dustless desk read, "Smiles given to the mentally challenged." These were reserved for those poor Negroes who were just not right in the head and had to acquiesce to the highly stigmatized impossibility of "needing to get help." Well, if he wanted a nut I would give him a nut. Besides, I was feeling a little high from the mingled smell of lemon Pledge and his generously applied cologne. He wanted me to speak to the first moment I began to believe I was being monitored. I cleared my throat. Began my monologue.

"Trashed the place looking for those damn surveillance cameras. You know, that whole eyes-everywhere routine . . . I'd already destroyed the main ones, they were sharp shards of glass at my feet." I jumped up on the faux-leather seat, did a practice swing with my invisible driver. "All with the swing of my seven iron. Mimicked Tiger Woods as he went off the tee. Stood on a low stool to get just the right angle. It sliced the air, a perfectly weighted pendulum. It's amazing how nicely boob tubes shatter, splinter, cracks spreading into a fractured spider web." After that performance, improvised from scribbles in my journal, I hopped down and slid back into the chair.

Bug Eye was playing with the chunky frat ring on his finger, same one that Brandon, my dad, wore. "You *are* a poet, aren't you?"

I woulda thought it was sarcasm if he weren't so proper, watching him wipe a handkerchief over his ardently sweating, roll-on-smooth bald head. The air-con wasn't working, and the fan in his office was useless against the midwestern summer heat. "Tell me, what happened next?"

I looked past Dr. Thomison at the light streaming through

the wooden-slat blinds. Was annoyed to be back in suburbia, spending the anniversary of the day I'd declared myself a suburban self-exile in his office. I mean, I had a sense of humor, appreciated the irony and all that. Still. The sooner I got out the better. I took a deep breath, told myself it was better to bite back the theatrics, but what did he want me to say? I looked over at him. I couldn't trust myself to speak without betraying a simmering insolence. Did he expect me to trust him? I remained silent. Dr. Thomison uncrossed his legs and crossed them again, jotting something down in his notepad before looking up. He tried to reach me again.

"Do you still feel as if you are being watched?"

Wouldn't you? I wanted to snap. The doctor's presence was redundant. He was a true representation of "beside the point" in the grand scheme of things. *Okay, maybe your office is my sanctuary*, I was thinking to myself. *Maybe. But as soon as I walk out this door there is a surveillance camera tracking me. If I go into the grocery store, there I am again, on tape. Walking down the town center . . .*

"I can assure you, you are not." The doctor looked at me in dead earnest, catching my eyes, reading my mind. I was impressed with his ability to say that with a straight face.

"Yes, you are positively right, doctor," I conceded. Just wanted to reassimilate as quickly as possible and leave Crickledown. If Bug Eye saw me fit enough, I could return to New York in a coupla weeks' time and begin writing. The sooner I wrote, gave them what they wanted, the sooner I was outta this mess. End of.

At the end of our hour Bug Eye said to me, "I know you don't believe it, Skye, but I *am* on your side."

◉

Walking out of his office after my final session weeks later, I flipped a middle finger at the CCTV camera in the reception hall. As I came out the automatic sliding doors, my dad spotted me before I spotted him, wheeled his black BMW around. My instincts kicked in—I wanted to make a break for it. But Crickledown was still in the Stone Age, no public transportation aside from erratic buses that went nowhere.

"Well, how did it go?" he asked with a concerned smile.

I was nowhere near forgiving him. I wanted to scream, but that would just prove his point about my "emotional immaturity." I rolled down the window.

"Well?" he persisted. As I searched my pockets for a packet of Kools I resisted saying, "'Well'? A well is a hole in the ground," just to annoy him. It was something he used to say to me while I was growing up here in the clean streets of Crickledown. He was waiting, his hands on the ignition key like a threat. *Answer me*, his stare said. I looked back blankly and shrugged.

"Use your words. I don't know what *this*"—he said, mimicking my shrug—"is."

"What do you want me to say?" I said, finally finding my cigarette packet. What would he have liked to hear? *Great, Dad, I'm cured!* I knew I couldn't say anything close to that without it being soaked in a sarcasm my father knew all too well.

My dad shook his head, looked disapprovingly at the packet of crumpled menthols, and started the engine. I was no longer the daughter he'd raised. I pulled out a cigarette, wishing to create a smoke screen, missing London, remembering New York.

◎

Now back in the Naked Apple, a.k.a. NYC, sitting on the bench with an old leather bag bulging with papers and wrecked journals, I file through random torn, crumpled pages, pull out one ratty-edged notebook. An old tube ticket falls out. My first journey through London's underground. Zones one through six. The black ink is fading, the print faint against the pink card. My first journey across the Atlantic had been seeded here in New York. Beside me on the park bench, another journal lies spread-eagle facedown. I pull out a cig nub from my pocket along with my portable recorder, push the button, and the LCD light flashes red.

"It began just this past March, the spring of 1992 . . ."

EXT. OUTSIDE NYC SUBWAY STATION

From a car radio, a presenter can be heard in
mid-flow rant.

          PRESENTER
    It's just discouraging, Tom, to believe
    that what happened to Rodney King
    could happen in this day and age. We're
    less than a decade away from the new
    millennium for Chrissake!

A traffic light changes. The car drives off
into the swish of several cars rushing to get
wherever they are going. An equally nervous
and excited SKYE exits the subway, grabbing
a pack of Luckies, a lighter, and a recorder
out of her bag. She walks with a slight slouch
and swagger. The wind blows through her baby
dreads.

It began just this past March, the spring of 1992. As I exited the Lower East Side subway into the mild air pushing New York litter into spiral dances around me, first thing I did was reach into my bag for a smoke and lighter and my recorder. I held the translucent light-blue lighter up to check its contents. Still empty. It had post-fluid staying power. Nothing in it, yet it lasted. I was at some magical crossroads. Yeah. Feeling the full force of my powers.

"My powers spiritual." That's what this post-punk praline-skinned voyager had said to me last summer on a bus on my way to Chicago. He'd said he could feel them. That we were somehow connected. I had to laugh at first, thought it was a creative pickup line, if that's what it was. Could only just about understand him under his accent. He was in his early twenties, I guessed. Seemed to be both younger and older than me at the same time. Wise—a fool in the king's court, me being the king.

"Where you from?" I'd asked.

"Well, I'm originally from London." He paused to let that sink in, his brown eyes catching mine before continuing his well-practiced mini-monologue. "Live in New York now, grew up in London. My mum's white English and my *daaaad*"—he said in a long, drawn-out, nasally voice— "African American. Or so I was told. I'm on my way to Chicago to meet some mates. And you?"

I told him that I was just escaping my St. Louis blues. It

sounded way cooler than the truth, which was I was coming to settle in for the summer before starting the semester at the university. He picked up on the St. Louis blues reference and started singing. *I left my St. Louis blues to live the life I could chooooose.* I smiled. It was a coincidence, but it was like he understood everything about me. Everything that mattered, anyway.

I plopped down in the ragged blue seat next to him, feeling for the first time, perhaps in my life, that I was on my way to meeting people who would get me. In Crickledown everyone seemed resigned to their assigned positions, predicated from birth on a social order you had no hand in creating but were obliged to maintain, then raise up your offspring to do the same. I often felt in between the in-between, where nothing in the realms of "this or that" seemed to stick for me. Maybe it was that this misfit wanderer fit all too well into the story I'd imagined unfolding for myself. On a Greyhound, leaving the St. Louis 'burbs for the first time to live on my own for the first time, with the desire to meet folks who were not simply characters in the same monotone flick I'd grown up in.

At a rest stop, he tried to light my cigarette with that lighter but couldn't get it to spark. He gave it to me, and I fired up.

"See, your powers spiritual manifest." He told me to keep the lighter. His name, Scottie. He was coming back from a visit with some folks in St. Louis. He was going to do a quick stopover in Chicago, catch a ride with some "aging hippie dharma bums" road-tripping back to New York, where he lived. I was attracted to this disheveled character. His slight, paper-brown body, though grungy and meager, had a lion-esque quality to it. I didn't feel exactly safe with him, even with his reassurance—"You're safe with me, mate," he'd said, "in spite of what some people might think"—but he was just dangerous enough. He was rattling on about the ignorance of the bus driver, who didn't want to let him back on the bus, accusing him of being a drug addict, and how folks were afraid and couldn't handle "real" people. "I'm the real deal, no carbon copy," he'd said. I soon understood his main (pre)occupation: masturbation, both mental and physical. I let him put his hand between my thighs. Most of the passengers were asleep anyway.

I thought of Damian, my boyfriend who lived in Chicago. He was going to get me a room with him and his friend. Neither the room nor Damian was a sure thing, and part of me was thinking all of this was crazy—leaving home so suddenly. Yeah, I'd been accepted into university. I thought I'd study communications. Had a plan . . . but was still taking a risk, moving to a strange city, into a stranger flat, meeting strange people on the bus into town. But it didn't matter. All that mattered was that I was on that hot-as-hell Greyhound with fifty-six other sweating strangers heading for a place that I'd never seen before, leaving a place I knew all too well.

In the end none of it worked out—school, the room, or Damian. We stupidly moved in with each other. Things got complicated. You know the whole "he wasn't the dude I thought he was" routine. I needed to find a new place to live. To make a long flick short, after several catastrophic months in Chicago, I dropped out of college and decided to keep moving, make tracks to New York. I was reading a James Baldwin biography at the time and fancied visiting the place he grew up in. Besides, by that point I knew someone who lived there. Scottie.

◉

Though it was my first time in New York, it was easy enough to navigate after catching on to the pattern: the gridded, slanted streets crisscrossing Alphabet City. I walked with purpose, like I belonged there, priding myself on having amassed some street cred. After all, I had lived some intense months in the Windy City. New York felt edgier, more alive and even more eclectic. People from all sorts mixing, melding—business suits alongside street vendors alongside bohemians. The neighborhood was staring gentrification in the face, which had not yet sunk its soul-sucking claws in. The Lower East Side was still considered "rough" by those who could afford to live elsewhere.

Standing outside an old falling-apart building, somewhere on Avenue B, I checked the address Scottie had scratched in my journal months ago and rang the doorbell. There was no response. The door was held ajar with a brick so I walked in and up some squeaky metal stairs to what I thought was Scottie's apartment. Cobain's voice whined through the cracked door: *But I swear that I don't have a gun.* I remembered Scottie talking about the last time he was on a Greyhound, how he'd been with his New York roommate, heading for Seattle. He went on about the grunge scene there, and about hearing Nirvana rock before they sold out their sound and got famous. I walked in. Cautiously. This *was* New York, right? Who would leave their door open in this city? Then I remembered that Scottie, who nearly left his wallet on the bus, was probably the kind of person who would forget to lock the door. After all, he wasn't really from New York.

As I entered the small dusty studio, post–Port Authority angst gave way to excitement. Half expected to see the short-haired, randy Scottie having a rebound shag, but I was probably inviting an instant replay of the Damian story. What if Scottie was really a jerk? What if I ended up with no place to stay? At least this time I carried no expectations. I didn't care, convinced myself this was different, and got ready for some innocent flirting. But instead I was greeted by *her*, or rather, *not* greeted by her . . . and my world fell apart.

She didn't see me at first, or hear my timid knock on the already open door. I walked into what could have been the Tardis, as the room was larger than it appeared to be at the entrance: an open space, cracked black-and-white tiled floors and raftered ceilings. The walls were concrete. To my right, a part of the room was curtained off to create a makeshift bedroom; a sofa divided the rest of the room into two parts. Left of the sofa border she stood, still apparently oblivious to my presence. Engrossed in what she was doing. Her disheveled dark, curly, dreading hair partially masked a determined face. She was pasting scrap paper of different sizes and shapes onto the white concrete wall, going at it so feverishly I was afraid to interrupt. When I finally got her attention and asked for Scottie, she gave me a quick once-over but otherwise seemed extremely disinterested.

"You can sit there and wait if you want." She caught me noticing the open bowl of pot. The room reeked of it. "Help yourself."

"Thanks."

I sat down on the sofa, suddenly feeling a little awkward, trying for an aloof coolness. Despite my tenuous attempt at grace, my bag landed with a resounding thud by my sweaty boots. I was suddenly aware of their mellow stench as I clumsily shifted on the anorexic sofa. Scottie's roommate went back to her canvas. The sunlight blasted through the window, casting her shadow on the wall in front of her. She began to outline it with strips of paper carefully, then again with urgency. I picked up a half-smoked joint.

"Naw, roll your own," she said without looking at me. Woman had eyes in the back of her head.

"Sorry."

The artist at work ignored me as I, now feeling as if I'd been caught stepping in shit, fumbled with the light-as-a-butterfly all-natural papers. Didn't look up again until I'd finished twisting a pregnant joint. Lit it with the light-blue lighter that Scottie had given me. After inhaling a healthy amount of smoke and holding it, I strained against the urge to cough until it flew out on its own volition.

At first she seemed not to notice, but then, sticking another scrap on the wall, she said, "That was three coughs—three coughs and you're off."

And I *was* gone. Purple sweat glistened along her long neck, light floated from her skin as she placed more and more paper, unsticking and replacing, sometimes ripping bits in half to fill a spot. Her wild head was spiked with electric strands of fractured white light. Wiry muscles pressed against honey-brown skin as she pushed against the wall. Her overalls just barely covered her clay-brown nipples. Hands. Lithe. Precise. I let my eyes wander from her strong fingers to her dancer's biceps. There, uncoiling its metal tail, was the snake. The one I'd seen before as a kid. This time its head turned and hissed, pointing its tongue in the direction of this strange and wonderful woman's work. Her paper-sculpted shadow walked off the wall and they waltzed to an orchestra of colors. The shadow's face was at first a phantom of someone familiar, then no face at all . . .

"Hey!"

Her face was two inches from mine. She grabbed the

joint. Mortified, I felt saliva nearly dripping from the corner of my open mouth. Could do nothing about it.

"Hey, compadre, ¿habla español?"

". . . Did . . . did . . ."

"¿Qué pasa, bonita con ojos rojos?"

"You were dancing with her—it—Sincara," I whispered, more to myself.

She looked at me long and hard before letting out a smoke-filled giggle. "YES!"

And just to prove it, she took an ink-sodden paintbrush and wrote across her paper-sculpted shadow, *SINCARA WAZ 'ERE*. She twisted the snake armlet on her bicep absentmindedly. "By the way, Scottie doesn't live here anymore."

Over herbal tea in the open-space kitchen, we exchanged names. She told me she was Pieces and updated me on what happened to Scottie. He had packed it in for London just over a month ago. She apologized for not saying so when I walked in, but she was afraid I was one of Scottie's floozies, coming to find him.

"Shit happens, ya know," she said, stirring thick white honey into my mug. "He gets a little punnani, leaves town; they come here looking for him. Then somehow I miraculously metamorph into Agony Auntie. In fact, one of them called about coming around here today, I thought you might be her." Her accent I couldn't quite catch. A mixture of flavors I couldn't quite recognize.

"Where you from?" I asked.

Either she didn't hear me (she had the effect of tightening my vocal cords), or she chose to ignore me.

"Here's your cuppa. Sorry to be rude, but I was in the middle of something."

"Yeah, I noticed," I said to her back. She was scrutinizing her canvas. "I really didn't want to disturb you, but . . ." She

16

waved her hand as if what I said were of no consequence and picked up a paintbrush, poised for that last stroke.

I moved toward her, catching a glimpse of the paper sculpture grafted onto the wall: numbers scribbled on backs of matchbook covers, ripped pages splattered with scrambled notes, cigarette packs from various places across the globe, all of which outlined a silhouette of her shadow.

Head still swimming in a green mist, I couldn't resist pulling out my recorder.

"It seems to be some kinda self-portrait," I whispered into the tiny protruding microphone.

Pieces placed her paintbrush purposefully in a jar of paint thinner. I wished I could stuff the words back down my throat. It had become an obsession, the tiny Walkman recorder. I'd bought it before leaving Missouri. A necessary tool for a journalism student. I used it more to document my "adventures" when the moment made it too awkward to pull out my journal. But I felt like I was invading this woman's private space. A very protected space. Her energy seemed to say, *Who asked you?* After all, we had only just barely met. Bracing myself for rebuff, I moved toward the sofa as if it were home base. Before I was able to get far, she turned so abruptly I froze. Her face eased into an amused smile, her eyes scanning mine as she lit her joint with Scottie's torch. Afterward she held it up to the light, checking its contents. Still empty. She put the lighter in her pocket absentmindedly, grabbed my arm, and led me back to the kitchen.

Figured I must have finally said something right, 'cause Pieces offered me the sofa if I needed somewhere to stay for the night. It was stupid, but I *was* counting on Scottie's generosity. Sussing that I wasn't one of Scottie's flings, Pieces relaxed a bit more.

"First time in the Naked Apple, love?"

I nodded, still trying to place her accent. "You know you sound a bit like Scottie? Are you guys, like, related?"

"'Are you guys, like, related' or something, maaan." Pieces laid it on thick, the surfer-dude routine. I shifted into defense mode. I did not sound like a surfer dude, okay?

Pieces smiled before I had a chance to get too annoyed. "What are you on about, girl. Relax! Stop trying to connect all the dots. Or is that what your recorder's for?"

It was my turn to smile.

U nder the dawn of the next day, Pieces sucked the morning dew from a baby rose at the park. "Me, I come
from nowhere and everywhere, and to the everywhere of
nowhere I shall return," she said. I was hooked, line and
sinker.

Earlier that evening we'd walked up and down Manhattan
until sunrise, sharing smokes and libations with the spirits of ancestors we barely knew existed. Sharing testimony.
Talking about everything from the war in Afghanistan to
the LA riots, from our favorite childhood boxed sweet
(Lemonheads and Boston Baked Beans) to the well-meaning
violence of being moved from the inner city to the predom-
inantly snow-white suburbia. She shared with me bits of
the story of her adventure with Scottie in Seattle. They'd
connected as some of the few alternative punk/grunge
Blacks—not considered Black enough for many of the gate-
keeper "Afro bots" who demanded your authenticity card at
the door, while simultaneously being a kind of trophy for
some of the white "friends" in the alternative scene who'd
say, "You are different from other Blacks" or "I don't really
see you as Black" and stuff like that, all of which I knew
and understood too well. The more we talked the more it
seemed we were telling the other's story, until it became
unclear whose story was whose. We both grew up in the
suburbs, both raised by dads who had served in Vietnam.
We both liked to travel. That is, I'd *wanted* to travel, for as

long as I could remember. Her passport was tattooed with various stamps from the UK, Brazil, Holland, and Germany. I didn't even have a passport.

I think Pieces could sense me moving toward the edge, ready for free fall. She found herself involuntarily slipping into big-sister mode. She *recognized* me. I'd always believed that I came from somewhere else, and now I was really beginning to feel as if I wasn't the only one. As a kid, to reconcile some kind of inexplicably deep loneliness, I used to imagine that I was somehow part alien. I mean, there *were* signs. I told Pieces this, and about the birthmark on my left thigh. That to me was proof that I came from somewhere out there. I'd been trying to decode the natural tat since childhood. Most people would have laughed at me. But Pieces didn't, she simply listened, both of us taking in the canopy of stars over Washington Square Park. Which is why when she'd asked me about Sincara, I fished out folded sheets placed in the back of my journal. Pieces took the sepia papers in her hands carefully, as if they were some precious artifact, and read them out loud under the spotlight of a streetlamp. I held my breath.

"'My First Escape,' by Skye, age eleven." Pieces cleared her throat and continued:

One minute past dusk. Darkness slowly falls over a white wood slat house, surrounded by a white paint–chipped fence. I lean against a white birch tree, a black-and-red sport duffel hangs over one shoulder. Digging into my jeans pocket I pull out a nicely folded sheet of thinly lined notebook paper, walk up the front porch stairs, place it in the mailbox, take a deep breath, and walk swiftly down the drive. I stop just at the bottom.

I just turned eleven. And I am making the most important decision of my life. To avoid a life sentence. For murder. I have to escape the scene of the would-be crime. It's not that I really want to kill my father. I want my freedom and this is where I am going. To wherever freedom is. I am not sure where that is but I walk anyway, crossing the line between the driveway and the sidewalk, my heart moves up to my head but my head is light. I feel like screaming. A smile won't leave my face and I am walking. Like I've never experienced what it is like to walk before. I go in the direction of my secret spot along the railroad tracks. Now I'm talking like I live in the country or something. No. But Daddy wants to move there. I live in the suburbs. When Black people move to the suburbs you know that you are moving up. Ha. It is 1983. We moved here from the city in 1976. For years after that year, I couldn't stand red, white, and blue for a while. Bicentennial-the-fuck-this and bicentennial-the-fuck-that. Back then, I actually believed I talked to Jesus. Now I know it's not Jesus I talk to. But back then, I read the Bible every day or some stupidness like that. Daddy's good girl. It was getting boring. I wanted us to be friends. But he had to understand that I didn't agree with his rules. I just didn't agree anymore.

I began to masturbate, right? I'd read about it in that book Are You There God? It's Me, Margaret. And when I did it, it gave me freedom. It was like looking into the face of all that IS and exploding with laughter. But of course I had to get on my knees and pray for forgiveness. I got on my knees a lot. But it became like . . . well . . . God's rules through Dad's mouth came out like a nightmare. Like I was in jail or something. I would have dreams about saving my mom from a dungeon. I wanted to save myself. Because my mom was really me. My dad seems to see that lately.

"You are getting just like your mother."

Sometimes it comes out like an accusation. I can't tell if he loved her or not. They were together for a few years before I was born. Not married. Just together. One day I overheard my aunt talking about my dad.

"That's just how he stay, just too intense. Brandon was like that since time, girl. Even with my sister before they got married. I think

21

it might be Nam that did it. I know he loved her though." Auntie Bernice paused to pull the thread through the eye of the needle with her teeth. "Shame how it all happened."

I was in my mom's belly before they got married. He called me a "love child." See, I don't get how he could talk all that hippie shit and then be so boringly Christian. I know I lost my angel wings when I asked if the Buddha was going to hell because he did not know Christ. These days he will slap me if I don't say "yes sir" with respect. I have perfected the blank look though. I imagine my mom musta been like a mute cooking machine. Forget him and his bologna-and-cheese sandwiches at lunch, anyway. Oh, I should be so excited to make them for him. Like I want to prepare for some life as someone's Christian housewife. I like softball. He threatened to make me quit the team 'cause it was making me too boyish.

"Do you always have to wear that baseball cap?"

A war zone was mounting in our house. But I am now on my way to peace. Adventure. I will just wander. Find a place like where the Artful Dodger lived; learn the craft of pickpocketing. I'll be like Robin Hood though. Take from the stinking rich. Give to the stinking poor.

It's scary following these tracks at night. But my adrenaline gives me courage. I puff on half a Benson menthol I stole from my dad's coat pocket and walk. Dad is out late tonight. Some neo-evangelical Christians meeting. He will go have coffee afterward. It will be late before he gets back and finds my note. I have some distance to cover.

As I walk, images from a recurring dream are on repeat in my head. Dad chasing me though the neighborhood with a belt. In his underwear. The cross he always wears, a burning-red choker. I walk faster. Hardly looking at anything but the tracks moving underneath my feet. Don't know how far I've walked, but I come up to what looks like an old train stop. It's deserted. I can stop here for a while. Catch my breath. Lunar beams bounce off the metal onto the track. So many stars. I lie back, look up, and go to the moon. I mean, I'm really close. And vibrations fill my face. And I'm on my way home. I know it because this is what freedom feels like. And colors, slanted prisms, fill my ears and love me. I see its face is like my face—it's a familiar face and then not a face at all. I look down and realize I hold a snake in my hand—like a staff.

"Go back," it hisses, its sliding tongue tasting the night air, one eye staring at me. I wake up sitting on the edge of the tracks. I hear the rumble of a train going toward the station not far from home, headed my way. I jump on it.

The note is still in the mailbox when I get back. No one is there. Just an incredible silence warming me. For the next few days I sit in that silence. Begin dreaming of a home somewhere out there. And someday I will get there.

After carefully refolding the lined and bent papers, Pieces gave them back. I found the story just before leaving Crickledown, folded up and molding under my mattress. It seemed right to carry it with me. Pieces stared at me intensely for a moment. Weirdly, I felt warmed by her gaze, like I was hers. Like I was a virgin being seen for the very first time.

"Me and you, you know, are sistuhs with a different mistuh, mate," Pieces said, her accent shifting from New Yorker to a British bend. "Like brothahs with a different motha." She pulled her locs down so they framed her tanned face.

"Yeah?" It was really more an exhale than a question. I didn't know this chick too well, but I did know I cared what she thought.

"I had those nightmares too, y'know."

"Which ones?"

"The whole holy chase scene."

"Oh."

"What happened to your mom?"

I shrugged, shoving the papers back into my journal.

23

"Sincara. So that's when you first had that vision." Pieces fiddled with the snake armlet that wrapped her bicep. "Why do you call her, it, whatever, Sincara?"

Suddenly feeling too open, I fumbled with my bag, dropped the journal inside.

"I don't know, sounded pretty. It's just a silly story."

"Then what are you calling me, hey?"

"What do you mean?"

"I liked your story." She took a swig of beer. "In fact, I *know* your story."

She handed me the bottle, still wrapped in a small brown paper bag. Elbows on my knees, I looked up at Pieces as her large hands gripped my shoulder. "NEVER. EVER"—she paused for effect—"NEVER ever justify yourself to ANYONE."

She jumped off the bench and we walked back to the flat, the sounds of New York waking up as our soundtrack.

INT. NEW YORK STUDIO

Skye, fully clothed and covered with a light sheet, is asleep on the sofa. She shifts from her side to her back, slowly opening her eyes.

Outside the window, someone's boom box is playing Jacob Miller's "Tenement Yard":
Dreadlocks can't live in a tenement yard too much su-su su-su su-su, too much watchie watchie you. Too much su-su su-su su-su, too much watchie what you are. Dreadlocks can't live in privacy . . .

The sun was low in the sky when I finally came to. My mouth had the taste of days-old socks. Below my hand, dangling off the sofa, was an overfull ashtray. A bouquet of old butts greeted me. I clicked on the recorder nestled in my chest, spoke in a whisper, half because I didn't want to wake Pieces but mostly because it was about as much as my cracked throat could manage.

The sky is the color of a black-and-white movie and I am on the run. I feverishly row a unicycle through the air, with a white staff. It morphs into a snake. It is Sincara, her one eye stares back, startling me off my unicycle. I am falling into a void of faraway sound; familiar, long blue notes, pulsing from plucked strings, sigh around me. I am falling forever and just as I am about to land, I wake up.

They were beginning again. Those strange dreams. Hadn't had them since I first saw Sincara about a decade ago. These were not ordinary dreams but felt like reoccurring hieroglyphics from many other lifetimes spent wandering through space. In straight language, they had that edge to them; felt more like memories, more real than reality. They would be on eternal repeat until I cracked them, or they cracked me. I'd talk to Pieces about the dream, see what she made of it.

Desert dehydration sent me to the kitchen. Mouth under the tap I lapped as much water as my stomach could hold before stumbling into the bathroom. There was a towel folded on the toilet. I assumed Pieces left it there for me

26

and took a long-overdue shower. Half expected her to turn up with some bagels or coffee in those generic blue cardboard cups. Didn't question why, seemed like something she would do. Walked into the empty front room, hair dripping and wrapped in a towel. On the kitchen table, water kerplunked from my dripping hair onto my opened journal. Inside, a note from Pieces: *Off to London. DON'T FORGET you promised to come along. Scottie's addie is below, with other domestically useful information. See you on the other side of the pond, my sistah.*

Whatever else was written after that was just a blur of inky symbols under the blow. She'd left. Just like that. I felt dizzy. I couldn't remember agreeing to come to London. But couldn't remember much of the night before . . . Everything was still murky under the razzle of Old E, green tea, and what I guessed was fatigue from a long bus journey. It wasn't impossible. I sure as hell *wanted* to go.

By the time I finished smoking a roach I found in Pieces's curtained-off bedroom, panic morphed into excitement. First I had a go at myself. What was I thinking? Alone in New-fucking-York. The only people I knew here were now in London. London, England. Home of the Artful Dodger. Miles away from here. And I was invited. Had showed up in New York without a plan and one dropped into my lap. This was a chance to leave the country. Once across the Atlantic, who knows where I'd end up, what I'd see. Shit. London. Had a place to stay. The only things I didn't have were a passport and the dollahs to get there.

In her letter, Pieces reminded me that I could stay on in the apartment. Rent was paid a month in advance. As for employment, her departure made for a sudden opening at Margaritaville. She'd worked as a host there, and pay was tips only. I looked around her bare room. The drawers were emptied, and her books were packed. Even beyond these details, her absence was palpable. A blank space in an equation where the answer should be. I reread the note she left for anything I might have missed. Everything seemed accounted for.

She instructed me to leave her books with Alex, the downstairs neighbor, and not to worry about anything else. I thought Alex was nice enough to help me carry the boxes to lessen the trips back and forth and up and down the stairs. But it was more an excuse to get into my business. He asked how long I'd been in town. Was certain that he'd seen me before. Heard that Pieces and Scottie had had a run-in with the police. Was I around then? He was *certain* he'd seen me before. I told him I knew nothing about it, hoping he would stop with the grilling already. He, with his too-clean, just-outta-college looks, was not my type.

"You guys sisters?" he asked as he picked up the last box.

"Sisters?"

"Yeah, you and Pieces. What's your name again? Didn't catch it."

"I didn't throw it."

"You could be sisters—"

That's how Pieces ended the note she'd left for me. *See you on the other side of the pond, my sistah.* Her words echoed off the page. "My sister"—I liked the sound of that. Never even knew how badly I wanted one until then. After I got rid of Alex, I sat down and began writing in the open journal about my first night in New York, filling in the bits I couldn't quite remember. I sat for ages in that Lower East Side apartment, holding the note from Pieces in my hand, just staring out the kitchen window at the weathered brick of the building next door. She was really gone, and the apartment felt empty, like an abandoned film set, still quietly reverberating with the memories formed there only hours ago. I paced around the room replaying the night before. I remembered walking through Manhattan, the park, her outburst, and then there was nothing but . . . blank. I guessed I'd had my first blackout. Picked up Pieces's note again, to scan it for further clues. Something to spark my memory. Nothing. Nothing. Nothing.

Well into the day, a sea of sounds: cars driving by, and people calling greetings; their yelling, laughing, cursing filled my ears. Nobody in my family had any idea that I'd even left Chicago. I considered calling home. For a minute I fantasized that Dad would be secretly excited about my adventures, but on the real I knew I would endure a blah-blah-blah lecture: Why did you drop outta blah-blah-blah opportunities gone to waste blah-blah, not safe for you to be in New York a-blah-blah-bladee-blah. But still, what could he do? I didn't want to come home. For a brief moment I wished that I could call my mother. Insane, that thought. My dad told me he had gotten rid of her ashes a long time ago and that it didn't matter where. That I carried her inside of me. He was a liar. I suddenly had the urge to tell him just that.

I stuck my pen into bed-sculpted hair and walked toward the phone, propped precariously on the windowsill on the other side of the loft. Exhaling slowly, the phone receiver now sweaty under my palm, I checked out the busy street below. Tompkins Square Park was just visible. Various people sat enjoying their lunch and one another, watching the passersby from park benches. The city soundtrack at that moment was sweet, peppered with Dre's "Let Me Ride" barreling out of a stickered, well-used but well-kept ghetto blaster, shrined by an assortment of teenage boys who sat and squatted on a park bench. Everybody was nodding to this track that tapped into a nostalgia most of the people my age didn't realize we had. I had some vague memory of my dad reluctantly tapping his feet, sinking into bass-driven outer-space melodies spinning from a worn record my auntie, his sister, slid out of a crazy-colored sleeve. "Uh-huh, see," she teased my father, "the P-Funk will get you every time."

Two Black, gray-bearded old men played chess in one corner; I could see my father, an avid chess fan, enjoying the spectacle. Putting the phone to my ear, I dialed the numbers quickly, without looking at the keypad. Let the phone ring once before hanging up. Couldn't face it. I was still too angry at him, though I kept the real reason why under lock and key from him. Also knew he would try to persuade me to come home. Tell me that New York was no place for a young woman just barely out of high school.

"You're not emotionally stable enough," he'd said when I first told him about the journalism scholarship. It was almost as if he knew—once I was cut loose, I would stay cut loose. "Chicago?! You have everything you need here, in Missouri," he went on. "Anyway, you should go to a community college first. Get a part-time job . . ."

I tuned him out. Concentrated on my game plan. My escape mission. Was getting out with or without his permission, but needed a little cash to tide me over until the first grant came through. His sister, Auntie Mich (came out like *Meesh*, short for "Michelle"), said she would talk to him. Auntie Mich and I had an understanding. Understood how hardheaded he could be. Sometimes she was able to talk some sense into him, get him to look at things from a different angle. Whatever happened, I was so outta there. Already had a place to stay. The official story: I would stay in the campus dormitory. Didn't tell Dad about my plans to shack up with Damian.

At that time I still believed I was In Love. Damian and I could've been classic high school romance material. Even better, we were pals as well. Hung out like buddies: jumping trains, riding theme-park rides, kicking the soccer ball around. We horsed around, and made out wherever we could find the tiniest privacy. He graduated a year ahead of me. Was accepted into the Art Institute in Chicago to study music. Played a mean sax. Mean enough to seduce a girl who had no interest in having a boyfriend. I'd thought he understood me. Both of us grew up in the 'burbs, though he lived in a different "village," as we liked to call it. He was the first Black person I could talk to about everything. Was even into what my dad thought was strange, hippie dope fiend music. Stuff like the Beatles' *White Album* and just about any Pink Floyd. Together we discovered jazz, reggae, and Black Power politics. He, like me, felt we had missed a revolutionary moment—stuck in post–*Brady Bunch* Bill Cosby land, customized shoulder pads and all.

Before him I was mostly a loner. My only close friends were the extraterrestrials I befriended when I was still riding my purple tricycle. They lived in invisible neighborhoods around our old apartment in the city: some of them stayed above the fridge, others behind the couch in the living room. After we left for the 'burbs, as I got older, these friends changed into true otherworldlies, living somewhere on the other side of the sky, a place I knew was my real home.

High school was the cliché of American high schools, with the socials, jocks, nerds, and losers that hung out in the campus smoking area. I probably would have ended up with the smoking-area crew if I didn't think it would get back to my father. He had people there in Crickledown High; Dad's cousin Patrick worked as a gym teacher. Kept an eye out for me. Eyes everywhere. I hated and assumed my "nice girl" image in order to survive high school and stay outta trouble, but in some ways, as that canned flick goes, Damian was the Bonnie to my Clyde.

I had a good rep at school with the teachers, so I could get away with writing myself passes and sneaking to my secret hideaway on the art building rooftop, where I'd smoke half a mentholated Kool and practice making clouds disappear. Damian also disintegrated cumuli. Understood it. I was that tomboyish girl swept off her feet in some old black-and-white fifties flick.

You'll like it here in Chicago, he wrote. *It is full of people like us. Conscious people, of all shades. There is one girl I'd like you to meet. Her name is Ava. She is a poet like you, Skye. The world is definitely bigger here.*

Dad didn't like Damian. At all. Didn't like his arrogance. It didn't matter that he was the son of a preacher, just like him. I thought it might please him to know. But it irritated him when I mentioned it. Even though he was always going on about how I should save myself for a man of God.

He knew Damian was in Chicago. Despite all her plans, Auntie Mich got NOWHERE with my dad. He insisted I stay in Crickledown and go to community college, scholarship or not. I put plan B into action. Too late for anyone to stop me. The day before I left I searched for a few ducats—knew he kept a stash in his sock drawer, but sometimes he moved it around. I ended up going through the entire dresser before I found a cent. But I also found some legal paperwork about my mom, and attached to it, a blanched envelope from her addressed to Dad. He'd told me Mom had died not long after my birth, but the bicentennial stamp commemorating the

American Revolution was postmarked the same year my dad packed us up to move to the 'burbs. This meant that my mom hadn't died when I was a baby, was maybe even still alive today? All I knew was that he hadn't told me everything. Had lied about what happened.

"I am so outta here," I said, feeling a seismic shift in the ground beneath me. I took a deep breath, put the unopened, time-stained envelope in the front pocket of my overalls, and felt immediately calmed—still on edge, but focused. First things first: get the fuck out as soon as possible. I grabbed the Yellow Pages and looked up the number for the Greyhound bus station. My feet were itching and had been for some time, but now they burned.

INT. MARGARITAVILLE - STAFF-ROOM SECURITY CAMERA

Skye is having a chat with a trendily dressed young man. He talks incessantly while Skye listens, smiling. He slides an apron across the table and offers her a cig. She takes both.

It was dead-easy getting hired at Margaritaville. Pieces had hinted to the manager, Toney, that I might want the job. Besides, most of the staff seemed to know me. Evidently Pieces and I had stopped in and gotten toasted. Wasn't used to being absolutely off my face, so I pretended to remember.

"You two lovebirds *were* a bit tipsy," teased Toney. "I was wondering when Pieces would come on out and bring one of her girls in."

"I'm not one of her girls," I corrected him. "We're like sisters—"

Toney gave a Black Power fist. "Right oooon! Sistahs doin' it for themseeeelves." He winked at me.

As annoying as Toney could be, it felt freeing to work at Margville. Compared to Crickledown, where there was barely a straight bar around, let alone anything close to a gay bar, it was something different. Toney was gay. And he assumed everybody was gay. Most of the staff here was gay. There was a huge gay clientele. It was the West Village. Soho. New York. On the rare occasion some asshole would come in and start making some homophobic remark about disease-carrying sissy cocksuckers, Toney would handle it. He spent his off time at the gym and had the guns to prove it. The chumps never saw it coming and rarely resisted as Toney stronghold-escorted the asshole out the door.

"We're here, we're queer, get used to it, honey!" he'd sing after them.

I was reminded of finding an old *TIME* magazine in the library as a kid. On the cover, two gay men held hands. I was attracted to it. Digested it slowly. Knew even then that love is love and gender is hit-or-miss. Still, the word "lesbian" hadn't ever occurred to me. I'd neither heard about nor ever *seen* one in real life. Sure, I knew they existed, but in another world, not in my reality. If there were queers at my school, they were as invisible to me as that other planet I imagined I came from. And folks always questioned my lack of dresses, the state of my hair, the way I walked. But working here, no one seemed to care. I could finally be myself. At the time I didn't even sweat it. Didn't think about the real reason I felt so relaxed.

And the tips were good. I began filling my cookie jar. Everything fell into place. Proof that I was on the right path. My powers spiritual were in full effect. All the dots connected. Even Chicago hadn't been a waste of time. If I hadn't been on that Greyhound bus, I never would have met Scottie, and if I hadn't met Scottie then I'd never have met Pieces. I saw Chicago as a transition. A bridge to the next 'verse. After all, Chicago is no kids' town, and I fancied I'd picked up some street savvy there. As opposed to the St. Louis suburb that I'd come from, Chicago was a monster metropolis. Building after building pierced the skyline through downtown Chicago. Walking past the John Hancock Center during the winter months, I sometimes actually did hold on to streetlamps to steady myself against the tunneling winds whooshing from the mouth of Lake Michigan.

And the Chicago ghettos must have been the first I'd ever

seen up close. Speaks volumes considering St. Louis ghettos have a reputation to rival Chi-Town's. Those ghettos I had been "saved" from when my dad moved us to the 'burbs. "Your mother was against it," he would say on those few occasions my dad spoke about her. She didn't want to be so far from her family and the church she grew up in. I often wondered what would be different about me if we had stayed in the city. Would I be tougher? Would I be *Blacker*, somehow?

In Chicago, I took the L down to the South Side sometimes to visit Damian at the Black publishing company there. It also sponsored an alternative school for Black youth, where he gave music lessons. One of the pillars of the Black community, the publishing company was also walking distance from a community-run vegetarian soul-food cafeteria, a sort of oasis in a neighborhood that not only looked but felt different from the rest of Chicago. It wasn't just the fact that the area was blatantly poorer—more derelict, rotted-out buildings, trash, liquor stores, churches, and barbecue joints—it was as if you were in a different town altogether.

We lived in Wicker Park. Not the best area, but it had affordable rent and was less run-down. Regeneration cycle in full swing, the neighborhood was increasingly yuppie white; meanwhile, the original Polish people who used to live there were either dying away or pushed out as property values increased.

On the way down to the South Side, the passengers on the train shifted to majority Brown. Off the train, I'd wait for the bus among nothing but Black faces. Something I hadn't realized I was carrying dropped from my shoulders; my skin color was not the thing, as it had been most of my childhood, that marked a difference. Even so I moved awkwardly among them, thinking that they must notice something not quite Black enough, that they probably smelled white all over me. Many stared curiously. Hadn't seen me around before.

"You remind me of that sister Lisa Bonet, the tall, more blacker-the-berry version," one dude commented, the edges of a colorful knit hat framing his milk-chocolate face. He was one of the few—checking my natty head—that nodded in my direction, like a fellow conspirator: someone of the Nubian tribe. It always ended the same though. Once they started talking to me, they realized I wasn't the ideal Nubian. Didn't fit the unwritten codes in the Afrocentric handbook: didn't do the African-wrap cowrie-bead routine and questioned Black Power rhetoric and wondered out loud why there weren't more posters of Black women revolutionaries up during Black History Month. One of the few things I had from my mom was a book by Toni Cade Bambara, *The Black Woman*. My mom's sister, Auntie Bernice, snuck it to me one day, saying she'd saved it for me 'cause "your mother loved this book. Use-ta piss off Brandon, so keep it to yourself, now." I felt like she was trying to tell me something, like there was something more she couldn't say. I read the book ferociously for clues. I'd shared it with Damian during our days in the St. Louis 'burbs. But in Chicago I went from being Conscious Black Sister to Hippie-Flavored Oreo in a matter of microseconds. Or at least that's how I clocked it. The campus was highly segregated, and most of the Black students were either already in Black fraternities or planning to pledge, Damian and his friends included. It was something I had absolutely no interest in—this disinterest enunciated a gap, real or imagined, between me and much of the African American student body. I also made "friends" with the "enemy"; to some, being seen hanging out with white students made me untrustworthy. On campus sometimes I'd spot some lone, funky-looking Brown person. Noticed them shyly from a distance; they seemed to have a confidence I found hard to approach. Kept to myself mostly. Spent a lot of time with Damian's friends but they soon bored me. I began drafting a Dear John letter in my head: *Dear D., It's not me, it's you . . .*

When I wasn't on campus or following Damian around, I would go to the water. The Lake Michigan shoreline cut across the city. The border between there and somewhere else; no land in sight, just water for miles. You could almost imagine you were by the sea. Gulls made homes on the masses of stone jutting around the angry waters. If you drove south along Lake Shore Drive you'd end up at a section everyone called "The Rocks."

There I sat and made plans to leave Damian, leave Chicago, leave the Midwest once and for all. Pulled out that faded envelope I'd nicked from my dad's chest of drawers from the inside of my denim. Couldn't bear to open it 'cause I thought I knew what it would say or what I hoped it would say—in any case it would only lead to more unanswered questions when in fact the mere existence of this letter told me all I needed to know. Didn't know if I should do something about it. Getting rid of the letter would be a good start. It could make a good paper boat. I started to get up and make my way to the lake's edge, but was distracted by two men sitting side by side just below me. If I sat up I could get a clear view. One had his hands in the other's denim. The fabric over his fly arched up and relaxed in rhythm with the waves licking the stones along the shore.

I couldn't take my eyes away. Heat moved south as the sun began to set in the west. I thought about my session with Scottie in the Greyhound. Started getting ideas about New York. More impulse than plan. A quick fix for a sulky heart. Could use the grant money I'd gotten for the new semester to travel there. There was no way I was going to stay with Damian, I wasn't sure anymore if I even wanted to be a journalist, and if I was going to have to find someplace to live I might as well do it in another city.

INT. PIECES'S APARTMENT
Skye grabs her bag and quickly shoves a few
bites of overcooked rice into her mouth.

                                    CUT TO:

INT. HALLWAY
Skye rushes out the door, nearly knocking
over her neighbor ALEX as she bounds down
the stairs. Alex opens the door to Pieces's
apartment.

                                    CUT TO:

INT. PIECES'S APARTMENT
Alex moves from room to room, checking for
pinhole-sized openings in the walls. Finding
one, he taps gently around it and pulls out
a small piece of plaster. Behind it is a tiny
camera. He pulls out a small cloth and he wipes
the lens before reinserting it into the wall.
Moving to the next room to repeat the process,
he notices Skye's notebook on the sofa. He
picks it up and thumbs through it.

In Manhattan everything is on the rapid. People move faster. Talk faster. Probably fuck faster. When ordering a bagel you have to know exactly what you want, no dilly no dally. Otherwise the man at the counter will sigh, look past you, and empathize with the line of folks waiting. Everybody is on a tight schedule. Grab breakfast, catch subway, eat muffin, inject caffeine, get to work.

My mantra those days was "make the dough and go." Keep moving east. Like the kung-fu barefoot wanderer. Could almost hear the theme tune. Do New York. Do London. Work and move on. Go to Morocco or Spain, or France. So I busted my ass at Margville, did as many hours as possible, spent as little as possible.

"Fake it till you make it," Pieces had said to me when I told her how uncertain I felt about being here, about what I was doing. And I became good at it. Even lost some of my clumsiness, or became better at disguising it. I mean, who would have thought that the same girl who was fired from her job at McDonald's after messing up so many orders (culminating and ending with the shake machine exploding all over my brown polyester uniform) would go from bussing tables to being host in such a short time? Was now sitting hundreds of customers a night in a semi-swank West Side restaurant in the Big Apple.

Being a host is not an easy job. Hard to be all smiles when the place is packed and you have an onslaught of people waiting to be seated, angry from waiting, trying to push ahead in line. Watching the others, I soon learned the art of being rude while making the customer feel they're always right, and how to do it all with a smile. I also learned how to sneak nearly a pack of cigs a night, share jugs of margaritas after-hours, and still get up to do a double shift the next morning. How to walk home twenty blocks at night, how to make eye contact and avoid it at the right moments like the best poker player, how to walk down those streets, which were still very new to me, as if I owned them. I fancied that within those months I was becoming a New Yorker, when in reality I had only cracked her shell.

Though the tips were good, New York was kicking my ass. The Big Apple gobbled money before it was possible to take a bite. It didn't take long to realize that I wasn't making enough to pay the rent and save for an airline ticket. I had to find a second job.

That wasn't the only thing messing with my mind. Sometimes I felt like a character in somebody else's movie who was somehow missing the plot. Kept finding fragments of my poetry written on the walls in various inconspicuous places. Pieces had to have read my journal to know this work. I didn't remember her reading anything but the "My First Escape" story. Had Pieces read it while I was sleeping? As hard as I tried, I couldn't recall any discussion about London except that Scottie was living there. Had this nagging feeling that I couldn't have been that drunk. But then again, it wasn't something I was used to at the time, drinking forties. And I'd smoked more weed that night than in my entire life.

Alex, the bloke living below me, stopped me on the stairway and asked me the usual: how was I getting on, had I heard from Pieces or Scottie blah-deblah-blah. I bumped into him a lot on the way to work. He always seemed to be just coming in or just leaving.

"Off to work again?" This time he was just arriving.

"Yep," I said, locking the door to my apartment.

"You get good tips there?"

"It's all right, you know, some days better than others."

"Got some extra work, odd-job kinda stuff, if you are interested."

It was the first interesting thing he had ever said to me. Times spent helping my dad tinker around the house came in handy: painting walls, doorways, windowsills, simple plastering. For the stuff I hadn't done before, I used common sense and healthy doses of bull to get through. Sometimes the work was literally shitty. Once I was stuck sucking sewage from some basement flooded with every excremental mix imaginable. Sometimes the odd jobs were absolutely strange. Like the time I had to build the rat cage underneath a health-food shop somewhere on the Lower East Side. I'd never built a rat cage before (which amounted to putting up a wire barrier between the roaming rodents and the stock), but pulled from memories of helping Dad build a fence between ours and the neighbor's yard. I was terrified of seeing the long-tailed creatures, but kept concentrating on the money.

Got my mind on my money, my money on my mind. Though I was prolly more of a Tracy Chapman kinda girl, I couldn't help but rock to *The Chronic*; guilty as I was singing bitches-and-hoes, I enjoyed owning it. I drilled holes.

On my walks home I would play a mixtape made from tapes and CDs found in a box Pieces left behind. Rodney King fresh on the membrane; against probability, the streets in LA were burning. I listened to an eclectic mix, from "Talkin' Bout a Revolution" to Snoop Dogg's "Gin and

Juice" to Bo$$'s "I Don't Give a Fuck" to Sade's "Is It a Crime"; they all made sense. I would play all these homemade tapes on my Walkman. I was tired of waiting for a "revolution" that never came so that I could get the fuck away from the AmeriKKKan crème dream.

Alex paid decently and kept me working. Often gave bonuses. "You like to smoke, right?" he asked, pushing a small but packed plastic bag into my hand.

I spent much of my off time high from his homegrown so I could endure him. He enjoyed watching me work. This was most annoyingly evident one day when he kept hanging around to "supervise" me as I sledgehammered the concrete floor in his bathroom. My job was to find the leak and fix it. It took me a few days to complete the job—one to find the leak, the other to repair it and the mess I created locating it. I'd often catch him watching me sweat from the doorway with a cup of coffee in his hand. I managed to smile at him as I pictured his balls exploding. When I finished this job, I would have enough money to buy a ticket to London.

PART II

*For Colored Girls Who Consider London
When New York Is Enough*

INT. PIECES'S APARTMENT

Skye stands by the door, army duffel stuffed to the brim. She checks her butt bag for her passport and ticket, says goodbye to what had become her home, and exits.

CUT TO:

INT. HALLWAY

Outside the door, Skye hesitates, taking a deep breath, and smiles before skipping down the stairs. Alex comes out of his apartment and watches her jump the last few steps to the bottom. He sighs.

> ALEX
> (whispering)
> Bon voyage.

He pulls out his cell phone, punches in a number. It goes directly to voicemail, so Alex leaves a message.

> ALEX
> Dr. Thomison, Skye has left the building.

I slept through much of my first plane ride like a natural pro, thanks to complimentary wine and whiskey shots. It was a bright June day when we took off. Staring out the window like a kid astounded, I watched New York disappear through the clouds. By the afternoon my stomach was a swirl of excitement—bland, rewarmed chicken tikka, a mélange of drinkable spirits, and the magic brownie Alex had given me, which was just kicking in when *Blade Runner* lit up the communal screen. I fell asleep before the opening credits finished. Before I could blink I was at Heathrow. Clad in army duffel, boots, and cap, I held a postcard between sweaty fingers. Had it folded in my back pocket during the entire five-hour journey. It was the last card I'd received from Pieces and Scottie. A crease dissected a blown-up Union Jack flag. I tried to reorganize my feelings around that symbol, but it stubbornly stood for the slave-owning racist South, no matter the angle. Those who sported the Confederate version of this flag in front of their houses or stuck it inside pickup truck windows weren't exactly allies. But I tried to see it as simply a British flag. Assumed that there were Black born-and-bred British people, though I'd never met one other than Scottie, who was half American. Also there was the butler on the *Fresh Prince*.

Standing in the long and slow-moving immigration line for All Other Non-European Passports, I reread the back of their card. It listed the address of the squat, somewhere in

Brixton, and how to get there. I put the postcard back in my pocket as my turn came up, and stared at my scuffed jungle boots.

The immigration officer looked at the virgin passport and then up at me.

"On holiday?"

"Yes."

"How long do you plan to stay?"

The ticket I bought was an open return. Scottie had advised me to make it clear to the immigrations officer that this was only a short stay.

I put on my best suburban American accent. "Just two weeks. I'm going to visit a friend studying in Oxford."

He stamped my passport, and I found myself on my first excursion through London's "finest" city transport, the tube. It had a very different feel compared to the L in Chicago or the subway in New York, but it immediately settled me. Public transport, no matter the difference from city to city, was public transport, a bunch of strangers pushed together for one common cause: trying to get somewhere.

Took a good look at the Londoners around me, what they wore, how they wore it, what they said, how they said it. The Queen's English was more foreign to my ear than I'd expected. Even the electronic female voice announcing the next stop, "Green Park Station," I found a little difficult to understand. After squinting at the colorful spaghetti-looped map, I decided to change for the Victoria line.

As I got off the train I heard an announcement: "Mind the gap. Please be aware that security cameras are in place at this station for your own protection." Making my way to the blue line that would take me to Brixton, I noticed strategically placed cameras throughout. There seemed to be more than I ever remembered seeing in the metros of Chicago or New York. I wondered why there was such heavy surveillance.

Waiting on the southbound platform, I got my answer.

"Any unattended bags will be confiscated by security. Please alert a member of staff if you see any suspicious unattended items."

As the train pulled into the station, I recalled reading about the IRA and bomb threats that had been occurring here in London. The automated voice over the loudspeaker didn't seem to alarm any of the other people waiting on the platform; everyone seemed to be getting on with it—the announcement was just a part of the London Underground soundtrack. It was a Friday night, and young people were dressed in trendy gear for an evening out clubbing. Laughed and talked in jovial tones. Some already getting lit, passing open cans of beer between them. No need for paper bags to cover the contents. *Dorothy, you are definitely not in Kansas anymore*, I thought to myself as I checked the tube map. Five stops to go. Excited, I reread Scottie and Pieces's postcard.

As I neared their place, I passed a housing estate that resembled a penitentiary, really. A prison block. There was a causeway connecting two buildings below red-tinted security lights. They curved with the corner of the street. There seemed to be only one entrance, and this was barricaded off by gates. Reminded me of some of the projects I had seen in Chi-Town.

Reached the flat at midnight. The thump of heavy bass hit me as I opened the gates and climbed up some creaky wooden stairs. The number 5B stared back in gold-painted metal. I breathed in deeply before knocking on the door. Nerves. It sounded like a party was going on. I wasn't good at the party thing and, after all, barely knew Scottie or Pieces.

If it didn't work out, I guessed I would find out how long my eighty pounds would last. Two hundred American dollars shrunk between beers, two cartons of cigs, a bottle of wine for the squat, and the airport exchange rate. Adjusting the duffel on my shoulder, I started to knock again but realized the door was open.

Unfamiliarly familiar faces greeted me, strangers nodded as if they knew me, all smiles. Just inside the doorway I dropped my bag and rubbed my sore shoulders. Out of the corner of my eye, I spotted Pieces behind two turntables. Her back turned, she was looking through crates of records. Heart pounding, with some effort I picked up the duffel and headed in her direction, pushing through a few dozen sauced but energetic bodies bouncing to a bassy tune. Pieces turned to find me standing in front of the decks. She grinned and gave me a hug.

"Welcome!"

My body relaxed. I barely knew this woman, but this was comfortable. Once released I felt other arms wrap around my waist from behind. Scottie.

"Welcome to Her Majesty's hellish garden." His greeting was a loud whisper in my ear, in time with the thumping music. He planted a wet kiss on my lips. We stood there for a few awkward seconds, grinning at each other before Scottie asked if I wanted a beer or something.

I nodded yes, and watched him as he went off to the kitchen-turned-bar. Another DJ came to relieve Pieces. We looped arms.

"How was your trip?"

I shrugged. "Got here."

"Is that all your luggage?"

She put the bag in Scottie's room. It was bare except for a DIY futon pushed up against a far wall. The mattress for two was propped on top of a flat wooden board, all held up by thick wooden cartons peeking from under a thin knit blanket. She would tell me later that, though Scottie gallantly insisted she take this room, she preferred to sleep in the open, near her work area. She found Scottie's room claustrophobic, and it didn't get good light. I plopped down on his bed, exhausted and more than a little overwhelmed. Pieces smiled wide—that wide smile that came out of nowhere from her typically stony face—and sat down next to me.

She said, "Welcome to the Trashed Palace."

I learned that Scottie had secured what they came to call the "Trashed Palace" before Pieces landed. They'd been planning to use the space for a rave for a while. It was only a one bedroom, but the front room was huge. The perfect dance floor, and the perfect excuse. Pieces pulled off my hat. Medium-sized locs sprang in unruly directions.

"You're looking well."

"So are you." She was. I did notice that she was a little lighter than I remembered her to be. But they say it's often cloudy in London, rains a lot. And she was still Pieces, the woman who, to some degree, remained an enigma to me.

She leaned over and kissed me on the mouth, passing a little tablet with the aid of a very agile tongue. The pill had a bitter taste, which I didn't notice as much as Pieces's tongue halfway down my throat.

I looked at her questioningly. "What was that?"

"Ecstasy. It's a mild one . . . will put you in the love vibe."

I hadn't been talking about the E, though it was my first. But hey, maybe this was the way the locals welcomed folks here. I noticed Pieces's pupils were slightly dilated. Swallowed the pill and started to confess that I didn't . . .

that I had never done anything like that before, but a syncopated knock interrupted my flow.

It was Scottie. In a way I was thankful—in a way. "Come on and join the party," he said. "Can't keep the guest of honor to yourself, Pieces." He handed me a beer and offered his hand to help me up. "Are you hungry? Could make some toast, or—"

"I'm fine," I said and took his hand.

He pulled me up. Our faces no more than six inches apart, I was reminded of how cute Scottie was. His newly grown mustache tickled my top lip as I planted a wet one on his. It restored some equilibrium in me, even if the tingle of Pieces's kiss lingered on my lips, tasting of coco and rum. Could definitely go for some on-the-rebound shag, even though my ex-boyfriend had left my mind long ago. Hormones going haywire, I thought to myself, if this was the "love vibe" Pieces was talking about, then that E was kicking in fast.

Artists of all sorts—musicians, poets, filmmakers, video sluts; some of whom were students and or slackers—moved to hip-hop anthems the DJ deftly mixed with what I soon learned was garage. The E came in gentle waves at first and soon moved through my body, my mouth frozen in a Cheshire cat grin. Scottie tried to introduce me to a few of the multiculti crew, consisting of mostly white people with a healthy sprinkle of African, Asian, Caribbean, and every possible mix. But I didn't get beyond a handshake and a "nice to meet you." I closed my eyes. Opened them. Self-conscious. The thought of looking stupid trumped the urge to move to the bass-driven music. The drugs seemed to have the opposite effect on the others, who were either dancing with abandon or embracing their friends. Heart racing, I felt myself having less control over my jelly-bone body, and

I had never really been comfortable dancing. Whenever I'd made an effort at school events, people would either give me pitying smiles or laugh outright as I awkwardly tried to mimic the latest moves. I felt the desire to escape as quickly as possible.

Headed for the bathroom, found a comfortable horizontal position in the tub. It was all too much. Ecstasy transmitting faint hallucinogenic light shows, a shimmering reflection of the naked low-watt bulb above me.

◎

There was a knock on the door.

"Hey, you okay?" It was Pieces.

Startled, I jumped out of the tub. Scrutinized myself in the bathroom mirror. I had fallen asleep for what felt like seconds, but might have been longer.

Pieces opened the door. "It's okay, everybody's left, you don't have to worry about any maniac fans," she kidded.

I ducked my head as I walked past Pieces, embarrassed to be caught out.

"If you're tired, the bedroll is over there against the wall and we can nick some extra blankets from Scottie's room. He won't be back till tomorrow. Or later today, that is."

"Where'd he go?"

"Out doing his street-minstrel routine."

After sweeping trash to one corner in the flat near the door, Pieces cleared a space on the kitchen-counter-cum-bar and rolled a joint mixed with tobacco.

"What are you doing?" In my short career smoking cannabis, I'd never seen it made this way.

"Skinning up," she said, licking papers together. "Making a spliff."

"A spliff?"

"Yeah, a spliff, a European joint."

"With tobacco?"

"Yeah, with tobacco. You'll get used to it."

I wasn't convinced.

"Believe the Yanks call it 'wake and bake,'" she said, handing over the fat rollie.

"Haven't been to sleep yet," I lied. Gave Pieces a curious look and accepted the spliff. "Anyway, what's up with this Yanks business?"

"I have no allegiances. I come from everywhere, remember?"

"But you were born American, right?"

"What difference does it make?" she said. "Border lines shmorderlines, binary shminary . . ." As she walked across the room, Pieces slipped out of her tank top and baggy, paint-splattered jeans, and tied a piece of brightly dyed cloth around her hips, still nothing on top. She hung a canvas on the wall beside her bedroll. Pulling out melted-down candles, she surrounded the mural in progress. What caught my eye was the snake tattooed around her arm. Remembered the armlet, but the tattoo? I'd sworn she'd had an armlet, but it was probably just the ecstasy and jet lag.

"Tea?" she asked, turning toward me, breaking my train of thought. I noticed myself noticing her nakedness, fascinated with the shape of her nipples as she walked past a few steps to the kitchen. "Do you want some?" she asked.

"What . . . ?"

"Tea," she said, raising an eyebrow.

"Yeah." I got up to follow her. It wouldn't hurt to stay up and chat awhile longer.

"I'll bring it over. Make yourself at home. Take off your boots, and stay awhile."

I pushed my bag against a wall in an inconspicuous corner, pulled out my journal, and considered going to the bathroom to remove my boots. My feet had been sweating profusely the whole journey there, not to mention the whole night long.

"I'm going to the bathroom for a minute."

"If you want a shower, I can get you a towel, but the water is probably cold."

"I just want to use the bathroom, I mean, I have to pee," I clarified, now self-conscious. "Maybe I could have a shower, though . . ."

"Here it's called 'the toilet' or 'the loo' or 'WC'—if you call it 'bathroom,' people will think you wanta get naked," Pieces said, rinsing a coupla mugs. I swore she winked at me.

After using the toilet, I went into the bathroom and turned on the faucet, but the water was freezing. Decided it could wait. "How do you heat up the water?" I asked, coming back to the front room, boots still on.

Pieces was back on her mat with her tea and spliff. "Oh, I just turned it on . . . I'll show you where everything is in the morning, er . . . when we wake up. Your cup is over here. Don't know if you take milk or sugar, but there is no milk or sugar."

I sat uncomfortably on the edge of her mat, knees folded into my chest. Pieces moved over and made room.

"Take your boots off and tell me about your trip. New York's the same as I left it?"

"I think it would be best if I left them on." I pointed to my scruffy shoes. "Maybe after a shower."

"You forget I live with Scottie and his crustoid feet."

"Okay, you've asked for it." I began undoing the laces.

Over tea and the spliff, I caught her up with happenings in NYC and my journey over the waters.

"It was a cinch finding this place though. Helps that it's close to the subway."

"You mean the tube."

"Yeah, the tube, right?" I chuckled. "That's right." Got off on the imagery; kinda sci-fi imagining a train snaking through a see-through tube somewhere in space. "It was way out, man," I said, trying to make a joke out of the Way Out signs. Pieces just stared past me blankly, her mind somewhere else, before passing the spliff. "And also it was weird, I don't think I have ever seen so many surveillance cameras. Has it always been like that?"

"Welcome to Big Brother a decade late." She looked up at me ominously. "Seems like Orwell was not far off the mark—spot on, in fact." She saw my puzzled look and smiled that smile that could make a nightmare seem just fine. "Don't worry, you'll get used to the Queen's Slanglish," she said as if it were an afterthought. Took a sip from her mug.

"Yeah. I guess." I fell back on the bed. "I still can't believe I made it."

"Yeah . . . but I knew you'd come."

"Really? How?"

"I don't know. You wanted to travel, see the world. That's all you talked about when we first met. Remember?"

She moved closer and put the spliff in my mouth before getting up to click off the light in the kitchen. "Scottie and I are chuffed you made it over."

"Yeah?" I said, half to myself. Was wiped. Pieces went to brush her teeth. I rolled on my belly, dug out a pen from my butt bag, and stared at a blank page in my journal. Too much to say. Nothing to say.

"You gonna read me some more'a your stuff?" Pieces returned from the bathroom, yanking me out of a daze.

Face and teeth scrubbed, she smelled of cocoa butter and peppermint.

"Nothing but nonsense. Uninteresting masturbatory ramblings."

"Liked what I read in New York."

"Maybe another time."

"Up to you." She shrugged. "I'm calling it a night. Or morning. You must be knackered as well. Though I thought the least you could do, as I am sharing my bed and my weed, is give us a bedtime poem."

"'Knackered'?" I avoided the issue. The last thing I felt like doing was reading. "What's 'knaaaaaaaackered'?"

"Tired," she said, yawning.

"Oh yeah. I guess I am knaaackered."

"Well, you want a T-shirt or something?"

"S'okay. I've got one."

Within seconds Pieces was under the blankets.

"Good night."

She rolled on her side. I tried to ignore the urge to touch her, ignore the heavy electricity buzzing between us. I stared at the ceiling, finishing my smoke. Curling into a fetal position facing the other way, I could hear Pieces lightly snoring beside me. I eventually drifted off into an uneasy slumber, giving in to the warm waves I assumed were the effects of coming off the pill Pieces had tongued into my mouth earlier.

Walk through the door into a déjà vu snapshot: Pieces stands in a white tank top in front of her canvas, brush stained white. A rhythmic hum escapes from her slightly parted lips. Simultaneously wanting to stay a fly on the wall and eager for her to see me, I freeze. Barely have time to wonder how long she's known I have been standing there when she pulls two fingers through space, wrist solid, gesture precise. Manipulating an invisible cord, she lassos me over to her.

We sit knee to knee on a dirty mattress covering a large square of the broken, cracked black-and-white tiled floor. I sink into the dingy foam, the chipped tiles, the concrete walls, the plumbing, and into her arms. Both on our backs, we stare at the peeling ceiling in silence. After a moment she answers me. Turning her face toward me, she whispers, "Yeah, I am really glad you are here." I turn and find my face centimeters from hers. And just like that, there is no distance at all. We make love and jam on toast.

INT. TRASHED PALACE

Hyped, SCOTTIE opens the door but stops abruptly when he sees PIECES and Skye asleep on the mattress in the front room. A strange look comes over his face, as if he's seen something he's not sure he understands. In another instant he is smiling. He quietly moves closer to them.

S cottie burst through the door with a strum of his guitar, shattering my dream just as Pieces licked the last of the raspberry jam off of my fingers. Wiping sleep from my eyes, I swore if he was the brother I nevah had I would've pushed his face into a toilet bowl by now. Scottie marched over to me before I could follow Pieces's lead and gracefully duck under the sheets. He planted wet kisses on my mouth and both of my cheeks, thin hair over his lip tickling my nose.

"And how is Your Highness finding it at the Trashed Palace?" Scottie inquired with a flourish of his arm, in a faux-posh British accent. "I trust your trip has been satisfactory thus far?"

"Mmmhmm," I managed, the room slowly coming into focus.

"And I am pleased to see that you seem to have made yourself quite at home." Scottie removed the guitar from his shoulder. Both Pieces and I ignored him. "Everything that is ours is yours; by all means, help yourself," he said, as if it could not be helped.

I wasn't sure what he meant but blushed anyway.

Pieces blanched. "Do you ever talk about things that you know about? I thought we agreed that you would leave your minstrel show out on the streets."

He responded by emptying his pockets with flagrant flamboyance. Sounds of coppers, silvers, and the occasional gold splashing against the wooden counter shook the remaining sleep from my eyes. "Made enough for the pasta, some vino, and—"

"I've got cigarettes." I stretched toward my bag, eager to be more bearer than burden.

"Give us a fag, then." Scottie dug through his pockets.

"A fag?"

"Yeah, that's Scottie for ya." Pieces sat up and yawned.

This time Scottie ignored Pieces, directing his energy at me. "You are in England now. It's time to learn English," he said, looking part court jester, part lecturer, misshapen Afro framing his salty, baked-bread-brown face. "'Fags' are slang here for 'cigarettes.'" Out of the lint in his leather jacket pocket he pulled an array of half-smoked butts with one or two mashed new ones, presenting the pile to me as if it were found treasure.

"That's okay," I said, rummaging through my backpack. "I'll stick to my fresh new American cigarettes." I opened the pack. "You sure you don't want one of these?"

"Maybe for later." He tucked one behind his ear. "But I prefer the recycled flavor," he said, emptying what was left of the scavenged butts onto an extra long, extra slim rolling paper.

"You smell recycled, mate," Pieces jibed, walking past us with jeans on and a white towel around her neck. "You can hop in the shower first, Skye, while I brush my teeth."

I got up and unpacked and repacked the stuff in my bag slowly, purposely, after finding my toothbrush. I took my time, was shy about getting undressed in front of Pieces and also felt a little out of sorts. It was already somewhere in the middle of late afternoon and early evening in London. Too early for dinner, but at home it woulda been just around lunchtime. I hadn't eaten since the plane.

"I'll have food ready when you're done," Scottie called

after me as I headed to the shower, as if reading my mind. "I hope pasta is all right . . . Otherwise, we can have pasta."

Our collective budget was tight, so from the day I landed I would find that "pasta" was our mantra. The meal of the day. With garlic and olive oil. Maybe some tuna and cheese on a good day. It was usually either that or beans on toast for the all-day breakfast effect. But what we ate really didn't matter; we would always make it into a party, a feast. And we were always laughing. Everything seemed perfect. We always managed to find a spliff or a bottle of cheap red.

That first day at the palace I slurped the noodles down like they were some gourmet dish, watching Scottie roll up from a healthy stash.

"Where did you get that?" Pieces asked as she started to clear the table.

"From Prof, as usual," Scottie said. "He is a generous man."

"Just be careful, Scottie." Pieces put the dishes into the sink and ran water over them. "That's all I can and will say."

"'*Will* say' is what I'm worried about," Scottie shot back. "When are you going to trust me? Prof is okay. A good geezer . . ."

Pieces sucked her teeth.

After our early Saturday-evening brunch, Scottie and Pieces decided to give me a tour of the neighborhood. Took me through the arcade entrance on Coldharbour Lane, into a maze of stalls, shops, and food stops. People sold everything from fresh fish to five lighters for a pound. Eyes wide, I was immersed in color: Brown faces bantering and bartering, a red-and-yellow sea of African peppers next to mounds of fat, shedding white garlic next to green and yellow bananas next to bright lemons and limes, oranges, pears, cherries, and avocados.

A Scottish family kitted up in white aprons, plastic gloves, and galoshes gutted and decapitated fresh snapper, cod, salmon, mackerel, catfish, tuna, and a whole load of other fish I had no names for. African and Afro-Caribbean folk stood in line in front of fresh fruit and veg stands, testing the peppers and plantains for firmness.

We strolled through the arcade, around the various stalls in the outside market. Stands selling videos: martial-arts films alongside classics with "Black" themes, from *The Harder They Come* to *New Jack City*. Next door, a dreaded man in a blue Yankees baseball cap stood behind a table covered with homemade CDs: reggae mixes, bootleg R&B latest. Playing out of his boom box, a sample of his wares put a backing track to the English farmer trying to hawk the last bits: "Box of seedless grapes one pound. One pound for a box of ripe strawberries. Two pound for a box of strawberries and a box of fresh ripe grapes! Two pound, two pound, two pound for two!"

Not far down from him, a caramel-colored young man clad in black combats, small Muslim hat, stood hands behind his back, speaking softly to the friend next to him. Their table was covered in pamphlets on Islam, oils, incense, and double-A batteries.

Scottie noticed me staring at a jungle hat displayed in the window of a secondhand army supply store. He took the worn and ratty one off my head and said he'd meet me in a bit at the café across. Pieces decided to join him. I waited. They came back within minutes, minus my old hat; Scottie was wearing a new one.

"I just traded it in," he said, placing it on my head and winking.

"Otherwise known as a five-finger discount," said Pieces in that dead-bored tone of hers.

"Instant karma," said Scottie. "They charge way too much for their gear."

"Order me a peppermint tea. What do you want, Skye?" Pieces seemed nonplussed by Scottie's antics, was giving him the seen-it-all-before look. I asked for a cappuccino.

"Must admit it was pretty impressive that he could just walk right out the shop wearing it . . . It's not like he blends in or anything," I said to Pieces. It seemed to me that Scottie must have been some kind of magician to get away with that.

"The best way to steal is to do it right in front of their eyes." She yawned. "Oldest trick in the book."

Scottie came back with our drinks and a white tea for himself. I offered to give him some change, but he waved it away.

"Told my friend Trent that this was your first coffee in London so it better be good." He added loads of sugar to his tea as he spoke. "Besides, it was free. I told him that if he wasn't nice to me I'd play my guitar in here." He laughed at his own joke. I smiled. Pieces looked resigned.

The three of us sat, not saying much for a while; sipped drinks, watched various people pass through the arcade. Sandwiched between Scottie and Pieces, I doodled in my journal. Scottie absentmindedly strummed his guitar. The café was packed with people now; a low rumble of considerate conversation cushioned the room.

Try as he might, Scottie couldn't resist the ready-made audience. He kicked into a song, a play on Mr. Rogers's "Won't You Be My Neighbor?"

Pieces stared ahead, looking annoyed.

"You guys get Mr. Rogers here?" I asked, admiring his nerve.

"No, watched reruns of it while I was in the States,"

Scottie said, continuing his song until one of the waitrons interrupted. Reminded him of the deal he made with Trent at the counter.

"You know the rules," she said, taking our empty mugs. Pieces shot Scottie a look and he pulled his guitar off his shoulder.

"Sometimes my hands have a mind of their own." Scottie smiled, but it seemed to wane against the tense silence that ensued.

A little wired on caffeine, I blurted out, "So where to next?"

"Yeah, what are we waiting on? We should move out," Scottie echoed.

"For Godot." Pieces lit the last cigarette, crumpled the empty box in her hand.

"'Godot'?" This conversation was either strange or I'd missed the point.

"Yeah, the geezer that never comes," Scottie explained. He leaned close to me, making circular motions near his temple and pointing to Pieces. He whispered, "Don't worry, she's usually better after she takes her medication."

"It's you that put me on the meds, mate." Pieces shrugged on her jacket. "Honestly Scottie, why do you always have to be such a show-off." We followed Pieces out of the café. Scottie, bringing up the rear, shouted goodbye to his mate at the counter. I stared at Pieces curiously, wondering what was going on between them. Guessed it just wasn't her style to be much impressed with anything or anyone, certainly not Scottie.

By that point it was getting late. Remnants of the day—empty boxes, slightly damaged fruit and veg—lined the curb as people slowly began to break down shop for the night. We cut across Electric Avenue, down Brixton Road past the police station. I popped into a corner bodega, which Scottie called an "offie," to buy some beer for the road at his suggestion. Outside I saw Pieces and Scottie at the bus stop talking to this skinhead, suspenders hanging from jeans tucked into his Doc Martens boots. I walked cautiously toward them, trying to suss if there was any trouble. He wore the uniform of disenchanted racist youth of the seventies and eighties, their violent distastes for anything non-Anglo known across the globe. But this skinhead was evidently a friend. He was telling them about the sound system playing at the Subterranean that evening. Had one free pass, which got two in. He couldn't make it.

"What are we gonna do with only two tickets?" asked Pieces after their friend boarded the 133.

"Could sell it. Be a shame though. King Dub is a nice system . . ." Scottie studied the free pass for the club in West London.

"Why not just show up and see what we can do," Pieces suggested, taking a swig from the newly opened can of beer. "Besides, it's Skye's first Saturday night in London!" She passed me the brew.

"Feeling restless, darlin'?" Scottie teased Pieces.

I cut in, trying to diffuse the tension. "I don't mind not going if you guys wanna go . . . I mean, I am a little exhausted . . . jet lag and all." I handed the can of beer to Scottie after taking a sip.

"Bollocks." Pieces put her arm around my shoulder. "You are too young to be worn-out already." She checked an invisible watch, then looked up at the sky. "The sun hasn't even gone down yet." She took the beer from Scottie.

"Well, I could get some cash from home. 'Sides, I am a little hungry." I studied my shoes and contemplated my next move, and right in between two well-worn boots, I spotted a shiny pound coin, as if some fairy had just dropped it there.

"Enough for a bag of chips! See, your powers spiritual manifest. Forget about going back, let us take you out," Scottie said, offering to go into the chip shop. He knew the manager and thought he could probably get a little something extra.

"Scottie's right, though," Pieces said, leaning up against the wall outside the chippie. "I do feel like something good is gonna happen. Maybe it's your friend Sincara come to look after us . . ."

I checked the tattoo on her arm again.

"Hey, didn't you used to have an armlet like that?"

"It's a good 'too, innit?" Pieces lit a rollie. "I got it done somewhere in North London. Yeah, I did have an armlet but I lost it. Can't remember where or how." She looked momentarily puzzled; she hesitated, a strange uncomfortable thought flickered across her face. "Probably somewhere in New York."

I frowned. "Didn't think it would be something you would ever take off."

Pieces shrugged her shoulders as Scottie returned with a large portion of chips and a chicken breast. In front of us, a gang of pigeons attacked a split paper full of soggy fried potatoes. Munching away, we three sauntered toward the tube station.

The evening was fattening up. Masses of people spilled from the carriages, so it was easy to skate behind ticket holders through the barriers at Notting Hill Gate. Heart pounding, I followed Pieces and Scottie's lead. They were experts at the craft of dodging fares, and schooled me on how to use the dud pass I carried just in case the guards were looking. Climbed the stairs up to street level into bright and vibrant nightlife: double-decker buses, headlights and back lights lining up on opposite sides of the road, streetlamps, vehicles, and streams of people—the swift bustle and stroll— some running to catch buses and others in no hurry to get anywhere.

We walked down Portobello Road to Tavistock Square and decided to hang there for an hour or so before checking the situation at the club. With the change we found on the tube seats after people had vacated the train we bought some alcohol, and still had enough to get home later. We sat on a stoop and popped open our beers. It had been a good day. As a trio we kept finding what we needed. Scottie, much to Pieces's irritation, kept going on about it.

"I'm telling you, together we can do anything," he said and strummed his guitar. "This is only the beginning." Scottie began to croon to a reggae riff.

"Can you play something on that?" A man with small demi-locs came up to us in the square.

"What's it worth to ya?" was Scottie's immediate and practiced reply.

"Russel! Man, how ya doing?" Pieces got up and gave him a hug. It lingered.

"Yeah yeah yeah, P! What's up with you? Long time no see . . . Didn't know you were back."

Pieces did the introductions. "Yeah, you know Scottie," she said. "And this is Skye." I shook hands with him. Russel and Scottie unenthusiastically nodded in each other's directions. Pieces walked a ways with Russel, leaving Scottie and I leaning against the concrete wall in front of a stack of council flats.

"Who is he?" I ventured curiously, wincing a little inside as he put his arm around her waist.

"An ex of hers," he replied with distaste. "Not worth the air she breathes."

I felt myself agreeing. He didn't look her type. I didn't know Russel, barely knew Pieces, but just from looking, wasn't surprised they were now exes.

The sun was an hour down. A few drummers still played in the square, but the stands once selling jewelry and other crafts had long packed it in. Scottie strummed a light rhythm on the guitar. I breathed in the fresh air and watched people walk by, sit, and hang out in the square. Many of them had locs. For the first time in a while I felt like I didn't stand out so much. I'd started growing locs in Chicago. Had been secretly not combing my hair my last days in St. Louis, hiding it under a hat. Once I made it to Chicago, Damian took me to a Black hairdresser in the South Side who twisted the already knotting hair. The twists didn't stay though. I didn't maintain them. Thought the point was to let hair do its own thing.

Pieces came back all smiles. "Guess what? Russel works the door at the Subterranean, so we can all get in."

"See, the power of three manifests again!" exclaimed Scottie. His glee was infectious. Even Pieces's glare didn't seem quite as harsh as he began to play a version of a topical De La Soul song. *Three, I said three, I said three . . . three is the magic number.*

I grinned cheek to cheek.

◎

The dance floor was hot and crammed with bodies dark, light, and every shade in between, dancing to the tunes a DJ spun from the stage at the front of the club. Most people rocked on the edges of the dance floor, leaving a few hardcore fans screaming "Tune! Tune!" to each new disc the DJ slid on the decks.

Scottie and I joined them, leaving Pieces to chat up Russel, which meant free drinks all night long. I swayed, feeling the music on the dance floor. Scottie pranced around, looking a little lost without his guitar. I caught up to him and offered him some of my beer, as his was running on empty. I asked him if he was okay. He seemed agitated.

"Absolutely splendid," he said dryly, then took a gulp of my beer and looked anxiously toward the door. "Did you see how the ignoramus at the door handled my guitar, as if it was trash? It better be in the same condition I left it."

"Hey," I tried to console him, "it'll be fine! Don't worry about it, enjoy the music, the free booze." I held up the nearly empty bottle.

"That's okay, you finish. It's getting stuffy in here," he said, walking away. "I'm going outside to see if I can blag a smoke, maybe strum up some change so I can buy my *own* beer."

Not long after that, he got into a fight with security. He tried to claim his guitar on his way out for some fresh air.

"You take your guitar with you, you can't come back in here," said the bouncer.

"What do you mean, I can't come back in here?"

"If you leave, you're gone," he said in a thick Jamaican accent.

Just then a few people he'd seen in the club earlier came back onto the premises.

"What about them, star?" Scottie said.

"Nevah mind them."

After that things escalated. In the end security finished it by throwing Scottie his guitar, yelling something about batty-man bumble clot get th' something-something outta my establishment. I had a hard time understanding him, but could tell that he was cussing Scottie down to the ground, and attempted to reason with the muscle-necked brother at the door. Both of us were kicked out.

We hopped on an N12 bus and walked from Camberwell to the Trashed Palace. Did my best to calm Scottie down on the way home. He wanted to go back to the club and insist that they let us inside. Trying to divert his attention, I asked him how he and Pieces met. That seemed to focus him, his face turned all nostalgic.

"I'd just gotten my first acoustic, new strings and all that. They—she and Russel—were sitting outside a bar. Pieces was more than a little off her face, pissed. I'd just watched her down the last shot of a long line of shots. 'Give us a song,' she said. So I did, but Russel was sour grapes the whole time. Pieces didn't care. She liked my lyrics. We chatted awhile. I gave her my number. We clicked, you know . . . like you

and I did on the Greyhound. Just easy. Made Russel green."
Turns out they'd hooked up at some point in London, and
Scottie decided to go to America with Pieces to check the
country out.

I could only take his word for it, but in the short time I'd
seen them together, could tell there was something between
Pieces and Scottie. Something intense. Something unsaid.
Though I didn't want to be on the wrong side of Pieces's
sarcasm, I envied their closeness. Could see how Russel
would as well.

We made it home to find Pieces mashed into Russel
against the wall near the door. She took her time before
slowly coming up for air and acknowledging us.

"He was just going," she said without an ounce of embarrassment. Russel and Scottie stared each other down
seconds before the demi-dreads took off, nodding goodbye to me.

"Nice to meet you," he said, blanking Scottie before heading down the stairs.

"'Nice to meet you,'" Scottie mimicked Russel. He took
his guitar off his back. "Never *could* see what you saw in
that wanker."

Pieces snickered in Scottie's face, more than a little
drunk.

"Oh, Scottie Scottie Scottie! Are we feeling a wee bit jeal-
ous? It's okay, sweetheart, I can share, I think the tongue of
some strong African buck down your throat could do you
some good."

I went to the fridge for a beer left over from the party the
night before. Scottie overdramatized his disgust.

"Anyway . . . why do you always have to act like a spoiled
brat?" Pieces joined me in popping open a beer with her
lighter. "Russel drove me here as soon as we heard what

happened at the club . . . Scottie, why do you have to always be so extra?"

"I don't understand why you insist on being such a slag." Scottie was in the toilet, gallons of pee splashing into the bowl.

A half smile formed on Pieces's face. "You'd think he was my wife or something." Clearly blitzed, she made slow movements. Pieces made her way to the toilet door and yelled, "Come on, hubby, we mustn't argue in front of the kid." Rubbed me the wrong way how she referred to me as if I were much younger, but I tried to make light of it. Feebly.

"All right, Grandma."

Pieces laughed, pushing buttons and enjoying it, then sauntered over to me and put her arm around my shoulder. "Skye. Sweetie. Babe. Didn't mean to hurt your feelings; you ARE getting to be a big girl, traveling the big wide world and all."

I shrugged her away. "Ha. ha."

Scottie came out of the toilet. "Don't let her get to you."

"Listen, lighten up, it WAS a joke and both of you are taking yourselves waaaay too seriously."

She swallowed what was left in her bottle and went to kiss "hubby" on the cheek.

I went to the toilet to release the beer bloating my bladder. It was one of those long ones. Gave me time to think. Sure, Pieces was drunk, but she didn't have to talk to me like that.

There was a knock on the door. "Come on Skye, I gotta go."

"It might take a while!" I yelled through the closed door. "I'm only now just learning to wipe my ass."

"Oh-ho!" Pieces laughed. "Put a lil alcohol in you and Ms. Suburbia turns boom banshee. Don't worry, I'll go piss in the baaathroom." She sounded like a sheep baying as she took the mick out of my accent.

I pulled up my trousers, brushed my teeth, and did all the rest of the before-bed routine, fuming the entire time. "How dare she call me 'Ms. Suburbia,'" I said under my breath, looking for dental floss. By the time I'd finished, both Scottie and Pieces had passed out. Scottie had put out a foam mattress for me and some worn but clean sheets. Earlier they'd designated a corner that would be my room. I lived behind a bookshelf made of stacked crates. Over a wooden bar hung a cloth, creating another wall. I took out a ragged copy of *On the Road* I'd found in Pieces's New York library from my bag along with a few clothes, and began folding them. And then something flittered to the floor.

It must have fallen out of one of my pockets; the folded card was stuck together. It had survived the wash, by the looks of it. I carefully opened it. Could just about make out the words *Remember . . . TAMT = The All Mighty They are watching*. It looked like Pieces's handwriting and sounded like something she might come out with, but I couldn't remember how I'd gotten it. Quickly decided it was just one of Pieces's cryptic jokes that I'd forgotten about that evening we spent getting wrecked in New York.

INT. TRASHED PALACE - AFTERNOON
Pieces and Scottie are in the kitchen having a
heated discussion.

Pieces paces furiously around the room, holding
her middle finger up to the camera and each of
the walls.

Scottie can hear someone approaching the door.
He grabs Pieces's shoulders to calm her and
puts his finger to his lips.

A moment later Skye walks in.

There was some unspoken contract between the three of us: we were creating the alternative family story. Pieces was the reluctant Morticia Cleaver, I was the rebelling *Leave It to Beaver*, Scottie was Rasta-fonzie cum laude in our alternative happy, dazed monsters scenario. Pieces and Scottie were more sarcasm than sweetness, and in order to stifle my imminent belligerence I held my breath, a well-learned skill, a pre-battle tactic to avoid immediate confrontation, if at all possible. To check the lay of the land from above.

The afternoon following the Russel and Pieces episode, we didn't really say much to one another until after our first coffee and spliff. Pieces and Scottie acted as if nothing out of the ordinary had happened and I decided I shouldn't be so sensitive. Pieces had only been teasing. Friends tease each other.

"Had a really cool time yesterday . . . Thanks for the tour," I said.

"Thank *you*, madam." Scottie's voice, still scratchy. "You made us three a holy trinity, it's the power that happens when—"

"Yeah yeah yeah," Pieces interrupted. "But I got some news. I might have a job." She got up from her stool to put the kettle on for a second round of instant coffee. "Won't know for sure until next week or so, but I got inside info that a space might be opening at the pub on Portobello."

"Cool," I managed, not quite sure why I felt disappointed.

"Yeah." Pieces looked at me. "Russel works there and he is leaving for Holland soon, so I could take his place."

Scottie was tuning a new string on his guitar. He purposely let it go sour before bringing it in line. "That's good news, but what about this week? We need cash now. Why don't you both come out with me this evening. Maybe we could do something."

"Like what?" I asked. "I don't play an instrument. 'Sides . . . I got a little bit of cash and—"

"You could do your poetry," Scottie cut in.

"No way!" I passed the spliff to Pieces. "I don't *do* poetry, I just write it."

"I'm not up for that today," Pieces concurred. "I say we relax . . . There's beer, there's smoke, there's food in the fridge . . ."

"If you want to call cheese and bread 'food.'" Scottie fixed the last string of his Yamaha and plucked it soundly.

◎

For the next couple of weeks we three went nearly every-where together. Russel's trip to Holland was delayed. Pieces's job would probably come through soon but until then, with no money to do much of anything else, sometimes we did nothing but just hang out. Bored and absolutely skint, we'd sit on a park bench or at a train stop or wher-ever. Just sat there. Did nothing, just waited. Scottie would pick at the skin around his fingernails. Pieces would move from bench seat to bench back, jump off, and pace around, before coming to straddle the bench again. She called this game "waiting for Godot." Since the café, it had become a theme. Usually we were actually waiting for someone, or something, like a train or a bus. Sometimes I would forget why we were sitting where we were sitting. I was ready to jump on any train I happened by. Scottie seemed resolute, as if waiting were an inevitable consequence of life. Pieces seemed very close to giving up on Godot altogether.

I never imagined London having so many parks. In almost every borough there was a bit of green and a bench to sit on and just watch the world go by. One day we were sitting in Kennington Park hoping to catch Scottie's friend Prof and score something smokable. We three had been waiting there for a while—the twenty minutes had turned into forty and then before long, an hour had gone by. It was an unusually sunny day for the last days of spring in this famously gray city, and I was content to write while Scottie worked out chords on his guitar, but Pieces was getting more and more agitated. On top of everything, Scottie had also somehow managed to lose his keys. Pieces now held the sole copy.

"We should really get a copy of these keys made," Pieces had said earlier that afternoon, plopping down after pacing around the bench we shared. "I got other things I could be doing than waiting around here."

I pulled my head out of my journal long enough to nod in agreement, though in reality I had nothing better to do. But there was a part of me that wanted to let them know I was independent, that I didn't need babysitting, that I might have my own plans.

We sat around, saying more of not much, until Scottie broke in with a slowly dawning epiphany.

"Yeah." His forehead wrinkled as if he was trying hard to figure something out. He snapped his fingers. "I am going to go and get a copy of the keys made."

Pieces looked at him and hesitated before digging in her pocket.

"Now? You've got cash to do that?"

"Don't worry, woman. I know what I'm doing."

"Right." Pieces eyed him and put the keys in his hand. "But come straight back. I don't want to be stranded here."

"I'm just going across to the key cutters next to the station and back again."

After a while, a guy with a just-woke mass of dark hair and a ring through his eyebrow happened by with some gear and a message from Scottie.

"He told me to tell you to meet him at my squat. He'll be back in an hour." Danny was his name.

"Where's your place again?" Pieces asked. She seemed to know him. "We'll be around in a bit if we don't catch Scottie."

"Suit yourself." He shrugged, passed us a tiny block of black hashish, and told her the address. "There's no buzzer so you'll have to yell up . . ."

"Fine," Pieces said. Once Danny left, she got up and headed out of the park toward the station. "I want to get home, or at least get you home. There's no point hanging out in Danny's den of death if we don't have to."

"If you have plans, I will be all right on my own, ya know."

Pieces ignored me. I followed her to the Oval station and waited while she made the call to Scottie's pager. We camped out at the phone for a while to see if he would return the call. After about thirty minutes Pieces called again, leaving another curt message: "Meet us in the park as originally planned, Scottie."

We shared a beer and a smoke, and waited. Talked about this and that; I filled her in on my time at Margville. Pieces doubled over when I imitated Toney, fist raised, chanting, "Sistahs doin' it for themselves."

"Yeah, I can just imagine it . . . They're all right, those lot . . . Some cool people come in there too."

I told her about the other jobs I did for Alex downstairs.

"That was wicked luck . . . finding that little extra," Pieces said.

"Yeah, I guess I was really meant to be here."

Pieces shot me a look that I couldn't decipher. "Yeah. Seems that way."

A chipped crescent blinked down at us from the sky, upstaging the streetlamps and random car lights. We stared at it for a beat or two of silence. Pieces asked me if I'd seen Sincara lately.

"The story," she said. "The one you called 'My First Escape' . . . it's stuck with me. Somehow I feel as if this tattoo is Sincara, and what you saw that day was real."

"That was some strong stuff." I remembered pulling on the pregnant joint in the New York studio. "But maybe it was you psyching me out, remember? 'Three coughs . . .'"

"'. . . And you're off.'" She chuckled.

"Yeah yeah yeah . . . Why do you always have to make fun of me?"

"I don't know, sometimes it's just too irresistible." After a second, Pieces leaned toward me, as if speaking discreetly in a crowded bar. "When was the last time you saw that snake armlet, anyway?"

"On your arm."

"Where this tat is now, right?"

"Yeah, don't you remember?"

"Weird." Pieces hopped onto the peeling wooden bench and sat on the back. "You didn't see it anywhere around the flat?"

"No. Why?"

Pieces, deep in thought, didn't answer right away. She

shook her head and inhaled slowly, exhaling through rounded lips, as if attempting to control her breathing. She then looked at me for a brief forever-second, as if trying to read me.

"It's been kinda fucking with my head. Like with a lot of things that happened before leaving New York, it's foggy. I don't ever remember taking it off." She looked gone for a moment.

"Yeah, weird, right?" I geared up to tell her that I'd also felt like I'd blanked on a lot of things that happened that night before she left. But before I could get the words out, she looked down at me and said, "Anyway, the armlet was a gift from a friend of mine that lives in Amsterdam." A slight smile softened her face. "Yeah, Eddie. She'd kill me if I lost it."

"Yeah? What's she like?" Anybody connected to that armlet and Pieces, I wanted to know about.

"You'll meet her sometime," she said, her mood getting lighter. "Hey! Maybe we could all take a trip down to Amsterdam together."

"Amster-amster-dam-dam-dam . . ." I began singing the summer-camp song that kids only sang when no adults were around. "They all went down to Amster"—at that moment I felt a bullet of bird shit land on my jungle hat—"damn!"

Pieces was rolling, nearly hiccupping with laughter. "You . . . you need help," she said. I smiled. I had to admit I was pleased that Pieces was finally confiding in me. And being there in the park with her, it felt like when we were together in New York. I was perfectly happy to sit there all night, but it was getting late. And still no Scottie.

"That lil shit better have a good explanation." Pieces flipped her cigarette into the darkness.

"Maybe the lil shit is waiting for us at Danny's?" I suggested.

She reluctantly led the way there.

Thick, musty, stagnant air filled our nostrils as we entered the freshly liberated squat near the Oval. The three-story flat had been boarded up for a while. Furniture, books, china, bedspread all sat frozen in time. Would have thought someone had just left to pick up a pint of milk if everything hadn't been caked in dust.

Scottie wasn't there and evidently hadn't been around. A group of punk crusties slumped in the front room, zoning to some trance music. We sat with them for a while and shared a smoke and small talk. It was hard to tell, as there was very little light, but the place seemed to have missed soap and a mop for decades . . . It smelled of mold. The crust-ies slouched, facing one another on two identical leather sofas; they were good quality, but were cracked, worn thin with age and use. In the middle was a thick, see-through glass table; emptied beer cans, bottles, smoked butts had been kicked underneath, covering a matted, dingy carpet whose true colors were indecipherable. A sole dusty light bulb hanging precariously from some twisted-together wires dimly lit the front room.

I whispered in Pieces's ear, "Was the Trashed Palace this mashed up when Scottie found it?"

"According to him it was just a little dusty, but since I've been back, I've made him take out about two dozen trash bags full of shit . . . the lil shit."

"Wonder what happened to him, anyway . . ."

"Don't know. Don't care. We are going back home, even if we have to re–break in to the place. I'm not staying in this dump."

One of the squatters tried to pass us a freshly rolled joint.

"No thanks," Pieces said, standing up.

I watched her pace the room over the clutter of odds and ends while I hit the spliff. I was cool. Enjoying myself.

"I wanna stay. I think Scottie will show up eventually." I was too stoned to move.

Pieces looked at me like I was mad and shook her head.

"Hey, I'll be all right. I know how to get back if he doesn't show up here." My eyes were slits.

"It's up to you." Pieces's face was close to mine. "But be careful smoking that shit. I hear rats like the sweet smell of hash oil on human skin." With that, she marched out the door.

I stayed up chatting a bit with Dan, or rather listening to him go on about squatters' rights, and how tough it was right now with regentrification of the area . . . which then moved into his ambitions of having a pot garden in the attic of this house. After the fifth spliff, feeling comatose, I started to fall asleep on the sofa but found out it was someone else's bed. I asked Dan if there was someplace I could crash for a minute. I couldn't face the walk back to the palace.

"Sure, mate, no problem, there's a spare on the top floor. Buzz is out for the night. Take his space."

Found the naked, mangy mattress in a closet-sized room situated next to the toilet. It was well used. A gray duvet, little more than two rags sewn together, lay like a twisted corpse on top. Hard to tell if it was clean but it smelled like the rest of the house. Stale. I pulled up my hood and curled up on the bed.

Tried to get comfortable but the stuff Pieces said about hash oil and rats was on repeat in my head. For most of the night, eyes wide, ears perked alert, I was convinced I heard the pitter-patter of little rodent claws scurrying over the unidentifiable rubbish surrounding the mattress.

What felt like minutes into a restless sleep, Dan nudged me awake.

"Thought you might like to join me for a cuppa, mate."

In the daylight I realized I'd walked over layers of cigarette butts, bits of paper, what looked like a condom, an old, empty, and yellowing syringe, an orange peel, flattened beer cans, soiled tissues—and suddenly a whoosh of stink burned my nostrils, making my nose screw.

"What is that?"

"The toilet doesn't flush," Dan explained through a yawn. "The only running water is from a tap outside . . . Someone couldn't be arsed this morning to go out and fill the bucket."

I joined him for tea out in the fresh air. Neither one of us said much. Both just waking up, but it wasn't long before we made breakfast out of another European spliff. Pieces was right. I was getting used to it.

Glassy-eyed, full of tea and biscuits, I decided to head out and make my way to the Trashed Palace.

"Welcome to London, mate," Dan cheered me as I left the stoop. "Say hi to Scottie for me. Tell 'im I said you guys should throw another party. The last one was wiiicked!"

I slowly walked back, enjoying the morning air, remembering the party at the palace when I first arrived. Dan had said he didn't see me there. I didn't tell him that I'd spent most of the time in the bathtub staring at a light bulb. But it was a good idea to have another party. Scottie was right. We could charge at the door and make a little dough doing what we liked to do. By the time I got to the palace I was high off optimism.

"Hey, guys!" I said, bursting through the door. Under the gravity of the silence, my excitement landed on the floor with a thud. Scottie had his hands on Pieces's shoulders. She shrugged them off. Ignoring me, she went to put some water on the boil for pasta.

"What. The. Fuck. Were. You. Thinking. Scottie," Pieces barely got out through clenched teeth.

Scottie said nothing, increasing Pieces's fury. I don't think I had ever seen her face so red.

"Just give me the keys. I need to get some air," she said.

"I don't have the keys."

"What?" Pieces spun around.

"Prof is on his way with them."

"What is Prof doing with—"

"He knew a man who could get them cut for free, someone who owed him a favor. Enough sets for each of us plus an extra set so we won't have to go through this the next time."

"'The next time'? I'm not gonna be here the next time . . . I'm sick of it, Scottie. Your little stories used to be cute but now they are getting old." Pieces sat down on a stool near the counter. "Why didn't you just tell us you were going to meet Prof?" She glanced at me and then back directly into his eyes.

"That's the beauty of it—I ran into him outside the tube station." Scottie looked away, revving himself up to tell his tale. "My first plan was to play a song for the cutter and see if he would let me owe him the money for the copy. He likes my stuff. But then I ran into Prof and—"

"And what? He had a lil present for you? Where is Prof coming from now?"

"Victoria station. He should reach any minute," Scottie said, cutting his story short. "I'll go outside and wait for him."

After he left I tried to change the subject, lighten the mood.

"Man, that was a mad evening."

"'Mad' is not the word, Skye," Pieces said. "I can't even begin to tell you . . ." A mix of exasperation and anger slid across her face. "Look, at the moment I just don't feel like talking, okay?"

"Okay." I nodded and went to join Scottie outside the flat.

Scottie's head was down, and he was picking the skin around his fingernails. He must have felt me approaching, 'cause when I got near, he lifted his head to reveal a sheepish smile, like a puppy caught crapping on the living room carpet.

"Look, I'm sorry about last night, I just—" he began.

"Shit happens," I said. In my mind, it had been an adventure. Even sleeping in the squalid squat was something new. Something I could say I did. It wasn't that bad; I met new folks, had a laugh. Besides, got a chance to hang with Pieces, just the two of us. I sat down next to him. "Who is this Prof character, anyway?"

On cue, a stringy-haired white dude, face covered in a long, gray-speckled beard and John Lennon sunglasses, appeared leaning on a wooden walking stick. I had to blink twice. Could hear a strain of a Jefferson Airplane tune as he approached, smiling. He was a sixties flick made flesh. He reached into his paisley waistcoat and presented to us, as if by magic, three shiny sets of keys along with the old one. Scottie stood up to greet him. Somehow the two complemented each other. Scottie in jeans and matching waistcoat, bare chest a smooth backdrop to the silver dog tags; Prof, with his patterned silk vest and leather trousers, also had a chain round his neck. Something heavy, most likely a timepiece, hidden behind the buttons of his waistcoat. Prof and

Scottie would almost be the same height if Scottie's Afro hadn't been canerowed, as he sometimes wore it.

Prof looked at me through his sunglasses. His stare was warm.

As Scottie introduced us, Pieces lurched out the door of our squat, grabbed a set of keys, and marched down the lane without saying a word.

"Want some grub, Prof?" Scottie offered.

"No thanks . . . Always get the feeling Pieces is not too keen on me," he said, giving Scottie a hug and slipping something into his pocket. "But call me and let me know how things go?"

Later, over an earlyish dinner, Pieces and Scottie barely said two words to each other. I tried to diffuse the situation.

"I guess I better find a job before I turn into a noodle," I said, slurping one through olive-oiled lips. "Pasta's good but . . . ?"

Both Pieces and Scottie managed a chuckle.

"I know what you mean," Pieces said, putting down her fork. "In fact, Skye, there is a woman I know that might need some work done. Gennie Jah. She works on All Saints Road, in West London. Rasta woman. She has a bookstore that also sells all kinds of Afrocentric stuff. You're always hanging out in those stores anyway. Maybe you could help her out, or something."

I brightened up. By this point I was broke. Skint. My stash dried up on a rapid.

"I'll introduce you," she said. "I know her from when I first passed through London."

"And if that doesn't work out, you'll find something.

Don't worry," Scottie said, stuffing his mouth with spaghetti. "Otherwise I might have to put you out on the street."

"Too late, you already did that one," Pieces hissed.

"Come on Pieces, I apologized," Scottie said, clanging his fork on the table. "Besides, you should be glad in the end. He managed to get us three keys cut. A replacement for me, one for Skye, and an extra . . . and—"

"If you hadn't *lost* yours in the first place . . ." The emphasis on "lost" insinuated that he'd been lying even about that.

"Pieces, that's beside the point."

"The point is that you don't keep your word," Pieces said fiercely. She waited for that to sink in before she continued, her eyes burning into his. "The point is we waited on you . . . You couldn't even be bothered to answer your pager."

"I lost the pager with my keys . . ."

"And why did you and Prof take so long?" Again she looked over at me, as if to say *Are you hearing this?* before turning back to him.

"He had to go all the way up to Victoria. I went with him. It just happened."

"Things don't *just* happen Scottie," Pieces said. "Either you keep your word or you don't. It's fucking simple!"

"It's not fucking simple."

Pieces got in his face. "It IS fucking simple. Either you fucking *keep* your word or you fucking *don't!*" The words were loaded, hit Scottie in the gut, but he got up calmly and strapped on his guitar and headed toward the door. Pieces was on a roll and he knew it. Before he left, he threw the extra set of keys and the package that Prof had given him on the table. It was chocolate-compressed weed wrapped in cellophane. Had a blue label stuck on it that said "grade." Later I understood it was short for "high-grade." Pieces wasn't impressed.

"What? Is Rude Boy Scottie going out to find himself one thing after another to use as an excuse for being a fuckup? Why don't you admit it—you're not Rude Boy Scottie, you're an asshole!"

Scottie responded by slamming the door behind him. I agreed that he could be a jerk, but thought she was being a little hard on him. After all, he did save us a few coins and he did do, in the end, what he said he would do. I watched as she took her plate and threw it in the sink.

"What's wrong with you?" she asked, turning around to find my head bowed.

"I don't know, maybe you were a little hard on Scottie," I tried to reason. "He was only trying to—"

"Look, you don't know Scottie like I do. You don't know a lot of things." She took the package of cannabis off the table and dropped it back down.

"And this Prof constantly *giving* him this shit. Does that feel right to you?" She looked at me, I shrugged. Pieces inhaled and exhaled sharply. "I've had enough. Period."

"Friends fight, right? You guys will work it out."

Pieces didn't look at me. She just grabbed the keys and mumbled something about needing privacy and going to clear her head.

I finished my pasta alone, staring out the kitchen window over Coldharbour Lane.

INT. TRASHED PLACE - EARLY MORNING

Pieces opens the door and shuts it behind
her quietly, so as not to disturb a sleeping
Skye. She walks over to her bed, plops down,
looks over at Skye's curtained-off space, and
sighs. She begins packing up some art supplies,
a colorful piece of cloth, a few T-shirts,
and a notebook, stuffing them into a bright-
blue duffel bag. Bag over her shoulder, she
starts to walk over to where Skye is sleeping,
hesitating before deciding to turn around. She
flings the camera a vicious middle finger before
silently slipping out the door.

After the key-copying episode, Pieces made herself scarce. When Russel kicked off to Amsterdam, she took over his flat and his job. Settling into Portobello, she concentrated on work, either at the bar or on her canvas, rarely leaving that area. She'd given me the address and I had her number, but it was impossible to catch her.

Ever since that night, Pieces had changed. I mean, she'd already seemed a little different than I'd remembered her from New York—but there wasn't much to remember. We'd only spent the one night together, and aside from exchanging a few postcards and the odd long-distance call, we'd had no contact whatsoever until I landed in London a little over a month ago. Somehow I felt I knew her less now than when I'd landed. That feeling of someone whose door was always open now locked shut. There was no real explanation beyond her needing what she called "brain space." I couldn't kick the feeling, though I had no right to it, that we had made some sort of pact . . . unspoken, perhaps, but it was there. I felt that she was somehow breaking the deal and I was desperate to know why.

One morning Scottie brought all of his unemployed, unemployable strong-brew crew to the Trashed Palace. Prof, Danny from the squat, and some other guy. They were all sitting around having tea after a night out, and were clearly agitated.

"I came back to the flat this morning to a bloody padlock

and a notice stuck to my door saying that it was private property, and that it is not only dangerous but illegal to enter the premises." Danny sniggered, then sucked down the spliff Scottie passed him. "Fucking kicked in the window, didn't I?"

Scottie roared with laughter and smacked fists with Danny. "That's right, mate, forget those bloody wankers."

"You and I both know, yeah," he squinted behind the smoke he'd just exhaled and passed it to Prof, "that it's only a matter of time."

I'd been hearing about police cracking down on the squatters. Margaret Thatcher had finally been booted out of office. Her legacy, nonetheless, left an imprint on the city. Things were tough these days. I passed by them, my eyes in a crust, heading for the bathroom.

"You've never introduced me to *her*." That came from the mouth of this small but husky, dark-mahogany man. His voice sounded millions of cigarettes old, and like Scottie, he carried a guitar.

"Wolf, this is Skye. She's going to be reading some of her shit-hot poetry at our next gig," Scottie said, putting his arm around me. I coughed, shaking loose from his arm as I covered my mouth. Wolf bowed, took my hand, and kissed it. "Lovely to meet a lady as lovely as yourself," he said. Cringey. It was way too fucking early for this shit.

I showered, and while getting dressed, I overheard Scottie going on about the gig we were planning to have in the flat. It was something that he talked about often but hadn't made any definitive plans for. Nothing was ever sure with him. The previous lightness of being I'd had when I arrived was quickly giving way to ennui. Everything felt up in the air. But not in a good way. I needed to see Pieces to get some grounding.

So I decided on a whim to pass by her place. Conveniently impromptu since she never answered her phone.

It wasn't too difficult to find. Though the flats on her street were somewhat uniform in style, each building seemed to have been there long enough to have earned its individual, time-sculpted character. I climbed the concrete steps to a fading white Victorian-style house and saw Russel's name next to the buzzer for the third floor. Just as I was about to push the button, a young woman breezed out past me, and I stepped inside. Maybe the doorbell wasn't working anyway, I thought to myself, though really I was afraid Pieces wouldn't answer whether she was there or not. Eager to see her, I dashed up the stairs. Reaching the top, I checked myself, catching my breath before knocking.

"Hey, Pieces," I said through the closed door of her studio. "Just thought I'd drop by. Make sure you're alive."

Pieces opened the door. Her slitted, slightly rouged eyes might as well have been two Do Not Enter signs. I spotted a joint in an ashtray balanced on the edge of an open window. With an inner shrug, I told myself she was just high.

"Hello." She left me to close the door and headed back toward her mounted canvas. I stood in the short hallway leading into the small studio, took a deep breath, inhaling the oil-saturated air.

"Yeah . . . I was just in the neighborhood and thought I'd drop in," I lied, following Pieces the rest of the way inside.

Pieces murmured something that sounded like "uh-huh" but she didn't seem to be listening. I continued anyway.

"I was getting tired of hanging around smelling all that testosterone at the palace. Needed some air. Thought maybe if you weren't working, we could hang out. Maybe talk about the gig that's going to happen."

She sighed. "I don't have the time or interest in planning anything with Scottie," she said. "And I'm working."

"Come on, Pieces. We all know that Scottie can be an ass, but his heart . . ."

Pieces's shoulders visibly tightened under the thin straps of her trademark white tank top. She turned toward me, a pointed finger knifing the air. "You don't know Scottie like I do, and frankly, my dear, I don't give a flying fuck. Why do you think I moved into Russel's flat? I am sick of Scottie, the Prof, the damn Trashed Palace, I am tired of *all* of it. In fact I need a break from this whole bloody island. I'm fucking off to Amsterdam. I might not stay with him, but Russel invited me up for the weekend." She stopped, took a deep breath. I think she saw the hurt in my eyes. I just about managed to stifle a gasp of protest but couldn't fix my face. I looked at the floor. With a resigned plop, she dropped herself into an old office chair in front of her work in progress.

"Listen, Skye. I just need some time to rethink things. I need space."

"Okay." I was gutted but tried to be diplomatic. "Maybe we can hang when you're back?"

"Yeah." She took another deep breath, swiveled around to face her painting. Her demi-dreads were tied up, the curve of her neck bared. I swallowed hard, looking for words, something that could break through to her, but it was evidently a lost cause. I knew I should have left, but my boots remained glued to the wood-paneled floor.

"Mind if I hang out awhile?"

Pieces gave up trying to concentrate on the painting and swished her chair around facing me, an exasperated sigh leaving her mouth involuntarily. "I thought you were just in the neighborhood . . ."

I avoided her eyes, pretending to check out the flat. The

place was sparse but nicely furnished. High ceilings, with a lot of light. Against one wall was a black-metal futon couch covered in a Jamaican flag. That *must* have been Russel's. Pieces didn't believe in flags. On the wall above it hung a photo of a nearly nude Black woman, a perfect Afro adorning her chiseled mocha face, posed against a blue backdrop. Bolded black curly letters below her bare feet spelled out the word "soul." I could see Pieces owning something like *that*, however.

"Not a bad pad," I said. "No wonder you like hanging here."

"Skye, what do you want? I'm working . . ."

I racked my brain for something to say that didn't involve Scottie. "Remember that woman who owns the shop not far from here? The one you said might be able to help me out? I thought maybe you could introduce us and then maybe we could hang out. But you're working, so . . ."

Pieces scribbled something on a pink Post-it. "Here's the address." She looked at me and for a quick moment, I thought I saw guilt flicker across her furrowed face. "Look, I am in the middle of this," Pieces said, pointing to the white textured canvas. Little waves of white jutting irregularly off the page. "But go see Gennie Jah without me." She told me how to get there, but I barely paid attention. Said thanks, wished her luck on her painting, asked her would I see her soon?

Outside I pocketed the Post-it and decided to head back to the palace. Something wasn't right. I could understand her wanting space, but something didn't sit well. Didn't sit well at all.

A week later, I moped over a can of special brew in the kitchen while Scottie took his fortnightly bath. He always washed with this special non-soap concoction in warmish water. It had to be the right temperature. He said it kept the dirt from sticking. Scottie, towel wrapped around his waist, came out of the bathroom muttering, "Still didn't leave any rings in the tub . . . Amazing." He sat down next to me at the counter. "Wolf and Prof are coming over soon, and then we are going to head over to Dan's, help them clear some stuff out . . . Wanna come?"

"Naw, I gotta bring Pieces her stuff. She's leaving right after work and wanted the few things she left here."

"Oh yeah. I forgot Mizzz I Need Headspace was leaving tonight." He mimicked Pieces with an unlikely princessly voice. "I wouldn't mind a holiday in Amsterdam." He got up to go get dressed.

Ever since she told me the news, it stung that Pieces hadn't invited me. I felt left behind and this confused me. A loud rap on the door and a strum on the guitar interrupted my brooding. Wolf and Prof strolled in carrying open cans of black-label beer. They both sat on stools around the kitchen counter.

Wolf turned to look at me, grinning. "You are so beautiful. But even more beautiful when you smile."

"Whatever," I said, throwing back the rest of my beer before tossing the empty can in the garbage.

"Skye's down 'cause her woman is leaving," Scottie announced. He was kitted up for a night out now, with some khakis stuffed into worn-in boots, a waistcoat over his bare chest, and the usual dog tags clinking around his neck as he moved to pick up his guitar leaning against the counter.

"My *woman*?" I protested. "She is *our* friend. This doesn't bother you?"

"Why would I be bothered," he said nonchalantly, stringing his guitar. "I'll miss her, but she'll be back. Besides, I could use a break from her nagging. Isn't that right, Prof?"

Prof was staring into space, circular sunglasses propped on his nose. He was in his own world.

"Are you tripping again?" Scottie looked him in the eyes.

"Life is a trip, my son," Prof said, taking off his glasses. "And leave the young lady alone. At least she's honest."

Scottie could say nothing to that. Wolf offered me a beer, which I drank greedily, ignoring the chemical aftertaste.

◎

On the way to the pub where Pieces worked, my anger surged—the more I thought about her leaving, the angrier I got. My original plan had been to find work, save up, then travel elsewhere. Amsterdam would at least be somewhere else. My feet had been getting a little itchy these days. And even if I didn't have the dosh to go, it would have been nice to have been asked. It was obvious. She wanted to get away from us, from me. I didn't understand it. The only thing I understood was that she was leaving me here alone to deal with Scottie and his beer-belching buddies.

Carrying Pieces's heavy backpack, and an attitude to match, I made it to the pub just before closing. It was one of those bars with enough swank to charge a little bit more than some of the other places in Portobello, and enough of that traditional-British-pub feel to make the tourist think it authentic. The last of the punters were walking out—a mix of the white middle class and the upwardly mobile working-class folks taking the ole lady out for a night, posses of nine-to-five workers sharing a pint after another soul-crushing week at the office, everyday joes laughing and playing darts in one corner. I walked in, pack hoisted like a mutated tortoiseshell on my back.

"We're closed, mate." A balding, middle-aged man in a white shirt, jeans, and pointy shoes, who I guessed was the manager, nodded at the door as he moved toward me.

"I'm waiting on a friend," I explained.

"I don't care who you are waiting for, we are closed. Nobody is in here." The manager came up to me, motioning me out. I took the rucksack off my back and tried again.

"Just here to pick up—"

Refusing to hear me, the bar manager took my presence as a challenge to his authority and switched into robo-bouncer mode. "I said we are closed, mate, which means you *cannot* wait in here."

I stood my ground. I knew that part of the reason he spoke to me that way was because I didn't resemble his usual clientele. If I'd been one of those yuppie American blonds, his tone would have been quite the opposite. He knew nothing about me, really, yet he'd made up his mind. And so had I. I was not going to be pushed around tonight. Had come all this way, aching shoulders and all, to accompany Pieces to the airport. I shrugged off his attempt to grab my shoulder, crossed my arms, my eyes daring him to try to touch me again. In the nick of time, balancing a stack of pint glasses, Pieces came up behind her boss and owned me.

"She's with me," she said.

The bar manager's eyes were dismissive, his posture relaxed into a reluctant tolerance. "I got work in the back. Clear up the rest of the glasses, break down, and wash up before you go." And with that, he walked off.

"Yes, General Dick," Pieces said under her breath before turning to me, motioning to the bar. I dragged the bag over to a stool and sat down. "Thanks for coming—the other bar slave didn't show, so I'm stuck closing!" Pieces snuck me a shot of Jim Beam and continued cleaning up.

I rolled the shot glass between thumb and finger, watching her systematically move the glasses to one table and wipe down the rest. She moved, as always, with a confident grace that I envied. My mood had been tempered, yes, softened by her gesture of thanks, and I was enthralled just watching her. She looked up at me, catching my stare. I looked down for a shy millisecond before toasting her and slamming the bourbon a second time.

"Hey," I said walking toward her. "Let me help." I pointed at the gold-and-black Roman-numeral clock hanging above the bar, which was always just a tad fast. "Time is ticking."

"No, that's okay," Pieces said, wiping down the last of the tables. "It's nearly done."

But I was already at the table of glasses, stacking them as I'd seen her do, way too high for someone of my (non)experience. A few drinks deep, my painfully awkward clumsiness surfaced again, and on my way to the bar I tripped over a bit of air—or a bit of string, depending on your angle—and the tower of eight pint glasses that I'd been carrying came smashing down, me with it.

"Damn it!" Pieces said, coming to help me up.

"What the fuck?" The manager rushed out of his cubbyhole, nose red, like he had helped himself to at least a few pints that evening.

"It was just an accident," Pieces said.

"'Just an accident'?" the manager snapped back, spotting the empty shot glass and bottle at the end of the bar. "And was *that* 'just an accident' as well?"

"What are you on about?" Pieces's patience was wearing thin. "I accidentally tripped and—"

"At least now I know who's been stealing my liquor, don't I?"

At this point, Pieces lost it.

"So now I'm a thief? Go fuck yourself, you bastard!" She dropped a few more pint glasses for effect.

Whether he fired her or she quit first was a draw from my perspective. We booked it outside, the manager slamming the door behind us. I was grinning to myself, loving getting into a scene with Pieces. But she wiped the smile off my lips as soon as both of our faces hit the air.

"You just bloody well burned that bridge for me, Skye. Brilliant. Absolutely brilliant," Pieces seethed outside the pub. My heart dropped into my stomach, anger resurfacing.

"What do you care? You're off to Amsterdam anyway and your boss is an asshole!" I was agitated, spoiling for a fight again. I was tired of her treating me as if I didn't know which way was up.

"YOU are the asshole, Skye," Pieces corrected me. "Who knows, if you had been cool and stayed OUT of it like I told you, you could've taken my hours while I was away."

Taken her hours? So this wasn't just a weekend—she had no intention of coming back anytime soon. I slung the bag hard against the ground, a sumo wrestler slamming his opponent. Already furious, Pieces grabbed her rucksack and continued walking. I ran in front of her, started walking backward to try and talk to her. Pieces stopped, more to keep me from banging into the light pole inches behind my egg head. She could see that I was more than a little pissed on drink and probably regretted sneaking me that last shot.

"You wanna yell at me?" I said. "Hit me? Go ahead, but don't just fucking walk away like a coward. Talk to me!" Desperate, I dug up my version of a James Dean *Rebel without a Cause* stance. Pieces was not stirred or shaken.

"What is up with you? I haven't got time for this. I've got a plane to catch."

"Time for what? What am I doing to you? I came here to help you get to the airport—"

"You know what, Skye, I don't need your help. I don't even know why you're still here." She adjusted the rucksack on her back and looked me in the eye. "In fact, I don't want you anywhere near me." She then trudged past me up the hill, leaving me there diminished, the wind knocked clean out of me.

Loneliness comes cloaked in many guises. The form it took then was unfamiliar to me, so I could easily ignore its presence, call it something else. But like the rain in London, it began to soak into my bones. Before I knew it, couldn't shake the cold. I became more and more introverted. A well-practiced exercise. Familiar. The world of lonely monotony I'd thought I'd escaped from? Well, I found myself in it again. Spent a lot of time walking. And walking. It had finally sunk in that Pieces was going to be gone until . . . well, until she was ready to come back. Scottie and I settled into a semi-routine, barely seeing each other. He was always chasing his next hustle. I'd venture out sometime in the afternoon, after a breakfast of a spliff and milky tea. Check pubs, cafés, restaurants for work. Quickly got fed up with one "no, sorry, mate" after another. Getting hired without a permit was trickier than I thought it would be.

The colorful Saturday-morning market experience I had when I first landed in Brixton dulled into the everyday. The reality of just getting by was evident with every step down those streets. The weekend rush of native London tourists, who flocked en masse to trendy nightspots, was blind to the day in, day out hustle on the streets. But it was serious. The air was thick with it. It was getting to me.

I started sleeping in later and later. My routine became: spliff, coffee, shit, shower, sofa fashioned from Pieces's mattress, folded and pushed up against the wall. If I was feeling motivated, I would sit down in Peace Park, or wander down to the Oval and go through Kennington Park. Spent a lot of hours in one park or another, writing in my journal, reading books secondhand, and found: Butler's *Kindred*, Orwell's *1984*, Lorde's biomythography, *Zami: A New Spelling of My Name*, Ntozake Shange's *nappy edges*, Barthes's *A Lover's Discourse*. Or I would just stare at the sky. For a long time, it seemed nothing happened, except in the worlds created on pages. Outside of that, I was lost.

Scottie was the breadwinner. He'd come back to the Trashed Palace in the afternoon with change from a night of busking and useful things found on the street. Well, useful-ish things: irregular hats, single gloves, a golf club . . .

One of the times we crossed paths, he walked in with the club over his shoulder and I asked him about it. "I used to imagine my dad played golf," he said, swinging the club. "I coulda been Tiger Woods. I always wanted to play, you see . . ." He chuckled to himself. "Whatever, at the very least it's a good weapon. I'm a lover, not a fighter, but"—he showed me a big raw bruise on his shoulder—"I need to be able to protect myself."

When I first met Scottie, he didn't seem at all the "thug" he was posing as. Sure, he was rough around the edges, living life pretty much on the streets, hustling. I guessed testosterone-fueled rumbles were part of the territory. Turf claiming.

"These guys were aiming for my head." He'd moved in time but a broken brick had grazed his shoulder. "I punched the wall, left a dent there, did more damage to my hand. They left me alone after that, didn't they?" He peeled off his leather glove and, from the looks of it, some skin with it. "As I was walking home, this seven iron dropped from the heavens." Lifted both hands in the air, pointing toward the cracking ceiling as if he could part it. The golf club had been, until then, hanging on one of the telephone wires.

I asked how the fight started. He told me some brother thought he was trying to chat up his girlfriend. He was simply sharing one of his new tunes.

"Sounds like folks are uptight," I said, thinking the atmosphere in Brixton could be as tense as the day is hot, and even worse if the day was not, as was the norm in London, depending, of course, on where you stood.

"Yeah." He pulled out a half-full can of beer from his waistcoat pocket, guzzled it down, and crushed the empty. I leaned against the counter and a sigh seemed to come out of its own accord.

"Hey, what's up? Skye blue?" He smiled at his pun, came over, and sat next to me, offering me a crisp new cigarette from behind his ear. "I haven't seen you much but you been looking down, down, beat down, what's up?"

I hadn't told him about the fight I had with Pieces. I'd tried to forget about it. Freeze out all thoughts of her and, as a consequence, all feeling. But after holding it all in, Scottie's genuine concern was enough to seriously threaten the fortified barrier I'd been hiding behind. I sucked in the cigarette smoke to dam up the inevitable tears. It had been a while since I'd talked and I needed to talk it out, so I told him everything—from the bar manager not wanting to let me in, all the way up to the grand finale that had left me shattered and speechless.

"She fucked off and left me there and I dropped down on the curb back in front of the pub until the manager threatened to call the cops if I didn't leave."

"Don't worry," he consoled me. "Pieces is the queen of disappearing acts."

"How do you know so much?" I asked, shrugging his hand off my shoulder.

"Well, you of all people should realize this."

"Why?" I sat on a stool in the kitchen, staring past him into space.

"Because you, darling, are her apprentice."

My head was too busy trying not to think about Pieces to figure out what he meant by that, or care. Point is that I didn't want to care.

"Look, don't get your knickers in a twist." He began building the first of many spliffs we would have that evening. He'd gotten his dole check and brought home some chicken breast and rice to cook for dinner for a change.

Scottie tried to cheer me up. "I used to mope around whenever she left, until I stopped taking it personally. Besides, she may run away, but she can never deny the connection the three of us have."

I nodded, decided he was right. From the beginning, Pieces was there and gone again . . . But in New York she'd wanted me around. We were friends. In London things were different.

I looked over at Scottie. He got up to turn on the kettle. Leaning against the counter, he looked back at me, waiting for me to speak.

"She doesn't seem like quite the same person I knew for a night in New York, Scottie. She was never easy but now she's . . . more distant." And that fight outside the pub just drove the wedge in deeper. "I don't know, I think I fucked things up."

"That little debate? That was nothing compared to the drag-out knockdown fights Pieces and I have had, Skye," he said, reminiscing as he let out a puff of smoke. He went to grab a box of tea bags from the kitchen cabinet. "I mean, when we first met, we argued a lot, but we're still friends. You are her friend. I am your friend. No worries, Skye." Scottie carefully stirred in just the right amount of milk and sugar, taking the bags out at just the right moment. "And she'll get bored with Russel, just like before." He set down two steaming mugs and passed me the smoke; some of it he was still swallowing when he said, "He's a twat, anyway."

◎

Lying on my mat later, I couldn't sleep. Kept thinking about the scene in the bar. If I had just kept my ass in that seat instead of trying to . . . to what? The "what" of it all was so obvious I had to look askance not to see it. I had perfected that technique. I resisted allowing a part of me I'd pushed down to overwhelm me. I could smell Pieces's cocoa-butter scent nestled in the pillow I borrowed from her bed, could hear her voice in my head. "What is up with you?" she had asked before walking away. The big "what" trampled through my brain, an elephant breaking china. I thought about writing in my journal. Instead I went to Scottie's bed and showed him how glad I was to find him awake. Wanted to feel something real, to fill the murky void of "what" with someone *there*. I held on to his body, a skinny life raft, but a life raft just the same, and with no shore in sight, something released, bathing my face in salt water. Scottie stroked and kissed me softly on the cheek and neck and I relaxed even more. Returned his kisses, searching for the taste of coco-nut—her kisses left that trace. She was there, yet just out of reach. Scottie looked down at me, smiling. I kissed him again before he could ruin it with some banal joke. Closed my eyes and moved onto his body eagerly. Flesh to hungry flesh. His mouth moved hot over my skin. Breathing heav-ily, I gave in to desire. But it was Pieces's tongue between my legs when I finally came.

My freshman year in high school I had a crush on my softball coach, one of the only single Black women in Crickledown, and the only one, period, that drove a two-seat jade lowrider. I remember dreaming about where she might've come from—certainly not this little town, with its neat, uniform lawns and Wonder Bread god. Missouri was known as "the Show-Me State," but it was also the buckle to the Bible Belt, as much as—if not more than—it was the gateway to the West. Anything that strayed from the straight Caucasian aesthetic was feared and squashed through a Play-Doh spaghetti grinder of conformity.

One day my coach gave me a lift home from school. I'd managed to sprain my ankle during practice and was embarrassed at my own clumsiness. Seeing me all droopy-lipped, she suggested that Ted Drewes was the best medicine for all softball injuries. Ted Drewes made the best concrete custards, thick and rich. If you turned the carton upside down, not a drop shifted. I got my favorite, chocolate-chocolate-chip, with chocolate syrup mixed in for good measure. That combined with going for a spin in the coach's car was heaven. I forgot my ankle and hoped she would take the scenic route home. She didn't, no matter how much I willed her to miss that stop off the highway that led to my doorstep. As she helped me out of the car, my arms around her shoulder for a split second while I caught my balance, I found myself wanting to kiss her.

I wasn't sure what that feeling meant, but it was different from anything I had felt for any boy. Different from anything I'd felt before. I became obsessed in some way, wishing to tell her about this passionate . . . Was it love? Maybe she wanted to kiss me too. That was the fantasy I had on repeat. But she was my softball coach. She was a grown woman, an adult with a sexy car and confidence that seemed unattainable to a fumbling chocolate-fudge-brown freak nerd of a teenager. I could never tell her how I felt! But she *had* to know . . .

Hopelessly infatuated and desperate for someone to talk to about my new feelings, I attempted to confide in my aunt Michelle's best friend Regina. My aunt and Regina had been friends since they were teenagers. Aunt Mich ended up marrying Regina's brother, so she was more or less my aunt too. Often they would burst out laughing simultaneously to jokes only they understood, much to the consternation of Auntie Mich's husband.

"Could you girls keep it down, I'm tryin' ta watch the Super Bowl . . ."

Aunt Mich and Regina would look at him and roll their eyes. He would be quiet after that, knew he was more than outnumbered. Wife and sister on the same team? Forget it.

In my just-turned-teen eyes, they were tops. Less uptight than most of the Bible-toting family. I felt freest with them. They were my confidants, and I could tell them just about anything. Just about.

When I approached Regina in the bathroom, she was washing her hands.

"Ah, hey, Aunt Regina?" I greeted her.

"Hey there, beauty," she said, carefully massaging the foamy soap between her hands. "What's cooking?"

"Well . . ." I wasn't sure where to start. I bowed my head, smiled shyly.

"Are you in love?" she asked.

In spite of all efforts to conceal it, my face reddened and my smile got bigger.

"I knew it!" She dried her hands on a navy-blue towel embroidered with my auntie Mich's and her husband's initials. She then hit me with a barrage of questions: What was the lucky boy's name? Was he in one of my classes? When I told her that it wasn't a *boy* from my school, she looked worried.

"Well, who is it, then? It's not some older man, is it?" She frowned. "You know you have to be careful . . ."

"It's not some older boy or young man, Auntie Re," I said, not sure how to explain. "And I guess it's more like a crush but it feels, it feels so . . . I don't know, right."

Tried to ask her if she thought it was possible for two women to fall in love, but she made a quick excuse and deliberate exit, leaving me there sitting on the furry toilet-seat cover to contemplate whether or not I should have brought it up at all.

Later that night I crouched on the stairs leading from the kitchen to the basement, eavesdropping on my aunties' conversation below. They always went down there to talk when they wanted a little privacy.

"So she caught up with me in the bathroom, M. Said she wanted to talk to me about something."

"Probably just some boy problem or something . . ."

"No . . ." Auntie Re said reluctantly. "It didn't sound like a *boy* problem to me, but I stopped really listening when—"

"When what?"

Regina lowered her voice. "It was as if for a brief moment I was talking to *her*."

"To Skye . . . and . . . ?"

"No, it was Skye's mother, M. I swear it was her *mother.*"

Pause.

"Re, you are crazy, so you are saying you saw a ghost? She is long gone and that was a long time ago!" said Aunt Michelle. "I know that God loves all his children, but I do believe that was Satan trying his hand with her, and God took her away from us so that her soul might be saved."

Regina made a low "hmmm" sound in agreement before pointing out, "True, but she never did come back, did she?"

Auntie took a beat before answering. "Only through the grace of God could she ever do that, in Jesus's name."

I had learned in church that Jesus could do just about anything, including raise the dead. Even though I wasn't the Jesus freak I used to be, I prayed for a while after that, that I could see my mom again, like Auntie Re had, though I barely remembered her. On the stairway, I tried to get up and close the door without making it creak, but they heard me. "You up there, Skye?"

The next morning Scottie and I had what I learned was a "snog." Not full-on sex but heavy petting, as they called it in all those old fifties sitcoms and movies I used to watch when my dad would allow me. Or when he wasn't around. He was so gung-ho bent that I not be influenced by "this world." I guess he thought sheltering me would help ensure I remained a virgin of clean mind, clean heart. As Scottie slid his hands into my underwear I began to laugh.

"What?"

"Nothing. Just thinking about what my dad would say if he knew where I was and what I was doing and with who . . ."

Scottie chuckled. "I know what I would say if I was your dad." He paused. "But your mum would probably like me, I mean, if you're anything like her?"

"I never really knew her." Left it at that.

"Oh." Scottie knew not to push it and instead went on to tell me about his.

Scottie's mom kicked the bucket about three years ago. He went to New York to try and find his real dad and ended up finding every oedipal replica of what he imagined or wanted his mother to be instead. I smiled to myself, remembering how Pieces first thought I was one of Scottie's harem.

"It was mad," he said, turning on his side, resting his head on his hand. "It was like I couldn't say no, or they were just there . . . I don't know."

"Did you end up finding your dad?"

"Tracked him down to Chicago. When I met you, I was on my way to see him."

"Really? What happened?"

"Well, I found his address. I went there and was knocking on the door, but no one answered." He turned toward me briefly and smiled mischievously, shrugging his shoulders as if it couldn't be helped. "I didn't want to come all that way for nothing, so; the top lock on the door was simple, I was able to jimmy it without much trouble, and the bottom bit was unlocked. I slowly pushed it open to find a run-down studio with a piano. And sitting on the piano was a folded note marked 'my son.'" Scottie sighed, scratched his head, folded his arms across his chest. "He wrote that he felt I was on my way. To make myself at home. That there was Chopin under the piano seat if I cared to amuse myself. It was one of those lidded benches.

"So I sat down at the piano. It was surprisingly in tune. I began to run my fingers over the keys," he almost whispered, his face maudlin and far away. "Then played each note . . . Then I felt something, some connection. So I stayed, squatted there waiting for my dad to come back . . . Spent most of my time learning the Chopin." Scottie smiled to himself. "A couple weeks later, some of my friends in the city were about to hit the road, so I told them I'd come along. Just before they arrived, I played one last Chopin interpretation, thinking the music would somehow leave a coded message in the piano, in the walls, wherever the sound waves could reach. And my father, if he really was blood, I figured he'd *feel* the vibe left reverberating. Like, he'd listen for it." Scottie paused. "There is so much music around us that we filter out. That we don't hear . . . Anyway, when I finally left, there was a man sitting there, gray haired, but with smooth, if stubbly, dark skin drinking from a bottle. He had on days-old clothes and smelled like he'd been sleeping rough. He smiled at me through strong yellowing teeth and said, 'Nice chops for Chopin.' He jittered slightly from what seemed more like nervousness than cold. 'Yes, yes. Nice chops for Chopin. One of my favorites.' I just nodded and thanked the man, and just as the slow elevator doors were shutting, the man got up and walked toward the door of my dad's studio. He said, stroking his scruffy chin, 'But I'm sure your ole pops could still teach you a thing or two?' And then the elevator doors closed."

I listened to Scottie's wild story, intrigued and understanding enough not to probe too much. "So who raised you?" I asked after a beat.

"Well, Prof adopted me," Scottie explained. "My mum and Prof had been seeing each other for most of my life. My mum was working-class, a social worker by day and often did extra hours cleaning hotels at night to help pay the rent. I never remembered being without, and Prof, though technically my guardian, always seemed more like a friend than a father."

I thought about my mom. My dad had never remarried after she died. I wondered what she'd ever seen in him. I didn't want to think about it.

"When she died, I just couldn't get my dad outta my mind," Scottie continued. "I guess I wanted to grieve with my blood. Get to know the only blood that I knew I had left alive."

His father never did look him up in New York. Scottie had left his contact details on the piano before leaving.

"I figured I'd leave the ball in his court. This time let him come and find me." Scottie started fidgeting with his finger. "I would like to think that whoever my father is, he isn't like me . . . always hustlin' for the next—but then again maybe I get it from him . . . Anyway, why would I wanna work in some place like McFuckery's for slave wages when I can make money playing guitar? Maybe he felt the same way about his piano . . ."

We both stared up at the ceiling for one of those small eternities.

Scottie turned to look at me. His formerly broody face turned hopeful.

"Hey, you know . . . I think this gig idea we've been talking about could really work."

"Yeah?" I said, relieved at the change of topic. All this talk about our folks did nothing to calm the turbulence in my head. So I was up for it. Up for anything. "When are you thinking?"

"Well, we should wait for Pieces to get back to properly plan it, but I've already started gathering forces. Met some people at Danny's. Said that they would set up their PA . . . And there are plenty of musicians around looking for a place to jam . . ."

He continued on about it, but I kept thinking about genes, what's passed down from your biological parents. My own father's voice crowded my head. Maybe what Dad used to say was true—I was my mother's child. And I had no idea who my mother was. Maybe she had a sense of humor that had disarmed my father and made him easier to deal with. She had fallen in love with him, hadn't she? I couldn't imagine that she would be the dutiful housewife, unless she was the version that would lose her cool and begin burning his eggs on purpose, especially if she was anything like me. She must have had a mind of her own. Any woman who read the book that Auntie Bernice gave me had to be about something. When my father said I was beginning to act just like her, I understood from his tone that somehow, becoming like her was unforgivable.

While Scottie was in the shower, I moved to the front room to put the kettle on, nearly knocking over Scottie's guitar. He'd left it propped against the wooden horse-leg table that posed as a counter near the cubby-hole kitchen. I got why Scottie would want to make a living his own way. It was a lifestyle for him. It took courage to do that. Both Scottie and Pieces were the same way. It moved me . . . Nobody I'd been close to had those kinds of guts. Everybody tried to make the fit somehow: Dad, my auntie, even Damian. I knew now that this was why I'd felt uncomfortable with them—just couldn't make the fit.

I picked up the guitar. I'd always wanted to learn to play, especially after discovering my mom's old steel-string acoustic. It was hiding behind boxes of records, books, and other bits and bobs my father had stashed there from when he moved us. A dust-caked graveyard of cartons lined one far wall. It was an unspoken law at home—those boxes were off limits. They held the mystery of all things untouchable. In my child's mind, those forgotten boxes were a crumbling old wall behind which lay a secret but cursed treasure. I was playing my version of *Indiana Jones* that summer, using a jump rope as a whip to break through the wall. I practiced spinning the rope, which was whistling through the air when, with a sling and snap of wrist, it hit my target. *Schlack!* I accidentally on purpose nailed one of the lighter cartons, precariously placed in between two other boxes. At that last crack of my make-believe lash, the stacked boxes came tumbling down. The guitar seemed to glow, like a sacred artifact, from under the rubble of spilled this and that. The strings were old but hardly used. I brought it upstairs to show Dad. He recoiled like he'd seen a ghost.

"Where'd you find that?"

"Downstairs in the basement. I—"

"You know better than to go through my private belongings." He grabbed the guitar from me gruffly, but once he had it, he held it as if it were the most delicate thing. He sat down on his chair in the living room, leaned it up against the old out-of-use combination stereo and phono-player. He was sweating.

"I wasn't looking through your things," I said. "It was an accident."

Caught up in his own memories, he picked the guitar up again and let his thumb fall over the strings.

"I didn't know you played . . ." I said quietly, hoping he would.

"It was your mother's," he said, putting it down again. "She played and sang beautifully . . ."

I was hungry for any and all information about my mother. He never talked about her, and forbade my relatives to talk about her in front of me. "What's gone is gone," he'd often say. "With the help of God, you gotta move on." He told me she'd died when I was still a baby, but why this had happened remained an enigma. The only picture of her I had was one I'd secretly pinched from my dad's drawers. Found it during a routine search for money. Kept it with me in my falling-apart wallet. Always. I had her brown eyes and thick eyelashes. Her hair was straightened. She had a half smile on her face, as if she were conceding or yielding to something she did not necessarily want to do. As if moments before the flash went off, she'd said, "Okay, go on and take the picture, if you have to . . ."

"Did she play it a lot?" I asked, rinsing out this rare opportunity to talk about Mom.

"She played a lot to you while you were in her belly . . ." He cleared his throat and abruptly got up and left the living room with the guitar in hand. I never saw it again.

◎

Scottie came in wiping his face with a towel. I was laid out flat on my mat, his guitar on my belly, strumming absentmindedly.

"Always knew you'd look sexy with a guiiitar," he said with a big grin.

A couple of days later he brought home a rough-looking steel-string acoustic, which we mended together. Evidently Prof had one at his house that he never used. Scottie pulled out an old Swiss Army knife from his pocket, invited me to carve whatever design into the guitar to make it mine. "Give it a little personal magic," he said. I told Scottie that I wasn't yet sure what to choose, so he told me to keep the knife, in the meantime. He then showed me a few chords and from there, I began teaching myself. It was something to do to pass the time.

"Hey, you're improving on the rapid." Scottie walked in on me working chord changes, his face the picture of someone with an idea dawning. "How about coming out with me tomorrow?"

"What?"

"Yeah, you know, watch my back. The vibe has been weird . . . Maybe you could give me a lil luck."

"Dude, I don't know if I'm ready," I said, smiling in spite of myself.

"Bollocks," Scottie said. "Cuppa?"

I put down the guitar and joined Scottie for a tea at the kitchen counter.

"You heard anything from that wench Pieces?" asked Scottie. I shook my head. Scottie nodded, taking a small sip. The silence afterward was comfortable.

At some point we made eye contact, as if we were reading each other's minds.

"Here's to Godot." He raised his cup.

"To Godot," I said, clinking his cuppa with mine.

INT. TUBE PLATFORM

Skye sits on a bench, head stuck in her book, writing. Occasionally she looks down the platform at Scottie, who is busy serenading a group of people.

My first few times out with Scottie, I stayed mostly in the background. Watching him. Watching people. Went up Coldharbour Lane, down Acre Lane, to the Clapham High Street. Sometimes we would blag a bus or jump a train to the West End, or do the underground shuffle: up and down tube platforms. I watched his performance. His technique. He could create his own stage wherever he went. Counting on being misunderstood, and making up lyrics as he went along, he was a street musician. Sussing people's mood, he was a counselor. A folk singer. Blessing the space. Priming. Looking for a target. A welcoming face. A settling place, to lay his lyrics. I studied the art. Of capturing souls, if only for a moment. Placing a smile there. And disappearing. Like an angel. I watched him as if I were in training. I romanticized his cause.

I would sit, write, and watch the trains swishing past me, pushing tube air through my hair and nose. Okay, before I go too far into creating some postmodern mixed-race Bob Dylan, it wasn't all peaches and cream. Scottie would come over to me occasionally with a handful of change, obviously on edge most of the time. Often he would end up in rows with less-than-enthusiastic punters.

"What I give them is more than whatever coins they throw at me," he said in his own defense. But he took the coins nonetheless. Always presented his hat at the end of a performance before giving it to me to hold. Some days we managed over ten pounds in less than an hour, other days we'd be lucky to pull in two quid. On those days Scottie supplemented his income by "recycling" used tickets. He taught me how and where to collect valid cards that commuters no longer needed, to resell them at a fraction of the cost.

I became adept in making something out of nothing. Using what the environment gave me. Began to see things that had been invisible to me before. Began to respect a way of life I had never known about, understood, always taken for granted, or just not seen. Lived off of what was wasted. Saw how capitalism killed any real possibility of everyone having what they needed: shelter, clothing, food. Even places like the greasy burger chains chose to mulch leftover double beefs before chucking them to deter dumpster divers and other vermin. Chad, everybody's favorite *Big Issue* salesman of the year, clued me in on this during one of our long chats while I waited for Scottie at the Clapham North station, one of his best ticket-touting spots. Scottie would always give him a pound. Chad would always give me a *Big Issue*. I'd always stand and chat, watching the steady stream of commuters with him while Scottie did his thing.

"Be careful with that lad," Chad joked one lazy afternoon. "Scottie's always finding himself in some kind of trouble. Here," he said, handing me a copy of the *Big Issue*. "Something to do while you're waiting around for that character."

I told him I didn't have any cash but as always, he insisted. The *Big Issue* vendors were homeless folks, and this was an "honest" way to make some dosh. Didn't feel right, but he wouldn't have it any other way, so I took the mag, bid him farewell, and walked fast to catch up with Scottie.

Chad's warning turned premonition, 'cause as I took

the corner I saw Scottie in a face-off with the some hulking white dude in the front garden of a pub. Jogged up to check the situation.

"Okay." The red-faced bar manager nudged Scottie. "No buskers . . . Move on."

Scottie jerked away. "Do *not* touch me . . ." he hissed like a cat.

"Move. On," the manager demanded. He was huge. Probably worked some night shifts as a bouncer somewhere. But Scottie was afraid of no one.

"The lady wants a song." He'd slipped into a tense but polite tone of voice.

The "lady" in question was a beered-up blond taking full advantage of happy hour, having a hen night out with her girlfriends. Not wanting to get involved, they remained quiet.

Give us a song, then, they had probably said as he sauntered past them. I knew the routine. As usual I sat just at a slight distance, observing. Would only jump in if necessary. It worked to his benefit if we weren't obviously together.

"You'll move on NOW or I'll call the police." The manager's face was pushing purple. He moved to shove Scottie. Scottie dodged, slung his guitar across himself so it hung on his back, and went into a titan stance. It was an odd face-off; Scottie with his thin, wiry body against ole Lobster Face, all pumped-up pecs and thick neck vined with bulging veins.

"Call the rasclot police then." Scottie wasn't moving. Wasn't intimidated. The bar manager knew that if he went in to call the police, Scottie would continue singing and the manager would have lost the match. So he played the only hand he knew and pushed Scottie back into the low wall surrounding the bar's deck. His guitar took a nasty scrape.

He jumped up, and so did I, willing him to walk away. Just go. But I knew that wasn't about to happen.

"I told you not to fuckin' touch me . . ." Scottie marched right into his face. "You have no right."

"Oh, go get a job, boy," the manager said before ordering one of his staff to call the police.

"Listen, you cunt . . . why don't you do your job and manage the bar and let your customers have what they want . . . Or is that not your job?" Lobster Face clenched his fist and Scottie squared away, ready to defend himself. He wasn't gonna be pushed again. "And I want compensation for damage to my fuckin' guitar!"

"In your dreams, mate." With backup on the way, the manager played it cool. Not wanting to get involved with the police, I went up to Scottie.

"Come on, let's go."

"Fuck that . . . I want compensation for my guitar . . . Let the police come . . . He had no right to push me."

Pulled him to me close enough to whisper, "Who the fuck do you think the cops gonna believe, Scottie?"

Managed to get him away before the fuzz got there, but it was close.

As we walked down Clapham High Street, it took Scottie a half a can of beer and a ten-minute rant to cool down.

"He was wrong, Skye. He had no right to do that." He pulled the guitar from his shoulder and inspected it. There was a long, deep scratch running down the back. "Fuckin' hell . . . I just take shit take shit take shit . . ."

"Maybe in that situation it woulda been better if you'd backed off a long time ago," I suggested hotly. Wrong move.

"What? I didn't do anything! He pushed *me*, and I still think I shoulda stayed—look what he fuckin' did to my guitar—I wanted to give a statement to the police, see if they would do their job for once . . . Hey?"

"You know they would've sided with Lobster Face."

Scottie laughed. "He did turn some interesting shades of crimson, all right."

We decided to chill for a bit in Clapham Common park. Scottie was as well-known on the high street in Clapham as in Brixton. A range of folks greeted him: shop owners, briefcase-toting suits, lil ole ladies. He chatted with the homeless beggars in the park before finding a patch of waning sun on a bench near the duck pond.

"I do good work, you know, Skye." He cracked open a can, courtesy of the strong-brew crew we'd just left. "Those lot . . . those beggars, they make more money than I do . . . I don't beg . . . I give something . . . People are just afraid of the truth."

I watched a duck float around a plastic bag, which nearly clung to the duck's head when the thrust of a sudden breeze carried the bag to its next destination. Scottie courted trouble. I saw how people reacted to him. Many would look him up and down like he was scum. His uniform: open, colorful cotton shirt, knit top hat, torn jeans, ripped leather high-tops, and guitar, which he often adorned with flowers. Twisted around his neck, his dog tags were a tangle of fading silver chains. He always smelled like beer. But for as many people who couldn't stand the sight of him, there were those who adored him. His fans would smile at me. "She's beautiful, is she your girlfriend?" some would ask. Other times people would mistake me for his brother, which both amused and annoyed me. I didn't look anything like Scottie. These people weren't really seeing me, only a shape in baggy jeans and a dirty denim jacket—saw what they wanted to see and reacted.

After the park we decided to try to take the train out to Brighton. Both blazing and in a good mood, we had been aching to get out of London for a while. Ticketless, in a practically empty carriage, we made friends on the way with a group of lads who back in the day might have been teddy-boy material.

Scottie broke them in with his classic "I hate Black people, don't you?" That usually scared them off or made them smile.

"You're all right, mate." They chuckled through their exhales of cig smoke. "Play me some Marley, mate . . . You sorta look like Bob."

The only similarities between him and Bob Marley were his complexion and the fact he had a guitar over his shoulder. Even so, he developed a good-natured comeback.

"I look like a jukebox to you?"

Scottie gave them an original he knew they'd get into— and they did, popping open cans of carry-on beer, offering me one. Then as an encore, he gave his own rough acoustic version of "Killing in the Name Of"—he stomped his foot down toward them on the first down stroke.

Now you do what they toldja!

He hit the chords hard, nearly breaking his strings and sending my head into a rock slam along with the other boys. Some guys at Danny's squat had been playing Rage Against the Machine while I was there waiting on Scottie that one time. I didn't know it then, but perhaps Scottie reminded those guys of the lead singer minus the locs.

Just as Scottie was finishing, a ticket agent came through the carriage door, chirping "tickets, please" in rhythm with the sound of the ticket-spitting contraption around his neck. The lads all had passes, but Scottie and I tried to plead innocence.

"There was no one at the station," I said, putting forth my best American-tourist-in-London act. Suddenly realized that, stinking of beer in my grungy clothes, I probably wasn't the kind of tourist they wanted in London, but tried to be convincing anyway. "How much are they? I'll take two."

As he printed out the tickets, I pretended to look for my wallet. "Oh jeez"—I laid the *Leave It to Beaver* on thick—"oh noooo! Scottie, did I give my purse to you?" His eyes were cracking up but Scottie shrugged, playing along, looking through his pockets. "Don't tell me I left it at the station."

"If you don't have the money, I'm afraid you'll have to get out at the next stop." This guy was a brick, or maybe I'd overdone it.

"You shoulda laid it on thicker," Scottie instructed after we got off the train. "Shoulda let a tear come to your eye. And if that doesn't work, then you should get irate and start slagging off Britain in the nasally-est accent possible," he joked as we waited at a deserted station in the middle of nowhere.

"Didn't wanna cause a scene," I said. Scottie looked at me and shook his head.

"What the fuck do you care, Skye? Why do you care so much what people think?" he asked me, exasperated.

As I pondered this, he popped open a beer the lads had slipped us, along with a small block of hash for the journey home. He was right, I did care. In spite of my outward fuck-you to the establishment, I was still highly self-conscious. I held back, knowing what people thought of us. It was even true that I would feel uncomfortable as he gave some punter an unwanted blast. Scottie did nothing to harm anyone, but for some, an unsolicited song was provocation enough to lash out. People did have the right *not* to want to hear him play, after all. But Scottie, the reluctant messiah of minstrels, blessed the people whether they wanted it or not. What was the harm in that? Every once in a while, some truly moved punter would push a five- or ten-pound note in Scottie's hand. Sometimes they might wink at me as they did it. It made me squirm, but for a while it was a rush when we got away with it, a laugh anyway if we didn't.

We made it to King's Cross, blatantly ignoring guards at the gates, and just caught the last Victoria line train to Brixton. Even managed to make some change along the way. Went to bed well sauced, and full off some chips scarfed on the way to the palace.

There were things we liked about each other, Scottie and I, traits we shared. Scottie—the kinda mate I almost found in Damian. We could swim all day in each other's reflections, resurfacing with some deep connection, but we were never able to completely fill the hole we both had in our chests. I couldn't talk to him about the same things I talked to Pieces about, and didn't want to. He wanted me to be more like her, and I couldn't. He told me stories of their adventures together, how she would sometimes bring her drums with her when they first met.

"She got me into this routine in the first place," he said. "She's changed, you know. Holding something back. She used to have that spark. The same fire you got in you, if only you could just see it."

"Have we finished with this Hallmark moment?" I joked.

Couldn't see it. I felt neither sparky nor full of fire. In fact, any excitement I had about our lifestyle was now beginning to dry up. I was tired. Of being broke, of feeling shit for being broke. Never experienced this kind of broke before. It was changing me. My father had always made sure I had what I needed, and when I wanted extra there was always the sock drawer. Now there was no sock drawer. And sometimes I felt like a pretender, sitting there with Scottie's hat in my lap, keenly aware of every inch of my father's appalled, disappointed, and embarrassed disapproval. Convinced myself it was better than being like him; he worked a job he hated just to pay the bills. Knew I didn't want to end up like that.

But I wasn't Pieces. I wasn't Scottie. I was me, brought up to be one of the proud, talented 10 percent, and was now practically begging for money. In the pit of my belly, I felt the old souls of the Black Renaissance turning over in their graves.

◎

One muggy day in some tube station, I watched from a bench near a candy dispenser as the off-work-at-five cattle pushed through. Studied the mirrors bolted on the walls near the tracks reflecting the masses of bodies on the platform, my eyes straining to see the rancher driving the herd. Shifted into a squat next to the bench to get a better angle. Was more invisible on ground level. After nearly trampling me with his black boots, one character spit right in front of me, his bag nearly swiping my head. Sometimes those that did see me would drop change, though I asked for nothing. Change I wanted to throw back.

Rush hour, which could be the most profitable time of day, was also the most excruciating. Watching the cogs in the money machine pushing into crammed tube cars, slinging "get a job" glances in our direction. Miss one day of work and you risked getting fired, your car could be taken away, you could lose the house. Homeless beggars, buskers, those living rough clarified all those fears in these people. Sometimes it was too much. And Scottie's relentless challenging seemed futile. Ridiculous. Stupid. Fuck it.

After the crowd had thinned, a creepy old man in a suit eyed me too hard. He squatted down, leaned his pasty face close to mine, and asked if I wanted to come with him, "little girl." I told him to fuck off. He laughed before moving on, unblocking my view of a sign across the track that read "Closed-circuit cameras are operating in this station to make your journey safer."

I looked for Scottie. He was somewhere farther up the platform. Without a word, I left him to continue his show alone. Needed air. Craved headspace. The pavement slanted before me. I lit a cig. Exhaled. Needed to walk. From Kennington station, I strolled past the Oval, down Brixton Road, ambling. No change for a bus.

With dusk scraping its eyelid across the sun, I hid behind my shades and hood. Numb to everything. Walking down those London roads, streets, ways, high streets, closes, and squares, I realized that it was the same ole, same ole.

Body and psyche know when you're in an unfamiliar place. Perceptions snap surreal, senses are heightened. Psychic antennae reach out and search for some crevice, groove, or nuance of the known, not necessarily the familiar but the internally and eternally known. It's an exchange. The landmarks, bent signposts, potholes, worn-in pavements, white walls tagged in spray paint and indelible super-nib markers—they give you an idea of where you are, a reference point, and your psychic antennae place their own marks there. Each time you pass. Each time some significant or insignificant moment is experienced there. The landscape somehow becomes a part of you and you of it. After a while the novelty wears away like the shine of a much-used doorknob worn smooth. You know that at the corner of such-and-such and such-and-such, there will be a graffitied wall, painted over every other month but only staying white for a few hours. You know that near the second traffic light, as you turn on the corner near the KFC, there is an uneven bit in the sidewalk. You know it so well that your foot automatically misses it without conscious thought. You even know where the dog shit will be.

I wanted to get somewhere else. Get that buzz of just-arriving all over again. That buzz I had when I opened the door into the New York loft and met Pieces. And Sincara again. Sincara. I started to pray for the return of Sincara.

Felt an electromagnetic temperature rise as I approached Brixton's center. Paused before heading down Coldharbour Lane toward the squat. Jazz riffs tickled my ears like the smell of food when you're hungry. The music was coming from a side street. I headed toward it, and there, positioned in a cubbyhole on Marcus Garvey Road, was Soul Food Books. There was a standard kit drummer and a saxophonist jamming with a poet. I stood in the back, along with a growing motley audience. Could just about blend in, which was a relief, and for a moment I relaxed, poetry sliding past my ears. Casually scanned the books as the first half of the jam finished. There would be a five-minute break before the open mic.

Conversation a low rumble, ebbing and flowing around me, I realized I wasn't the only person there on my own. Avoided one man's eyes as he nodded, making his way toward me, and continued scanning the bookshelf stuffed with Black literature. I wasn't in the mood to make polite or political conversation so I headed for the toilet. Somebody's feelings might get hurt. Those of the melanin nation weren't always allies—you could be diminished under the interrogative eye questioning your "realness."

In Chicago I'd been excited to finally meet other "conscious" Brown-skinned folks. Others who opposed imperialistic slavery posing as the American dream. Being in that bookshop clear across the Atlantic reminded me of Damian and the "Black consciousness" meetings he had with his "brothers." Had a similar atmosphere, but different. Damian's meetings had been dominated by a bunch of ego-induced Black Power rantings—the few women there were introduced as the girlfriends of brother so-and-so. They sat there saying little or nothing at all. The boys went on and on about a number of Black male revolutionaries— how the Man killed *their* men, *their* leadership, *their* positive role models. At the time, I was jazzed to hear so much dialogue around Black history, but felt invisible.

"We have got to learn from our leaders before us, brothers," Damian had said, licking his lips the way he did when he was about to put his saxophone in his mouth or make a point. "We have to strengthen ourselves because the Black maaaan is an endangered species. Especially the *conscious* Black man."

I couldn't hold it down. "And we should also learn from our sisters. Right?" Silence. I continued, "Black women revolutionaries like Angela Davis, Assata Shakur—hell, Harriet Tubman was a revolutionary, an activist." The brothers looked at me like I'd clearly missed the point. Damian seemed embarrassed.

"Assata who? Baby, Black women pose no threat to the Man. He uses her against us," Damian "corrected" me. "It was Rodney King, not Rhonda King, that got beat down by the pigs, remember that."

I checked the room to see if the lips of the other women were forming words of protest. They looked down and away. Damian closed the meeting asking if anyone wanted a beer. I looked up at Damian in disbelief. How could he treat me like that? This was not the guy I horsed around with in Crickledown. This was not the guy who spoke to me as his equal in debates of everything from passive resistance to extraterrestrial life forms. Damian gave me my first copy of Alex Haley's *Autobiography of Malcolm X*. It had whetted my appetite for more. Sent me on a search to find the women revolutionaries. The boy who'd encouraged me to open my mind was now a Black man engaging in a dick war with the Man, and had just effectively shut me down. I was amazing in Missouri, but invisible in Illinois. I was revolutionary material in St. Louis, but Uncle Tom in Chicago. I stopped talking to him about my visions and sharing my writing, and he stopped talking to me, period, about anything real. Patronized me as if I were no more than "his woman." He even had the nerve to walk over and peck me on the cheek after the last meeting that I would ever be present for again came to a close. "Do you want a beer, baby?"

I nodded my head anyway and watched as Damian went to join his brothers. And my sisters . . . well, my sisters, my sistahs, had their backs to me now, talking among themselves. I was thinking for two seconds about joining them when I overheard, "Who does she think she is anyway, talking that white-feminist malarkey." "And what about our *sisters*," one of them sneered, mimicking me. "She needs to get her priorities straight. They are murdering our men out there!"

I decided to head for the girls' room instead. Went in and did what I always did: studied my face and whispered, "Yeah, still here, but what am I doing here?"

In Soul Food Books, I walked out of the toilet I'd escaped to and looked for a back door. Wanted to leave before I found myself stepping in it. But the back door was locked and the only way out was right next to the stage. Slipped my journal in my back pocket and made my way through the thickening crowd of largely Black faces. I was near the stage, brushing past the tight audience, and I felt my journal jostle a bit but was in such a hurry to get out, I didn't bother to push it back firmly into my pocket. Seconds before my hand reached the doorknob, I heard the journal hit the floor with a flat thump. Damn. I'd succeeded in doing exactly the opposite of what I intended to do. Eyes were on me. Having trouble getting volunteers, the emcee scanned the crowd. Her adept eye caught me fumbling with my journal.

"You with the book," she said, waving me up. "You look like you have something to say."

There was no spotlight but I felt heat shooting through my crown, turning my face into a sweaty mass. The emcee smiled at me and teased, "Looks like there are a lot of words in that book. Are you a poet or not? Maybe you're a poet and didn't even know it." The drummer did a rat-a-tat splash, some folks in the crowd laughed.

"Don't be afraid, it's a safe space," she said in a loud whisper to me, her hand outreached. As much as I wanted to dash it seemed wrong to leave her hanging. Before I knew it she'd managed to get me behind the mic. I opened the bent notebook to a page I knew well. Still, it took me a minute to catch air. I began almost inaudibly, throat swollen shut, hands slightly but visibly shaking the book in my hand.

> *Homogenized, colonized, and sold as advertised . . .*
> *the revolution is NOW! A sleek new car with revolutionary gas*
> *   mileage . . .*
> *the revolution is NOW! Edited for your viewing pleasure on*
> *the national news with Big Brothah having big-stick Peace Talks*
> *My bomb is bigger*
> *Making the world safe for democracy and*
> *revolutionary soap pop-pop . . .*

My eyes didn't leave the pages. And as I picked up steam, the drummer found a place in my cadence to drop a rhythm. The sax came in and out with five-note scales.

Rumor has it Uncle Sam fucked Betsy Ross
though many still insist that AmeriKKKa is an
immaculate conception
founded on some white man's erection
I mean freedom of expression

Beginning to feel carried by the sounds, I resisted looking directly into the eyes of onlookers. Except for some shy glances, I was focused on something way beyond. Midway through now. The journal found its home in my back pocket and I chanted the rest of the piece from memory. I lost myself in the *all* of it all. I'd gone into another realm, a place that felt as right as any right place I had ever felt and that kind of right was rare—I was exactly where I was supposed to be.

And how many young homies wearing the Malcom X hat
really know where the revolution at
where the revolution at?

The sax trailed off, a line of notes chasing the text to an ending, and I parachuted back to earth on that stage in front of all of those faces. The room was silent. Claps came slowly. Hesitantly. Like scattered pops of a firecracker. *That's it*, I thought, *time to sail*. I jumped off the stage and exhaled. The next poet was introduced. An excruciating self-consciousness enveloped me. Pulled out my tobacco to make a cig, headed for the exit. Definitely needed air like smoggy skies need rain. To clear my mind and escape the curious glances. Pushed through the door and lit my narrow, fluted rollie.

Outside, a skinny guy with a mass of dreads smiled at me while talking to a group of people. I hadn't intentionally looked his way, was only deciding which way to walk. Wasn't sure I should go back home. But might as well. Hitched up my collar, sucked in the cig, and put one foot in front of the other. As I approached, the dude with dreads held out his fist.

"Yeah, yeah sistah . . . Dug your stuff," he said, smiling. "MJ." He brushed his thumb at his chest. "And you?"

"Skye." I touched his fist, imitating what I'd seen others do.

"Yeah, I saw you at the jam at Scottie's squat . . . You're not letting him get you caught up in any trouble, are you?"

Taken off guard a little, I did vaguely remember him from the party at the palace when I first arrived. It seemed a lifetime ago.

"You know Scottie?" I threw out noncommittally.

"Yeah, I've known him for a long time. . ." He looked past me. "Speak of the devil."

Scottie was strolling down the road, guitar strap loose like an undone tie. I realized I was actually glad to see him.

"You should come down to The Venue and perform sometime," MJ offered. "In fact, next week there's a spot open there. It would pay a little bit, and give me a chance to hear more of your stuff. What do you think?"

By this time, Scottie had caught up with me. MJ coolly greeted Scottie and gave me his number.

"Call me and let me know." He left us to talk to someone else he knew.

Scottie grabbed my arm and pulled me away. "I don't trust him aaat aaallll."

"Who, MJ?" I shrugged. "He asked me to do stuff for some gig he's organizing."

"Be careful with him . . ."

"Why?"

We started walking. "He uses people," Scottie said, putting

his arm around my shoulders in the way that pals do. His mouth was close to my ear. "He's pseudo . . . a pretender."

"What makes you say that?"

"One time I was laying some lyrics on some folks outside the shop. They wouldn't let me onstage with my guitar. He came out and told me to take my rubbish elsewhere."

"Well, you can be a little aggressive."

"'*Aggressive*'?" He stopped in his tracks, took a step back, forcing me to stop walking and turn round toward him as he spoke. He looked like a wounded cub. "I wonder about you. Can't you see that what I do is good work? Subversive work. I am *real*."

"What do you mean, you wonder about me?"

"I mean, are you with me or not . . ." He started walking again, taking long strides past me, barely looking at me.

"'Course I'm with you . . . What are you goin' on about?" I double-stepped to catch him and keep up.

"Never mind . . . It's just that sometimes you remind me a little too much of Pieces," he said. "What happened to you, anyway? You just disappeared."

"I needed some air," I said, not wanting to elaborate. I couldn't stop thinking about the buzz I'd felt reading onstage, and I wanted more. I let Scottie march on ahead of me, put MJ's number in my pocket, and smiled. Things were looking up.

INT. TRASHED PALACE - EARLY AFTERNOON

Skye moves about the flat restlessly, plops on
her bed, and flips through her journal, but
writes nothing. She jumps up and moves to
the window above, where Pieces used to sleep.
Her futon is still rolled up under one of her
colorful cloths. Skye notices an old canvas
stuck behind the roll, pulls it out, and looks
at it for a while before stuffing it back where
she found it. She grabs her bag and guitar, and
heads out the door.

The next day I got up early (so before noon) and took an instant coffee, my journal, a pen, and my guitar to the park. I had work to do to prepare for the gig, and though I didn't plan on using the guitar, as shabby as my playing was, it seemed to free me up for writing. I would strum, practice chord changes, pick around, and hear a poem before I wrote it during the quieter moments of the day. I would leave the park when the lunch crowd got too thick. But sometimes, when I was lost in my own world, people caught me unawares.

"Keep at it, young lady." Lines framed her ageless, bright brown eyes peeping out from under a swath of draped cloth, its pastel colors muted by time. She took a few steps toward me. "Open your mouth more when you sing." Lifting her arm, she revealed a cane hidden under her layered cloak, tapping it on the pavement in my direction to make a point.

It writhed in her hand and for a glitch in time, I swear I heard it hiss-whisper, "Sincara . . ."

She flipped a shiny coin in my direction. I caught it.

"Hey, I don't . . ." but by the time I said "sing" she had already walked away.

I shook my head and rubbed my eyes. Pocketed the pound coin and rolled a tiny spliff for the road. Whether or not the woman was real, the message was clear to me. And I had a one-pound coin to prove it. Maybe Scottie was right. Maybe I *could* do this. Decided if I could do what I did at the bookstore and manage a gig, maybe I could have a go at busking. Better than a life working for McFuckery's, and hell, I couldn't even get a job there if I wanted.

I kept reminding myself that I had little choice if I wanted to make some kinda dough and move on. Psyched myself up, traveling from one end of the Northern line to the other, and the same again with the District, Victoria, and Hammersmith lines, my guitar a silent witness. I couldn't muster a single chord. Instead I would scribble down weird visions in my diary. I got little sleep those days but whatever shut-eye I caught was intense. Sometimes I'd doze off on the tube. Vivid dreams would drip and splatter onto the page. I'd wake up at the end of the line and walk to the opposite platform, travel back the way I came.

One time the train paused at the platform at Clapham Common longer than usual. An undercover metro cop jostled his way through a crowd of waiting passengers to the car in front of me, catching the arm of a youth exiting. Flashed his badge and read the boy his rights. The youth raised his arms in the air, as if to say, *It wasn't me*. The cop pointed to a CCTV camera perched above the mirror at the end of the platform. The youth hung his head. With the situation under control, the train took off.

I waited for the next train, looking up at the surveillance camera that had busted the young man moments before. Felt like a poser with the guitar on my back. Made the decision to take the Central line from Notting Hill to Oxford Circus, then the Victoria line down to Brixton. The windows of the tube, like a movie screen, flickered ghostly images of passengers standing, sitting, staring into space, leaving, boarding. Cables twisting along the tube walls fell into streamlined sequences behind my reflection.

At Oxford Circus I decided to go up for some air—dancing

behind one of the many commuters, I managed to just get through the gates. Took exit number fifteen toward Piccadilly Circus. The retail shops stood side by side; mannequins displayed the latest fashions, high market and trendy. Tourists zombied from one shop to the next while frustrated nine-to-fivers pushed past them. They had to get back to the office, rushing to where they didn't want to be in the first place. Monday's the longest workday of the week, next to Wednesday.

Piccadilly Circus: it was a mini-slice of Times Square; advertisements blinked slogans flogging brand names while pigeons scavenged among the tourists sitting on the concrete-island roundabout. The angel Eros stood sputtering water into the metal-and-stone fountain in the center. I had to sit down. Get my bearings.

A nearby busker began playing a Dylan anthem.

How does it feeeeeel to be on your own. A complete unknown . . . like a rolling stone . . .

I made a rollie, wishing I had some spare change. For a moment I felt disconnected from the mad space around me: detached, though sitting in the center of consumption junction. Then two things happened; some pigeon shit landed on my shoe and a group of white American tourists deposited themselves right in front of me, blocking my view. I mean, their asses were literally in my face. I moved over a bit closer to the busker.

They held a Central London map between them.

"Greg, honey, I think Oxford Circus is that way, honey."

I thought, *Oh Christ, it's the Brady Bunch on holiday*. Complete with video and disposable cameras. The ditsy daughter could've been the same one I'd sat behind in history class my sophomore year in high school. Cheerleader, popular, most photographs in the yearbook. She'd flip back her Farrah Fawcett hair every five minutes, leaving yellow strands on my desk. When we got to the two paragraphs that covered slavery in our American history books she came up and asked me, the only Black kid in the class, if I could help her with her paper on the subject. I knew I was supposed to be thrilled that the most popular girl in school finally saw me, but had never felt so humiliated.

I had an overwhelming urge to stick my boot up the ass of the girl who was blocking my view of Piccadilly. Before I could follow through, the busker, seeing possible punters, began his rendition of an American classic. He had them locked in by the time he got to *and they were singing, bye, bye, Miss American Pie*. Bobby Brady, dressed in hippie surfer gear, was bopping the hardest. He went to drop some change. The busker said, "Thank you very much."

"Nice guitar playing. Can I have a go, man?" the over-confident surfer dude asked. The street musician seemed reluctant but the prospect of more change made his decision for him. Surfer Dude began to softly strum the guitar before coming out with a James Taylor tune. He apparently impressed his girlfriend or sister (it was hard to tell), Marcia.

"This is so cool. I should get a picture!" she squealed.

"Yeah, okay, but it's gotta be with this dude here." He slid the busker a fiver, making sure his girlfriend caught his generosity. "Thanks for letting me have a go on your guitar, man!"

"Oh, I wanna be in the picture," Marcia whined, tossing her blond hair back. She turned to me, suddenly visible, and asked if I minded taking the picture. Keeping my words to a minimum, I took the camera. I didn't want them to suss that I was American too. I pointed the camera in their direction and clicked. And I don't know why, but I started walking, then sprinting, away. Still holding the camera, laughing as I went, I snapped shots at random, catching who knows what. I heard the inbred Brady family screaming behind me, "Oh my god, I can't believe he stole our camera, somebody stop him!" as I tore down into the tube station and got lost among the crowds. Luckily there was a gate open. I sped through, ignoring the cries from security. I think I even stopped to snap them before sliding down the escalator, guitar in my lap. Managed to duck onto an overcrowded Bakerloo line train to Elephant and Castle. Made it to the end of the line exhausted but elevated. Decided that before mashing myself in with the others, I would wait it out. Northern line. Elephant and Castle.

It was rush hour and the platform was packed. Masses of stressed-out worms squirmed and pushed into tins of transport. The platform heaved a sigh of relief once they were all safely on the train. Snapped a picture of myself in front of the blue-and-red tube symbol. I then pointed the camera into the dim, dusty, rusted tunnel, tracks dropping off into the darkness. Felt calm, the same way I felt when I smelled a library or a secondhand bookstore. Everyone else was looking in the other direction, the way the train would eventually arrive. I leaned over closer to the edge, trying to imbibe the image whole, so that I could call on it during unbearable moments.

I would have sat out the hours between 4:30 p.m. and 7:00 p.m. either in a café or pub if I'd happened upon some loose change left on the seats from unlucky passengers. Back when we'd first gone out together, Pieces had called it "offerings from Sincara." But I hadn't found any change. So I sat on the platform and pulled out a scrap of paper. When I wrote, I breathed easier. Began writing about my *Brady Bunch* adventure. Knew that when I told Pieces she would tilt her head back slightly and release that out-of-nowhere laugh of hers. When. The melancholy attached to that one word, "when," spread through me like the flu, dissolving all the muscles in my body.

A while later, I decided to head to the surface. By this time another northbound train had opened its doors to let out a horde of nine-to-five zombies. They pushed me into the lift.

"Mind the closing doors."

My nose was nearly touching a poster advertising legal help for immigrants. Underneath it in ballpoint ink, the words "go home nigger" were scribbled. Dark-brown bodies were poised for the opening of the elevator and then bustled past me to the nearby barriers. I couldn't move. Even as I heard the Englishwoman robot repeat, "Stand clear of the closing doors." Above me a surveillance camera blinked its eye. I stared up at it as the lift took me down again.

By the time I did come up from under, it was dark out. Night always crept up on me. I jingled a couple coins I didn't realize I had deep in my bag and decided to get refreshments. Took the usual route home, down Coldharbour Lane, under a wash of after-hours street vendors whispering, "Got green, got white, got that skunk, mate, that grade, Rasta . . ." This time I walked right past the Trashed Palace to a run-down kids' playground nearby. Sat up in the small hut over the slide with my guitar, and played to the night air. Tomorrow, I decided, I would go it alone. Again. Try to busk. As I downed one of two cans of beer, the hum of distant traffic blurred into an ocean of sounds. Crushed the can under my boot and finished the other one, which left me heavy-lidded and almost calm. Slumber hit me sledgehammer thick.

INT. TRASHED PALACE - EARLY MORNING
Scottie comes out of his room stretching. He
looks over into Skye's area and sees she is not
there. Her recorder is peeking out from under
her pillow. He picks it up, pushes play. Skye's
muffled voice comes out of the speaker.

> SKYE
> (V.O.)
> The sky is the color of a black-and-
> white movie. I am on the run through the
> streets of London. But there is no place
> to hide—a monitor stands in every corner
> shopwindow, projecting every passerby.
> I am riding a unicycle. Flying through
> the air, I use a staff as a paddle, and
> one beat after a lightning rod of sound,
> bluesy guitar riffs stabbing the air, the
> staff turns into a serpent in my hands.
> Sincara. Startled, I fall off my bike and
> when I land, I bump my head hard.

"Wake up, wake up! You can't sleep here."

I woke with a jerk, smashing my head against the low roof of the kids' hut. The sun was blending blues in the sky. It was early.

A middle-aged groundskeeper holding a black bin liner in gloved hands stood over me, glowering.

"Sorry." I slung him a half-abashed smile before making my escape via the slide. Guitar in hand, I exited the playground to the beat of my pounding cranium.

Back at the palace, Scottie was having his wake-and-bake breakfast when I walked in.

"You coming out with me today?" Scottie asked, taking a sip of his first cuppa. "It's been a while . . ."

"Naw . . ."

"You sure?" He took it personally. A slight pout formed on his lips as he cleaned his nail with a makeshift plectrum.

"Yeah . . ." I went over to the fridge.

"Wow, you are hardcore these days, yeah?"

I popped open the can, licked the foam from my finger. "Learned from the best. Want some?" I grabbed a glass and poured.

"Maybe after my tea." He eyed me suspiciously. "Rough night?"

"Try rough week . . . rough month, year . . . take your pick."

"What's up?"

"Nothing's up, that's the problem."

"What's eating you?"

I swallowed the rest of the beer in my glass and took the can. I walked over to the kitchen window and stared out onto the street. A balding, thin Black man dressed in white carried a white wooden cross down the road. I'd seen him before, in different neighborhoods in different parts of London. He never said anything. Just walked past, solemn expression stitched to his face. Nobody ever bothered him, no one ever mentioned him. He looked the part of a saint. No one could escape the feeling that his presence was an omen. A sign.

"What's up with you?" Scottie came up behind me and touched me on the shoulder. I moved away from him.

"I'm not in the mood."

I took the beer with me into the bathroom and started a bath. Sat on the tub's edge and watched as it filled up . . . the water splashing and filling the tub . . . I closed my eyes. I coulda been sitting at the creek in Crickledown, Missouri, listening to the water rush over all those pebbles, glossing them up. They dulled once in your hand and under the sun. I would search for perfectly flat ones to skip over the water. Had a seven-skip record.

"I'll see you later." Scottie popped his head in the door. "You sure you're okay?"

"Scottie," I said switching off the taps, "could ya just give me some headspace?"

I heard the door click shut behind him. I stripped and sunk into the almost boiling water, beads of sweat forming on my forehead under the blanket of steam rising and filling the room. It felt a little like a baptism when what I needed was an exorcism—I was feeling that mean. Wrestled with a twisted guilt that I carried with me from childhood. That everything was my fault. From my mother's unhappiness, to my father's frustration, from Damian's embarrassment, to my "sistah" Pieces's cold shoulder, from the bar manager's belligerence to the reason that old man asked me if I wanted to come with him, "little girl"—it was all my fault. Not so much because of the way that I am, more *that I am*. An ancient ache became more pronounced in my belly. So much was knotted up in my gut. No matter how much I wanted to, I couldn't unscrew it. The mechanism was deeply entrenched. I needed to design a suitable monkey wrench. Slid down into the steamy water until I was fully submerged. Let out a sigh, watching bubbles rise and trouble the surface.

EXT. OUTSIDE TRASHED PALACE

Scottie stands chatting with PROF. They both
walk across the road.

Skye exits the palace, adjusts the guitar over
her shoulder, and starts walking.

Prof lets himself into the building.

Scottie, keeping his distance, follows Skye.

After the bath, still in an iffy mood, I psyched myself up and left the palace, guitar hanging off my back. Grabbed another strong beer, ignoring the disapproving look of the old Jamaican man tending the shop. Settled on making a home on some tube platform for a while. Maybe I would play to myself as I had on the playground the night before, if nothing else. The gig that emcee had offered me at The Venue was tomorrow, and I didn't feel ready.

Guitar strap molding itself into my shoulder, I realized the poison I spent my last pound on was beginning to work. It took the better part of the 9-percent black-label can to get me close to playing the first chord, but I started. I ignored some passing requests for songs, mumbling something about being only an apprentice. Took another sip from the can before placing it next to the wall behind me. My fingers pressed against her metal strings. An imperceptible vibration sang from her neck and out her belly. I dug in my pocket to retrieve a makeshift plectrum Scottie fashioned for me out of a used phone card.

I looked up across the platform and saw Pieces. Silent. A train was rumbling in, the front lights casting slanting shadows between us. A miracle. I looked up to smile in victory, but she wasn't there.

I blinked and opened my lids only to see the advertisement wallpapering the graying underground intestine. I wasn't missing her, anyway. Who gave a fuck if she never came back. The brew circulated through my bloodstream, warming up an anger, pushing down a pain. Gripping the makeshift plectrum, I began the only three-chord pattern I knew well. Breathing in the tube air, I bent my ear to catch the tune in rhythm with the departing train. Felt something lodged in my chest go with it, catching the bluebird sparks spinning from steely friction; a wailing came from my gut.

And then I was singing.

I got the blues
running round my heart
moving down to my shoes
and now I'm walking it off.

My eyes were closed and I went in. Oblivious to the clink of coins dropping in front of me, oblivious to the muffled warning coming over the intercom, sentencing unlicensed buskers to maximum penalty charges and/or arrest.

I played and played and played until I forgot about playing. I was so out of it, or into it, that I didn't even see Scottie's natty 'fro bopping up and down among the crowds passing through; he had been standing there listening for some time. Later he would say that it was a cool kinda reversal of roles. Usually I watched his back. This time he was watching mine.

About a beat after my last guitar stroke, first I saw Scottie then I saw the cops approaching. Scottie saw them too.

"Time to move on," Scottie stated the obvious, hurriedly gathering the change that had been tossed in front of me. "GO!" he hissed.

Coming out of my trance, I slung the guitar over my shoulder and started in the opposite direction, only to eye metro-security muscle making their way toward us with determined looks on their faces. The only way out was through the boys in blue.

When they arrested Scottie and me, my reaction was somewhere between bored annoyance and angry fear. I'd had a few run-ins both in Chicago and New York. Mostly for fare dodging. You never know what the cops are going to do: let you go with minor humiliation or go the whole way. These London Bobbies were on a mission. Seems that Scottie's interference didn't help things. That, and their finding me with no valid travel card, was enough to get us both a night in a holding cell.

As we were cuffed, I practiced the Fifth and said next to nothing. I wasn't sure what my rights were in Britain, but I'd heard about the ramifications of the British suss law in action back in the eighties. I knew I had rights, but in my bones, I knew they could do whatever they wanted. Survival instincts came into play. I held it down. Hoped the Bobbies would realize that we weren't hardened criminals and save the cell space for the murderers and rapists. I had to chuckle to myself, at first, because in the beginning it was hard to take them seriously, growing up in a country where the cops were armed. I learned, however, that the artillery was not far away and even without guns they were just as intimidating, and racist. On the way to the station I heard them calling the arrest in: "One male and one female, IC3 unknown." I later found out that "IC3" was code for a person of African and/or Asian descent. The "unknown'" I assumed was because neither one of us had ID on us.

"Where are you from?" a bushy, dark-haired cop asked, trying to make conversation while taking my details at the station. I told him "from America" and he was like, "Yeah, yeah, but where are you *from*?" He went on proudly: "My girlfriend's a Black. Her mum's from Nigeria. You kinda remind me of her."

"Does she know you refer to her as 'a Black'?" I asked, unimpressed. He said nothing else after that except the perfunctory questions for his forms.

My cell, a sleeper, was just about a paceable distance. Step one-two-three, turn; step one-two-three, turn . . . There was nothing to do but wait. The dark-haired man at the check-in desk wouldn't allow me my phone call. Insisted he would call anyone I wanted to reach. I decided against it. I was terrified of being left here alone with no one knowing where I was, but I didn't trust the cop. Besides, who would I call? Pieces was in Amsterdam, Scottie was in here with me. There was no way on earth I would call my father. I found a comfortable position on the hard concrete bed and waited for sleep to find me. And somehow it did.

The sky is the color of a black-and-white movie. I am on the run. I swim through the air using a staff as a paddle. It turns into a snake. Sincara. Startled, I fall for forever before landing hard, knocking my skull on the pavement. When I come to, a crowd of white coats stand around me: Do you remember your name? What's your name? Everything is a haze. I have no idea where or who I am. But I recognize a sound now breezing past my ear, that familiur blues riff. I try to lift myself up to see where it's coming from, but fall back immediately into a deep, soundless sleep.

INT. TRASHED PALACE

Prof takes down the mirror in the bathroom and
removes a small square of wall. He pulls out a
small camera and cleans the lens before putting
everything back into place. His phone goes off.
It's a voice message from Scottie.

                    SCOTTIE
                    (V.O.)
          Just got out. Maybe headed your way.

Guitars strapped onto our backs, looking like the Bobbsey twins, Scottie and I left the station the following afternoon.

"What annoyed the transport police"—Scottie was all rant as we left—"was that the punters were actually *enjoying* it. You know, you were there!" He pulled a cigarette butt from the inside pocket of his jean jacket. It was speckless. I wondered how he did it, especially with all the rough sleeping and situations he found himself in.

"I don't really remember," I said, trying to picture the night before.

I didn't tell him about the dream in the cell. It freaked me out. All of what had happened in the last ten hours or so freaked me out. I wanted a beer. Kinda wondered when I'd started drinking so much. Kinda didn't care. In about five hours I was due to perform at MJ's poetry reading and I wasn't sure I could face it. I felt emotionally exhausted. On the other hand it was paid, and I needed the cash.

"Hey, let me play guitar with you?" Scottie offered. "We could go through what you are reading, right? And whatever fire you were playing in the tube, I am sure I could find a riff to make it even sweeter."

"I'm not playing this guitar," I said, just then noticing that I had managed to bust the G string. "Not even sure I'm up for this, man."

Scottie stopped mid-step and shot me a look of amused

incredulity. He then swung his guitar from back to front in a graceful arc and answered me through Curtis Mayfield.

People, get ready, there's a train comin'. You don't need no baggage, you just get on board.

And just like that, it went from being my show to our show.

"You got any beer money, Scottie?"

"No, but you do." He pulled out a plastic bag full of coins, some one- and two-pound discs glistened against the copper and silver. "I picked it up before the police got to us," he said proudly. "They didn't see me do it, too many people. They couldn't prove it wasn't mine, so." He handed the bag to me.

"I made that?"

"Yes," Scottie said, as if he had won some major victory. "You made that."

◉

Spending the night in a jail cell affects your metabolism. Your BPM changes. The first few steps you take outside are slightly outta sync with the rest. Reality takes on a new glimmer. Not to pretend I had in any way been a bona fide jailbird—I only spent one night in there, after all. But now I had a performance to get through. I would later find out that it was a local council–funded event, one of three planned for the summer, specifically to showcase Black talent in Brixton and beyond. Each poet would have ten to fifteen minutes onstage. It wasn't a lot, but it was the longest set I'd ever done.

As we approached The Venue just in front of All Saints Church in Brixton, bats' wings began to pound in my gut. I'd never done a real live gig before—a planned live gig, on a stage, and paid—but more than that, I was entering the domain of London's Black poetry scene. I felt as if I was about to undergo some initiation. I had the urge to have that inverted Lacan moment in the bathroom. What would they see? Would they see what I saw when I looked in the mirror? Could I fix my face in a way that would make them see me as I wished to be seen? I had to stop thinking. I was beginning to realize I could only go *there*—the place I had been the first night onstage at the open mic and then later in the tube station—when I turned off the chatter.

I decided I would shoot from the heart but keep my journal in hand, like an ammunition belt. Scottie and I rolled into The Venue smelling of our strong beers. The punchy odor preceded our entry. Maybe we looked a bit out of sorts, Scottie and me in crumpled, slept-in clothes, both of us complete with battered guitars. Maybe some thought we came in off the streets.

Those that greeted us pulled up distant smiles. Most of them knew one another from other gigs, from the scene, as fellow Black literati, struggling Black artists. I wanted to believe in the air of unity about, I wanted to be a part of it all. I searched for MJ's face. And when he saw me, his smile, too, was distant.

"How are you, sistah?"

"Could be better, could be worse. You know Scottie."

"Yes, you okay?" MJ asked Scottie.

"As good as could be expected."

"Yeah, we just got out from a night in a holding cell," I said, eager for a sympathetic ear. "We were picked up by the cops last night for no real reason."

MJ's face remained straight. He retained neutrality. But underneath that was an air of not being surprised or impressed. He had well-practiced riding-the-fence skills.

Never changed his expression, even when being (happily) distracted by someone (else) he knew.

I overheard folks talking about what they were up to, their work, the weather, tonight's lineup. "Oh, you're performing tonight as well?" Not far beneath the brotherhood-and-sisterhood smiles and demeanors lay the subtle tension of competition.

I listened to the poets before me perform. Each one was introduced onto the stage after some witty words by MJ. The stage was huge, and a spotlighted single mic and music stand lay exactly in the center of a space big enough for a full band and their dancers. The poets started making their way from "next up," often arriving at the mic just in time for "and give it up for . . ." Well thought out and organized—MJ knew his job well.

Scottie and I would be up close to the end of the first half. I don't remember MJ calling my name as much as Scottie taking my arm. Stinking of super-strength black-label brew and operating under post-jail shock, Scottie and I swanned onstage, beer cans in hand. Scottie insisted on introducing me, but not before paying homage to the other poets. Seemed like MJ felt as if Scottie was fucking with his rights as part of the Union du Emcees or something. I saw sparks fly from his eyes in Scottie's direction.

I put my journal on the stand, but the words were a blur of ink—swishing through the beer goggles that seemed to have sprung up over my eyes. Scottie ended his introductions with a loud *ZI-ZANK* strum on his guitar and turned to me with a "ready when you are" smile. I looked out at the public, a myriad of skin tones in the stands looking back expectantly. Before me, poets had waxed (and waned) lyrically about Africa, racism, love, self-evolution in cloned cadences. I knew that I couldn't do what they did how they did it, understood that I didn't know what I was doing, and in that moment, just before panic set in, someone yelled out:

"Speak, sister!"

Scottie did his version of a Hendrix chord slide, fingering punctuated by his signature guitar strum. He assumed a Jim Morrison swagger and I started off the set Public Enemy–style—"fuckthepolice fuckthepolice fuckthemuthahfuckingpolice"—disrupting the general mood. "I said fuck the—" then held the mic toward the crowd. Behind me Scottie had my back, yelled, "fuck the—" and, encouraged, I did it again. "I said fuck the"—a few in the crowd joined in with a feeble "fuck the" in unison with Scottie, who was grinning by now—"motherfuckin' police!" I rounded off the phrase and just went into a meltdown, a torrid stream of "fuck the police" after "fuck the police," as if I were consumed with some kind of rage and punching the person who had triggered me, over and over and over again. My mind was blank to anything else. Scottie, in his element, rocked out, mixing some kind of James Brown rhythm guitar with some discordant chord changes that echoed how I was feeling.

I took it for granted that it was a space to talk about what was real. What was immediate. What was happening day-to-day, right now. That's what poetry, hip-hop, improv, and rock 'n' roll were all about. So I thought. But the emcee decided we were too drunk to finish, that we ruined the sanctity of the poetry stage with our beggars' beers.

MJ came onstage, cut me short. "And that was Skye, ladies and gentlemen! Let's give her a hand." He whispered to me, "Go get some coffee or something and maybe we will have *you* on again."

Scottie didn't look too pleased as we shuffled offstage.

"What's going on?" he asked.

"Apparently we're too drunk."

161

"What?!"

"This is not a rock concert, but a poetry reading . . . No beer onstage," I said, approximating MJ's voice.

"That's bullshit."

"I know, but . . . maybe I was a bit, you know, shaky."

"No reason to cut you off . . . You were fine."

I looked at the beautiful Black faces in the audience. This generation's international Black Renaissance, spiritual and lyrically nimble. I belonged there. I didn't belong there. A couple of would-be poets swung self-satisfactory smiles my way as I lurched toward the exit. *Good riddance*, they seemed to say. Then the Cypress Hill lyrics began pumping from the inside of my eardrum, *I ain't goin' out like that . . . ain't goin out like that*. Before I reached the exit, I did a U-turn.

Sitting just behind the front-row middle chair, I patiently listened to poet Afro-disiaca read her queengoddessmother poem. At the end of two poems she announced that she felt uneasy.

"I am feeling much negative energy," she said in her high-toned voice, looking straight at me. Damn, I wasn't doing anything to her. Felt my neck itch. If she didn't feel she had the strength to go on, I would. I jumped back onto the vacated stage.

"Are there any real artists in the hooooooooooouuuuse!" I screamed.

One of the beautiful crew came up offering to buy a beer if I'd come offstage.

"I don't want a beer." I stared at her. Then she offered me a mic. I asked the audience if I needed a mic. "No!" came roaring back.

Encouraged once again, I continued, tearing apart egos. I went on about fake unity, challenged the posers and pretenders to keep it real. I didn't realize that a bunch of the beautiful ones were trying to subtly encircle me as I ranted. And then Scottie stepped in: "I used to love you. But not anymore. Before I head on out the door, I'll say see ya . . . but I wouldn't want to be ya . . ."

By the time he finished his line, I was standing outside The Venue, heart pounding. My gut churned with a strange mixture of indignation, a dash of victory, and a splinter of alienated loneliness. Somewhere deep inside I knew I'd blown it royally.

"Forget about them. They are pretenders. *We* are real," Scottie said, lighting up a fag end. He seemed to be enjoying it all. I grabbed him playfully and took the cig away from him.

"We'll never work in this town again." I passed back the stub. "And I doubt MJ will have two words to say to either of us now."

"You forget MJ, how he met you. You were shooting from the heart then just as you were tonight. It's real for us . . . not just about putting on a show."

I mused over my time in London so far. My brain clicked back to the Trashed Palace party when I'd first arrived. Then, I'd spent the majority of the time in the toilet; now I'd been kicked out of a bar, spent the night in jail, and done a drunken purge over an unsuspecting audience of artists and the general public.

"I think it was quite a show, in the end," I said, digging into my pocket to see if I had any more change. Downing another beer, I decided that I wouldn't allow myself to be pushed about anymore. Fuck guilt. That wasn't even a *real* emotion. The days for apologizing for not making the fit and all that mess were over. Giving a fuck—that was over.

"Yeah, we should finally throw that party. I could do with a *genuine* jam."

INT. TRASHED PALACE

Pieces walks in cautiously, goes over to the kitchen to pour herself a glass of water. She looks around suspiciously before smiling to herself. She looks directly into the camera. After finishing her water, she pulls down her trousers and moons each wall in the flat. Then she walks over to the wall closest to Skye's bed and begins knocking on it. Satisfied, she scribbles something illegible, moving inch by inch until she's covered the entire width of the wall at eye level.

Post-blowout at the poetry gig I threw myself into jump-starting the idea of having the jam at the Trashed Palace. We'd been talking and talking and talking about it, and the time was now. Besides, it was probably the only chance I'd have to perform my stuff again. These days MJ iced me whenever we crossed paths. Needless to say, he didn't hand over a cent after we nearly "ruined" his gig. He and a few folks held a grudge. But a few others had a different, more interesting reaction. A friend of Scottie's had filmed the event and put the audio on an online university-student collective bulletin board. It was a mercifully short clip of me chanting "fuck the police" and Scottie's exit line, "Wouldn't want to be ya." We set up an email address linked to the site and advertised the Trashed Palace's Jam on Toast. While surfing online in Amsterdam, Pieces had stumbled upon a post about the jam and sent word that she would be around to help us organize it. YES! Scottie was right. This was proof that she was as connected to us as we were to her. I was walking on air, juiced up in a way I had all but forgotten was possible. Reaching euphoric. Pieces was coming back!

The closer it came to the time that Pieces was due in London, the lighter my mood became. Shifted upward. It all became clear to me: In this world you have to do things for yourself. To keep it real, it was better to ignore the rules and make your own game. I began to feel my powers spiritual reinforced. Everything was coming together again. Pieces was coming back.

When she arrived, I went to pick her up from the station, my head exploding with nothing other than the thought of finally getting to see her again. It seemed longer than usual as I held my breath all the way there, and not until she was exiting the station did I give a good exhale. I had so much to say, but when I saw her I could barely get two words out. I helped her with the djembe she'd borrowed from her mate in Amsterdam. Her rucksack looked full and heavy.

"How was your flight?" I asked after an awkward greeting.

"Short," she answered. A smile briefly graced her face. Good. She was glad to be back, it seemed.

"It's good to see you."

"Yeah," she said, somehow managing to secure and light a fag.

"Can I get one of those?"

She nodded and pointed to a pocket in her denim. I helped myself. Silence. I'd spent so much time wishing she was around to talk to and now couldn't think of a single word to say.

"So what's th' coup? What have you and Scottie been planning?" I filled her in on what we'd been doing.

On the way to the Trashed Palace we passed a pile of TV sets, computer monitors, keyboards, falling-apart desks and stuff. Pieces paused in front of the office graveyard. She looked perplexed.

"I wonder if any of this shit works," I said, slinging the djembe behind my back. I squatted down for a closer look, and asked, "You okay, Pieces?"

"Oh yeah, yeah . . ." she said, straightening up. "I'm cool, it's just that . . ."

"What?"

"We should come back with Scottie to pick these up. Some of this stuff probably does work. We could create some kinda video installation for the party."

"Yeah. That's a cool idea. We could set up videos and maybe even some cameras."

Pieces arched her eyebrow.

"What?"

"Nothing," she said, pulling another cig from her denim jacket pocket. "Just good to see you again, that's all."

◎

For the next couple weeks we were all jazzed. Everything we did was centered around the gig, the Trashed Palace Jam. Turned out most of the TV sets and computer monitors that Pieces and I had picked up actually worked. We found, begged, and borrowed videotape players and more monitors. Held open rehearsals, mainly between the three of us, but other random musicians would drop by, meaning they went more like jam sessions because we never practiced the same song twice. Pieces organized video material, including the loan of a camera, and made sure we all kept a grip. We even got a computer hooked up. I set up an online message board and flypapered stickers in conspicuously inconspicuous places. If I was in the mood I might adorn it with the lyric: *TAMT = The All Mighty They are watching*. The idea came from that tiny bit of paper I'd found folded in my pocket when I first got to London.

Pieces was in charge of decorating the flat, and seeing the TAMT note stuck to the wall near my mat, she spray-painted the text in big letters in various places. Also: *TAMT vs. TAMU*. She'd explained that it stood for "The All Mighty They versus The All Mighty Us." She seemed obsessed with the interior of the palace. Especially the walls.

Since The Venue, in a way I felt I had something to prove. The Jam on Toast wasn't just a party, but a political act. It would be illegal, unsanctioned; we'd be breaking government licensing laws. Most of the people chipping in to make it all happen were also squatters, activists, and/or artists. There was Danny, from the Oval squat, who was also an internet geek and put together a simple temporary webpage for the Trashed Palace. He compiled footage from jam sessions and other Trashed Palace shenanigans. Jackie, a British-born Black woman from Reading, organized the sound system. The night before the gig she was busy soldering wires and testing amps with her colleagues, the centipede crew. They worked together setting up sound systems throughout London, so we left them to do what they knew best. Pieces found old VHS tapes thrown out near some dumpster or at flea markets around town: everything from Bruce Lee, Jackie Chan, and *Super Fly* action flicks to kitsch sitcoms like *Rising Damp* and *Charlie's Angels*. She and I worked together on the video loops with the help of Kenneth, a guy she met through Russel. It was verging on utopic—a mixed band of misfits, artists, musos, slackers, punks, homegrown Londoners Black, white, West Indian, Asian, German, Portuguese, Italian, and every blend imaginable. We were an unofficial collective. Inspired. It was all happening. We believed it would set a precedent for things to come. There was talk about putting on live events, exhibitions, maybe even opening a part-time café. It was gonna be something.

We got hundreds of greetings on our online message board, salutations as well as cussings. We advertised the street name for the Trashed Palace on all the flyers, but not the address. Only those we knew well had the full address. But even if only our friends and their friends came, there would be a crowd, and word was spreading fast. Scottie and I became famous in certain circles. Sometimes people we didn't know came up to us and said that they saw the site, wanted to come to the rave.

We asked for four pounds at the door to cover expenses, but it seemed we might even make a profit. Everything seemed good to go, but Pieces was concerned.

"We may need security, with all this equipment and it basically being an open party."

"All we need are eyes," argued Scottie, changing a guitar string. "That and to put a spell of love at the door."

"You mean include an ecstasy tab with the price of entry?" she countered.

"I think we could count on a few of our core friends to help look after stuff. Besides, we don't have to let in anyone we don't want to," I suggested.

Pieces crossed her arms. "And who is going to play door-man? Not me."

Scottie put his guitar over his shoulder. "Eeeasy now . . . Things, they will work out, man," he said, sliding into a Jamaican accent, and out the door, avoiding the inevitable volley.

Pieces mimicked him. "What, does he think he is pure Rasta now?"

I smiled to myself and continued to hook leads from the VCR to the TV and tune them in.

"Do you need a hand with that?" Pieces was standing right behind me. I jumped.

"Naw, I think I got it," I said, picking up the remote. "But you can grab one of those tapes from your bag."

She handed me a tape. I put it in without looking at the label. It didn't take long to tune in: a mix of movie clips of various action heroines, from Wonder Woman to Pam Grier's Coffee Brown to Eartha Kitt's Cat Woman.

"Is the other VCR hooked up?"

"Yeah," I said, double-checking the leads.

Pieces put in another tape: on it a video clip of Scottie and I going at it at The Venue. I went a little red.

"I wish I had been there," Pieces said.

"I guess I was a little off my face . . ."

"Yeah. My first thought was that maybe you were a little . . . well, that maybe you fucked it up."

I switched off the TV screen and with my back to her, I exhaled audibly, busied myself with unplugging and wrapping up cables, that self-righteous rage I had when I left The Venue post-performance surging to the surface.

"I mean, that was a paid gig, Skye . . . and Russel heard that—"

"Yeah, but they were also assholes. Whatever *Russel* heard."

"It wasn't professional."

I looked at Pieces sideways. That was great coming from Miss Skip Town incarnate. She came over and put her hand on my shoulder.

"Look, you are talented. Smart. Don't let Scottie get you into all kinda fuckeries."

I shrugged off her hand and walked toward the kitchen.

"I thought he was supposed to be your friend."

"He is my friend . . . Doesn't change the fact that he is a fuck-up, just as I have been . . . But that's not you, Skye." She leaned over the counter. "Anyway, don't let Scottie fool ya. He came from a bourgeois family. Prof has dosh and hasn't always been so out of it. Scottie just adopted street shit since he moved back here." My mind flipped back to Scottie telling me about his mom having to hold down two jobs. Didn't sound very bourgeois to me.

"What's fucked up about living this lifestyle?" I asked. "What's so fucked about refusing to pay for a roof? What's so fucked up about refusing to be caged in? Moving? Staying fluid?" I was on a roll. "You yourself told me you didn't believe in boundaries. We have a community here. Everybody's got their fucked-up-ness. But everybody is trying to be something outside this . . . this fucked reality. To not buy into it. Like the rave you guys had when I first got here. The people there were all vibing nicely from different cultures, spaces, backgrounds, classes, boys-and-girls and girls-and-boys and boys-and-boys and girls-and-girls and no one giving a shit."

Pieces clapped her hands in mock applause.

"Your speech is moving and all, but let's deal with reality . . ."

"This *is* reality," I said, fuming. "What was happening that night was real."

"Everybody was on E."

"Then let the whole world be on E if that will help, but don't chastise me about my behavior. I thought you'd be proud of me for sticking up for myself."

"If that's what you were doing, I am."

By this time I'd made my way to the kettle.

"You want a cuppa?" I asked. I didn't like arguing with Pieces, wanted to change the subject.

"Oh, you know how to speak the working lad's Queen's English?" she joked with me.

"Nevaaaaaaaaaaah," I said, pushing the button on the kettle. "I could only possibly go posh, dahling."

Pieces's laugh had a way of pulling a smile out of the

depths of my uncertainty, putting things into perspective. Over mugs of peppermint tea, we replayed the video clip.

"You know, Skye . . . you are mad." From Pieces, that was a compliment. "Maybe I will take a copy of that tape back to Amsterdam with me."

"You're going back?" I nearly choked.

"Man, I can't wait to get back to Amsterdam . . . It's cheap to eat well. And a tomahto tastes like a tomayto there."

I tried to hide my disappointment. After all, she was here now, and I still had time to change her mind.

"Are you hungry?" I asked, pulling some pasta down from the top of the fridge. Pieces, not too impressed, pulled out a ten-pound note from her pocket.

"Let's expand your understanding of British culture, or should I say British cultural appropriation." She smiled. "I'll take you for a curry."

**EXT. OUTSIDE A HOUSE SOMEWHERE IN THE
COUNTRYSIDE**

Scottie is sitting with a new guitar. He looks
up to the camera.

> SCOTTIE
> That last bash at the palace, you see,
> I only knew one thing, that this could
> be our last hurrah. I was mad, steaming
> inside, and I just thought, *Fuck it, I'm
> going for it.*

WOLF peeks his head out from the door of the
house, a spliff in his mouth. He stares in the
direction of the camera, annoyed, and blows out
smoke.

> WOLF
> Scottie, we're ready to record this tune.
> Let's get this done, yeah? Ya ready?

Scottie strums his guitar.

> SCOTTIE
> Born ready, brother.

The flat was transformed: street signs, traffic lights, graffiti, plus six or seven TV monitors transmitting eclectic visuals. The plan: start off with a DJ, do a live set at about midnight or so, then continue with the DJ. Just go with the flow. Somehow Scottie managed to get a whole load of booze on credit. We devirginated one of the cases, popping open a few bottles. He insisted that we make a toast to the power of three returning. Pieces acquiesced. I was hopeful. The bottle necks clinked together like the top of a pyramid.

People started trickling in about ten-ish. We still weren't ready, the sound system was stuck in a stalled van somewhere on the other side of town. Scottie went to help get things moving. I tended the bar while Pieces played host, greeting folks and catching up with some of the usual heads. The door was handled by a long-legged brunette Tank Girl replica, Eddie from Amsterdam, the woman who gave Pieces her snake armlet. She smiled at me, easing out of a ripped and worn leather jacket, dark hair a grown-out Mohawk surrounding her cherub face.

Her blue eyes pierced mine as she held out her hand. "Heard a lot about ya," Eddie said in a strong accent I couldn't quite catch. It sounded English but not quite Londoner.

"Really?" I resisted the urge to say, *Heard nothing about you.* I played some CDs from a shabby boom box in the kitchen. People drank and waited. It wasn't long before Scottie got back with the centipede crew's sound system. They started slinging cables and with the help of Scottie and Pieces, everything was soon nearly good to go. More people trickled in. I sold more beer.

"You guys gonna play live?" asked one raver; his pink face had that pre-sweat glisten.

"Yeah, later." I gave him his change.

After a while the door was locked down, and Eddie began her DJ set. I wasn't sure yet what I thought about her. I watched her chat with Pieces from behind the bar. They seemed close. Eddie caught me staring, smiled, and pointed me out to Pieces. They waved at me. Embarrassed, I went to empty an ashtray before lighting another cigarette.

At some point Scottie took over the bar with a few of his mates and I milled through the thickening crowd. The palace was approaching sardine-can packed. I found Pieces chillin' on the floor near the DJ box. Had a relaxed smile on her face. I sat down next to her. She broke a small pill with her teeth, handed half to me and half to Eddie.

I was already on a buzz. Adrenaline. The rave was kickin'. Pieces was pleased. She gave my hand a hard squeeze and smiled, bopping her head sedately to the beat. Good. Maybe she saw what wicked work we could all do together and she would stay.

I studied the crowd. A mix of every age, color, gender, sexuality; something I had only witnessed happening here in London. That old seventies lick, "One Nation under a Groove," began to make sense to me. Eddie mixed one heavy bass beat after another. "Jungle," I found out it was called. The crowd went mad.

I hadn't eaten much and the pill was slowly beginning to take effect.

"I'm gonna dance, you wanna dance?" Pieces asked me, feeling the music. She looked contented, at home. I decided to swallow my fear of drowning and take her up on the offer. She grabbed my hand and led me to a spot close to the speaker. She began moving her hips and I did a two-step, closing my eyes and soaking in the bass line.

Folks were lost in their own personal grooves. Spiritual revelations were sparked and nurtured through music. There was no stopping. Once I started moving I forgot about time. I forgot about being broke in London. I forgot that Pieces was leaving. She and Scottie came and sandwiched me. We danced like that awhile before Pieces spun me around so that she was in between me and Scottie. While holding eye contact with me, she used her ass as a weapon, Scottie couldn't keep up and eventually danced away. She moved in closer to me, holding eye contact, grabbed my arms, and put them around her waist. If I could've smiled any wider my whole face would have cracked open. We boogied together through a few glorious tunes before she was up to tend bar for a bit. She left me on a high that sent me dancing in exaltation. I was mostly in my own world. Had never let myself go like this before. And I felt a part of something larger than myself, like what the sanctified must have felt in church. No one was posing or caring about anything. Just the music. Everybody was vibing on instinct, connecting, whether dancing alone or in loose groups; pockets of spontaneous combustions lit the dance floor. People lost it. Just because.

Time slipped well past midnight. Sunrise was not far off. Pieces pulled out her djembe from behind the DJ's table and started a simple beat, complimenting and completing the ambient house Eddie now played. She mixed it with a scratched sample of some Afro beat. I was still out on the dance floor. Pieces's rhythms fed my movement, my movement fed her beat. I began chanting. An ivory-skinned dude, his short-sleeved button-up tucked in to the waist of his straight-legged jeans, brought out a muted silver trumpet. Husky brass notes jazzed in, punctuating and sliding over the rhythms. Celebratory sounds tunneled out of my throat. Eddie passed me the mic. I had forgotten that I was there with other people. Or it felt like we were one people vibing on the same energy. There was only "us." I hit a lyric. Grooved with the sounds, pulled from text I'd scribbled down while in New York.

It's a mad, mad world
and I'm sitting on this A train
riding into the madness of Manhattan
with all these mad people
but most of them don't know they mad.
Me, I revel in my madness, find rhythm in my badness,
yeah, my bad Black ass,
and the only reason I'm "Black"
is because I'm not white
or I think that's why.
See I've been called a "nigger,"
a "spade," a "jigaboo," an "Oreo," a "coconut," a "freak,"
I've even been called "atypical"
'cause I practiced alongside Hepburn,
the rain in Spain stays mainly on the plaaaain.

Squeezing through my teenage years,
spitting blood I swallowed my fears,
and when time came for me to fly, I flew
with ratty bag and
needing to stay nappy-head

I left my St. Louieeee bluuues
to live the life I could choose
But wasn't prepared for the gap
Between not being white and being truly Black . . .

Someone joined me from the dancing crowd; all baggy pants and Tommy Hilfiger T-shirt, his thin toffee face was hidden under the crisp, curved Cubs baseball cap. We kicked lyrics back and forth; the ravers were still in. I kept going until there was nothing left. And somehow between me, the dude on the trumpet, Pieces, and Eddie, we rounded off the set together in synchronicity. The punters went wild.

Scottie stepped in. "I know you *must* be feeling it."

Affirmation came from the crowd.

He began strumming his guitar. "Are you feeling it?" he continued and began a call-and-response improv with the crowd, working them up further, and then as if on cue Eddie slid in some beats mixed with a Kurt Cobain sample—*I like it, I'm not gonna crack . . . I like it—like it—like it*—slowly building it up as Scottie smashed his guitar on the floor. Everyone went mad. Pieces and I looked at each other for a suspended moment before simultaneously breaking out in laughter. Scottie came over to where Pieces and I were standing, flashing contagious ear-to-ear grins. We hugged each other, spinning around under fractured disco light.

It was creeping up to 7 a.m. the next day and the place was still thumping. Spontaneous jams between musicians, mixed in with the DJ's groove, took place organically, without an emcee. Pieces caught my eye from the DJ booth, where she was keeping Eddie company. There was an intensity about her stare, like there was something she was burning to say to me, then it changed into something indecipherable. Pieces walked over and suggested we go out for air. On our way to the door she told Scottie that it would probably be good to start winding down.

"No worries, Pieces, things are under control," Scottie answered.

There were all manner of ravers spilling out onto our doorstep: crusties, E-trippers, acid-droppers, ketamine-snorters, straight-edge vegans, and old school hippies who hadn't stopped partying since 1968. We kicked empty cans off the bottom step and started down Coldharbour Lane. Sunday morning Brixton was waking up.

"Wicked party, innit?" I said, breathing in the fresh air.

"Listen to you. 'Wicked, innit.'" She laughed. "You'll be sounding like a true South Londoner soon enough," she said, leaving the *h* silent at the end of "south."

I ducked my head down to hide a smile. I glanced over to her then down to my shoes then back over to her. A million thoughts in my head matched the meter of my heartbeat.

Go ahead and tell her, I said to myself. *Go ahead and tell 'cause* she needs *to hear it. She must feel it.*

"Pieces, listen, it's *good* to have you back," I said, starting in on my "please stay" speech. "Scottie and I hold down the fort well enough, but you make up the balance. There is something to that power of three and all that."

"Yeah, maybe . . . but that's what I wanted to talk to you about. I'm going back to Amsterdam tomorrow—I mean today. Later on tonight I've gotta catch a plane."

"Damn Pieces, I knew you were going back, but you've only been here one hot minute."

"I know, I know . . . but I can't stay here anymore. I've outgrown this scene. Been there done that, you know? This will be my last blast, hurrah hurrah, before I get down to sorting out my life. I'm more chilled in the Netherlands. Plus I kinda got something going there." She smiled to herself and my stomach dropped.

"Like what?"

My gut was scraping the sidewalk. I concentrated on swallowing the lump that was growing in my throat.

"Let's just say Amsterdam is giving me what I need. Things are too crazy for me here and it's bound to get crazier . . . I need headspace . . . something stable."

"Who is he?" I left the "or she" in my head unsaid for some reason.

Pieces looked for a minute like she wanted to correct me but within the same split second changed her mind. "Does it matter?"

I wanted to say, *To me it does. I love you. Scottie loves you. And I know you love us. So, what are you doing?*

Instead I said, "What the fuck do you mean, 'Does it matter?' I'm supposed to be your friend. I know we haven't known each other for years or nothing but—"

"Look, let's just leave it. I'm going back, just accept it."

"You don't wanna talk about it? What's up with that, Pieces? Thought me and you were sistahs and all, but maybe you are like the rest."

"'The rest'?" Pieces challenged. "What's 'the rest'?" I said nothing. "Who are 'the rest,' Skye?"

She must have known what I was talking about. All those folks pretending to be real. *We are*—that's what Scottie had said. What you see is what you get and all that. She was just playing with my head. We sat on a bench in the park opposite the church.

Pieces sighed. "I'm not chatting rubbish . . . You have to trust me," she said, leaning back. "Later on you are gonna understand some things."

A few zombied ravers and members of the strong-brew crew passed through the park, somehow mingling in with a few Sunday churchgoing Christians, all shined and polished for God. I concentrated on making a rollie. Later I was going to understand some things? What was left to understand? I had nothing to say. What could I say?

"Anyway, we'll see each other." Pieces broke the silence. "Think of it as a place you can come visit."

I didn't respond, waiting for what I knew I would never hear. *Come with me.* I laid my head in her lap and watched clouds pass.

◉

"Hey guys, shit's going down at the palace." Eddie ran up to us, out of breath. She took her time to catch it. Though the message was urgent enough for her to come find us, her tone of voice was blasé. "Just thought you should know. Cops came, shut it down, and rounded up a few of the frisky ones, to boot."

I sat up. "Scottie?"

"Probably him too," Eddie said matter-of-factly. "He was refusing to move. He knew they would lock down the place once we were all out."

"Fuck!" That was Pieces, who was by now walking purposefully in the direction of the Trashed Palace. I started to follow but Eddie put her hand on my shoulder and told me I should stay. Wait till things cooled off.

"Patricia knows the scene," she said. "She knows how to stay out of trouble."

Patricia?

"Come on. Let's walk up to Tulse Hill to the park and chill. I don't know about you but it's nice to get some air and enjoy whatever buzz is left that the cops didn't kill."

As I got up and started walking, I realized that though I was coming down, I was still high. We must've floated up to Brockwell Park, with the amount of drugs racing through our bodies. I'd seen Eddie pop another one earlier. We found a patch of grass at the top of a hill. It was a nice day out, some people were already passing frisbees, kicking the ball around, chasing down toddlers, cruising on bicycles. I thought about the good ole days . . . When I first came to London. When we three hung out in the park. Especially that first afternoon. Magic. Scottie was right, we were magic together, we three . . . Fuck Pieces or Patricia or whoever the fuck. Deep down I was determined somehow to make her stay.

For a long while Eddie studied life in the grass we were lying in. I stared at the clouds passing. I imagined scenarios in which Pieces would somehow miss her plane or, during her time walking around the city to clear her head, she would realize that she loved me. Loved me and Scottie both. But clearly she had something or someone pulling her back to Amsterdam. I turned to look at Eddie, who was sucking on a blade of grass.

"So you came over here from Amsterdam to see Pieces." I stated the obvious. Suddenly I wanted to interrogate this woman Pieces never said much about.

Eddie giggled.

"What's so funny?" Either her laugh was contagious, or the drugs made me more empathetic. I couldn't resist a grin.

"You guys call her 'Pieces,'" Eddie said, propping herself up on her elbows. "It's just a lil weird, but in a strange way it suits her better than 'Patricia.'"

"You say 'tomahto,' I say 'tomayto.'"

"Yeah, a fruit by any other name is still a fruit."

We laughed again. I didn't really wanna like her but I did. Could see why Pieces did too.

"I suppose she is a bit, I don't know, difficult . . . loopy, even," I said, slowly and meticulously rolling a cigarette. The cocktail of E and booze set everything in slow motion. Every action required the utmost concentrated care. "But I suppose we all are."

"Man, she's chilled out a lot though," said Eddie. "I hardly recognize her. Talking about settling somewhere, taking it easy on the drugs, maybe going back to school to study art. Which is good 'n' all, but she got a little sanctimonious about it. You know how she can get."

I knew. Eddie rolled over on her back and continued.

"In a way I guess it was some kinda relief when she lost it a bit in Amsterdam."

"What do you mean?"

She gave me a look, surprised I hadn't heard.

"Well, she got into this big argument with Russel. Decided to move out. Found an empty boat to squat in."

For a moment I felt extreme relief. So she wasn't going to see him. Or was she? I tried to pretend that I could care less.

"But they've patched things up since then . . ."

I played detective in spite of myself. "Have they?"

Eddie grabbed my cigarette. "No, I think Pieces is just freaking. She's worried that too many drugs have done her in. She claimed there was a whole block of time she forgot about. Russ told her she should check into an outpatient clinic; that's when things got ugly."

"Why is she going back, then?"

"Headspace? I'm not sure. I guess she needs some time to process everything. Get sorted." Eddie passed the fag she was holding more than smoking to me.

Headspace. That was it. Nothing personal. I needed to get a grip. But then again, a grip on what exactly? A grip on reality? "It's all in your mind," I overheard Prof saying to Scottie one of those times Scottie had teased him about being on something. He'd alluded to him being disconnected from reality. Reality is all in the mind. He was right. Pieces was pretending that all would be okay if she could just get away. I'd thought so too. But in the end you can never really get away. In the end the reality we were all expected to consume was no more real or less real than anything drug induced. I pondered on this for a small eternity, as scenes from my recent past flickered through. The moment before I let loose in the tube station singing my heart out, I was there. Present. Scottie smashing his only guitar at the jam, with no dosh for a new one. He was in the moment. The moment was not about the guitar, but the act itself. Plans didn't matter.

"I hope Scottie's okay?" I said.

Eddie turned on her side to face me. "Yeah, I'm sure he's fine. Prof was there looking after things."

"Hey, ladies." Enter the original hippie stage left, burning ears and all. Prof walked up smiling. He sat down next to us. Chitchat with him helped distract me from the war zone in my head.

"Nice rave you guys put on there . . . nice vibe . . . sweet energy." His speech was drawn out and measured.

"Yeah, up until the pork came through, hey?" Eddie turned on her side. "What happened to Scottie?"

"No worries." Prof sucked his cig. "I broke down the bar and stashed the cash so there was nothing to get him on but disturbing the peace."

"And squatting illegally."

"No, your smart friend Pieces had it registered with the council as an occupied spot. Under law, cops have to give notice before closing it down."

The paperwork was on the door of the place. Trouble was that their notice could be just twenty-four hours. Prof crossed his legs.

"And Pieces?" I asked.

"Oh, she's fine. By the time she got there most of the noise was done. Police put a lock on the place, mostly to make sure the punters didn't come back. She went for a walk to let things cool down. Said to tell you if I saw you to meet her back at the palace in an hour."

Eddie stretched out on her back and did an E yawn. Contagious. I was yawning too.

"Tired already?" Prof asked. "Been up since yesterday. Didn't sleep much the day before either." Then he said, as if it had just occurred to him, "I haven't shut my eyes in over forty-eight hours. Must be three times your age."

I smiled. "What are you on, ole man?"

He pulled out a bag of several tiny black dots. "This is special. The real thing. Bends the brain. Helps release

185

psychic toxins. LSD of the highest order." He made it sound as if those tiny inky dots were black gold. "You wanna try some?" He gave me three. "You, a friend," he nodded toward Eddie, who was in her own world, "and maybe another friend." His glazed blue-gray eyes locked on mine for a moment. He acted as if he was sending me on some rite of passage. I laughed to myself and took them for later. Maybe if Pieces stayed, the three of us could do them together. I mean, she did refer to the Trashed Palace as "our" squat, so maybe there was still hope that I could convince her to stay. She would see in the end that she belonged here with us.

Prof decided to stretch a leg, as he put it, and left Eddie and I lying head to foot in the grass. We were silent for a long time. My head was spinning with the whys of it all, why things were happening the way they were. Why I even gave a fuck. Couldn't keep my mind off of Pieces. Something more than just wanting a change of scene was going on. I could feel it. Two and two resisted making four. Well, if nothing made sense then, as the Talking Heads say, "stop making sense." I fingered the plastic baggy from Prof in my pocket. I had a bright idea.

"It would be madness to take them," I said, dangling the bag over Eddie's smiling face. She sat up.

"Exactly why we should!"

I knew I already had too many chemicals running through my body, but other than that I couldn't think of a clear reason not to.

"Would be cool if Pieces could join us," I said, putting the trip under my tongue. I was on a roll. Best to stay way out. Roadblock thinking too much. If I allowed myself to do that—think—I would risk crashing into the rails and getting too close to something that didn't want to be discovered just yet. I knew deep down it wasn't really about Pieces, it never had been, but I held her responsible.

"Yeah, well . . ." Eddie said. "Let's just take back the third one and see if she's there, hey?"

"Doesn't she have to catch a plane soonish though?"

"Oh, Patricia's hardcore. By that time she'll be coming down and doing the airport scene on a nice buzz." Eddie had a monkeyish grin on her face.

I laughed in collusion and jumped up off the ground, extending my hand to Eddie. "Let's see what's going on," I suggested. We strolled, coconspirators arm in arm.

G ot back to the Trashed Palace to find the place locked up and Pieces using bolt cutters to get through the lock. Eddie and I waded through empty bottles and cans and packs, cig butts, dead lighters, a piece of shoestring, and other unrecognizable rubbish up the stairs to the door.

"Hey, Pieces . . . what's happening?" I asked.

"The police fucking raided the place, didn't they?" she said, snapping the lock. "At least I'm lucky they only used this poxy lil lock." She threw the padlock down among the other clutter. It clanged against an empty bottle. "My fucking bag is in there and I have to be at the airport in a few hours."

"Shit. Prof told me about Scottie."

"Well, surprise surprise" came a monotone murmur from under Pieces's breath. I noticed the squatters' rights notice was ripped from the door. We followed Pieces into the flat.

"So they took him on what charge?" I asked, only half-way still in my right mind.

"Possibly doing an illegal rave . . . disturbing the peace. Evidently Scottie didn't leave willingly, called for a sit-in. Everybody else just left peacefully. So much for our little collective, hey?"

Inside as outside, the Trashed Palace was living up to its name. Empties littered the floor along with cigarette butts, spilled brew, and in one corner a special present from one satisfied raver: a rainbow pool of vomit.

"I'm glad I won't be here to deal with this mess." Pieces located her bag.

I looked around me, nothing registered. I felt a little dizzy and needed to sit. Found a stool. As I moved, traces of light followed.

"You guys want a beer?" Pieces headed to the kitchen.

I stared straight ahead, trying to maintain focus. Regain some equilibrium. My eyes landed on the collage of spray-painted eyes on the wall, blinking around that "The All Mighty They" note I'd stuck there.

I looked at Eddie, my eyes in a dilated spin. Feeling the acid, I wilted into my stool while Pieces caught her breath and calmed down.

Popping open a beer, she checked Eddie and me, suspicious.

"What are you guys on?" she asked, a half smile threatening to break through a reprimanding face. I think she already knew.

I pulled out the plastic bag with the remaining hit. "Want one? We just dropped twenty minutes ago."

"You must be mad."

"Aw, come on. It'll be fun. Anyway, why can't you postpone leaving until tomorrow?"

"I have the tickets in my bag, Skye," she said, as if speaking to someone a bit slow. "Tripping on an airplane is not my idea of fun."

For a moment I panicked and wished I hadn't dropped. But it was too late, and if Eddie could do it so could I.

Eddie was mesmerized watching the fractured light that came through a crystal hanging in front of the kitchen window. I breathed in deeply and watched Pieces's face change. An eyeball on her head bled through her furrowed brows and took over her face before shrinking and disappearing back into the bindi she had stuck to her forehead. I blinked. There was no bindi. Blinked again and I began to catch the room around me in frames. Focus pulled from Eddie to Pieces leaning on the kitchen counter beside me, playing with the beer cap. Cut to her fingers moving the cap through her fingers and back again.

"I feel like I'm in a movie," I finally said, my own face turning into a ball of silly putty.

"Yeesh, Skye." Pieces looked at me closely. "Have you ever dropped before?"

"Plenty of times," I lied.

Pieces laughed, walking past me and disappearing into Scottie's room to finish packing. Eddie looked up at me and we both broke out in giggles.

Eddie and I spent a long moment just smiling at each other . . . playing with and tossing each other colorful balls of energy floating between our hands. I found a Pink Floyd CD, or it seemed to appear between my fingers. I slipped it into the ratty boom box, which to my ears magically transformed into heavenly speakers. We let the bliss of it move our arms and legs. Yes, the sound had colors. Eventually we both ended up flat on the kitchen floor, which I realized was not cold but warm and breathing.

Pieces peeped her head over the counter, took one look at us, and shook her head, holding back a smile deeper than she could hide from my now-sharpened eyes. Sharing a kind of telepathic link, Eddie and I both got up and gave Pieces a hug. Pieces was patient with us for a few seconds before patting our backs and gently shrugging us off.

"Listen, Psychedelica Number One," she said, briefly holding my shoulders and looking into my eyes. "I gotta go . . ." She slung her bag over her shoulder, picked up her drum, and turned to Eddie. Then glanced at me before turning her attention back to Eddie. "And *you*, Miss Drug Slut. You still coming?"

Eddie nodded, her saucer-sized pupils entranced by Pieces's aura.

I somehow helped carry Eddie's DJ bag to Brixton station. Pieces led the way. Moving through linked and fluid energy masses, I was a hunk of warm clay melting into my surroundings. Everything made sense. Nothing made sense. Cold and empty structures folded across the landscape: office cubicles, banks, factories producing neo-food wrapped in plastic, money-box institutions, passing off worthless pieces of paper as something of value. Souls suffocating inside shells.

I watched people walk, stand, sit, live in their bodies. Some looked comfortable, wore their skin, muscle, bone like a well-worn T-shirt. For others, their bodies were ill-fitting uniforms. They covered their awkwardness with cut suits, or off-the-shelf trendy gear. Outer layers of conformity made them into something. Spoke an image. Said nothing about who they really were.

I watched the way Pieces moved. Every inch she was there. She didn't bother with much conversation. I caught her at times snatching sideways glances at folks as they boarded or left the train. Occasionally her eyes would shift up, reading the underground map. For the first time I saw a shyness there. I saw Patricia, and I saw Pieces desperately trying to hide her, or was she trying to protect her?

"Stop staring at me, Skye," Pieces whispered. "You're giving me the creeps."

I turned to look at Eddie. Mistake. Machine-gun giggles

rumbled in her throat as she sang, "You say 'tomayto,' I say 'tomahto'?"

"A fruit by any other name," I shot back. A tight grin held back an imminent burst.

"What's up with you nuts?" Pieces feigned annoyance.

"I don't know, what's up, Pieces, I mean, Patricia?" I could no longer hold back my own dammed-up giggles. Pieces resisted at first, but eventually laughter broke through that sometimes-steely face of hers. Some of the passengers around us also began chuckling. By this time Eddie was in spasms on the floor.

"Will you guys just get up and chill out?" Pieces, trying to keep a straight face, glanced at some of the passengers whose humor seemed to be wearing thin. It was obvious we were off our faces, obvious we were foreigners. But you know how it goes. The more you try to hold it, the more you can't. Many stops and several deep breaths later, Eddie and I calmed down. Pseudo-serious expressions thinly plastered to our faces as we refused to look at each other. Eye contact would break the tissue-paper skin of composure. Pieces looked at us both and shook her head.

"Come on, you hippies, it's our stop," she said, picking up her things.

Then time seemed to move in fast-forward, everything around me was sound and form. All I remember clearly is holding Eddie's hand. We were principal characters in a sped-up Spike Lee–esque dolly shot, from the platform through the airport of whizzing activity. Next thing I know we were saying our "see ya laters." Pieces's voice snapped me back into real time.

"Be careful what you do in here, they're always watching." Pieces pointed to a surveillance camera in the terminal near her departure gate. Her eyes searched mine before pulling out some papers and a pen from her waist pouch and handing the bits to me. "You are going back to the palace, Skye." It was more of a command than a question. Giving me a long hug, she said, "Have fun, write what you experience, but make sure you make it back safely, yeah?"

I watched their plane take off and then others, searing through the sky for what seemed like a slice of forever. I studied the angle as they lifted off the runway and arrowed through space. Counted how many seconds before the huge planes were reduced to specks, and then disappeared to the other side of the sky. Several hours passed.

And I didn't feel bad. Just felt like I was missing somebody. Someone I knew like my own heartbeat, but had only just met. It was an oddly comforting feeling, like an old blanket or worn duvet. The sun started to set and I stood up and walked slowly through Heathrow, getting my bearings. A hallucinogenic light show ebbed in flow. Low tide. *The trip*, I thought, *should be wearing off soon*. I could just about face the tube, if my legs weren't so rubbery. I slid into a booth in an English airport pub. Hall and Oates crooned, *She's gone, oh why* . . . I'd walked into a cliché movie scene. An overworked, underpaid, mousy-looking waitress came over to me and asked if I wanted anything. I couldn't speak. Hadn't spoken since the plane took off. Didn't know if it was because I didn't want to or had forgotten how to form words. I pulled out the scrap of paper and pen Pieces had given me and wrote down "whiskey sour."

Flipping over the paper, I realized that Pieces had shoved me a handful of flyers advertising some club in Amsterdam called the Boa. One woman carried a staff that looked more like a snake. It had a single eye painted on its back, which spread out like a cobra. Its mouth spread into a smile. I began doodling oblong circles near the mouth of the snake absentmindedly. A spiral led to the pupil in the snake's eye. I concentrated on the paper because I couldn't face what people might look like under the influence of the microdot. But I was also in a sort of trance, I felt Sincara was near. And poof. I looked up to see Prof. He slid me the whiskey sour I'd forgotten and sat across from me. I caught his amused eyes before barfing up Walt Disney onto the barroom floor.

Prof handed me a packet of tissues he had in his vest pocket.

"On second thought, your irises tell me maybe you don't need that drink." He pulled a banana out his sports jacket pocket. "Fruit?" He went to the bar to get a glass of water and something to soak up my puke sculpture from the floor.

The waitress's mousy face had transformed into that of a seething hamster. She followed him with mop in tow. Put my head on the table, hidden under folded arms, more out of visual overload than embarrassment. My elbows melted into the varnished wood and I became the table. Fixed to the airport pub floor. The sounds around me blended into one noise, sometimes zipping past me like the sound of cars on a freeway. I had the feeling of being that cat in the movies, numbly walking through a swishing series of near misses. The trick was to focus on the other side—or was it that each step that took you forward revealed the path through?

I felt a tap on my shoulder.

"Drink this." Prof set the water in front of me and sat, watching me curiously as I reentered the "real" world, rubbing the glaze from my eyes. I took the glass in my hand, willing it into a solid object.

A few sips and we left the pub. I held Prof's arm as we walked toward the underground, and he told me that he sometimes came to the airport to think. He paused, playing with his speckled gray beard as if he were waiting for some profound wisdom to bless him, before explaining how he'd been hoping to catch Pieces before her flight left. Realizing he'd missed her, he just hung around until he saw me.

I was glad to see him. Felt better since vomiting, but drained. I probably would have just passed out at the nearest convenient spot if not for him. Prof paid for my tube ticket. We were headed in the same direction as far as Victoria. There, I decided to take him up on his offer to crash at his "pad," as he put it. I couldn't face the Trashed Palace, not alone, not in my current state of mind.

◎

At Prof's flat I'd nod off then jerk awake. Each time, I would dip into that dream I kept having in variation. The details of the story changed, became more elaborate each time I closed my eyes, but they always carried the same theme. I was being tracked. I was on the run. Sometimes I'd run into billboard-sized monitors linked to CCTV cameras. The images seemed to imprison me. I'd sprint in the opposite direction. I'd fall. I would always hear this strange bluesy riff, picked strings resonating from far away, and I would always feel Sincara's presence, as if she were trying to make me *see* something that was right in front of my face, just before I bumped my head and jerked awake.

Daylight broke through Prof's dingy curtains. I stretched as I got up, shaking off the residue of those disturbing dreams, and stared momentarily into space. Getting my bearings, I checked the couch for anything that might have fallen out of my pockets. Spotted the little plastic baggy. Still one dot left. The one meant for Pieces, who was now gone. Again. Not one to waste, I dropped the dot under my tongue. This one was for her. Prof shuffled into the room wearing a well-worn smoking jacket, feet in old leather slippers.

"I was just leaving," I said hastily.

"Don't worry, you're safe." I don't know if it was the light or what, but for the first time I could see Prof was in fact younger than I'd thought. But he looked tired.

"Did you enjoy your trip?"

I nodded. "Just did the last one."

He eyed me before going to the other room. Brought out a long plastic bong. I would have to stand on his sofa to hit it.

"That should bring you on sweetly," he said, a doctor talking to his patient. "Fix you something to eat, cuppa tea?"

I surveyed his small, one-bedroom flat. It was crowded with books, newspapers, old albums, lava lamps, and the odd African wood carving. Rays of sunlight piercing through the window above the couch I'd slept on illuminated thick dust moving through the air. A smelly mix of sweat, cigarettes, and weed stood in there, stagnant. He opened a window in his small kitchen and waited for the kettle to boil.

I could see why Scottie'd adopted him. Or why he'd adopted Scottie. They had the same measured pace about them. They even made tea the same, stirring the milk in slowly, as if creating a meal. Could tell they'd spent a lot of time together. Scottie, the younger version of this man in a lot of ways. Both did everything with extreme care. It was then it came back. Scottie had been arrested.

"So, what happened to Scottie?"

"Oh, he's out now." Prof passed me a steaming mug of milky tea. "That boy has always been in trouble."

"I heard you practically raised him."

"Just about. He mostly raised himself." He looked down, shaking his head for a moment, deep in his own thoughts.

He suddenly snapped out of it and offered me a biscuit from a freshly opened pack of Hobnobs. "You should put something in your stomach."

It was that morning that I began to realize why he was called "Prof." Over tea he gave me long-winded advice on how to use LSD, including a history of its development. He went into some drawn-out conspiracy theory. Said the CIA experimented with the drug on human guinea pigs. Wanted to see how it could be used as a form of mind control. Told me it could be therapeutic, help me see things I needed to see. Separate the wheat from the chaff. The surreal from the nonreal. He told me to write down everything I could remember and as much of what I was seeing as possible.

"You're a writer, right?" he asked.

I shrugged, uncomfortable.

"Use this as an exercise in emotional and psychic cleansing . . . You might even get the answer to things you forgot you had been asking," he said while breaking down the bong and placing it on a shelf next to a stack of yellowing magazines. "Most of all, pay attention to the signs in your dreams." He pulled a gold chain from his robe. On the end of it a small clock swung before his shaded eyes. "I still haven't slept so I think I will do so now. You can stay as long as you like." He hesitated for a beat before adding, "I have some of my best breakthroughs here, in solitude with no distractions. I dig in deeper," he told me before quietly clicking his bedroom door shut behind him.

The bong hit made my eyes heavy. If I sat any longer, Prof's old couch would swallow me up. I did not want to dig in deep. Distraction was what I needed. Answers always led to more questions. I needed to move, and keep moving.

After collecting myself, I quietly left Prof's house. With the sun an open-palmed smack across my mug, I searched for my shades, remembered I had none. There was a stand near the Victoria bus stop that sold them. I replicated a trick I'd learned from Scottie and walked away with some new glasses on my face, tag and all. Before moving to London I would've never thought to do that. The most I'd ever stolen had been from my Dad's sock drawer. But then again, I'd never been to London before, drank so much beer before, smoked so much weed before, binged on so many drugs before. I wasn't the same girl from Crickledown, dreaming of escape. I was becoming an expert at it. But now my own mind was the cage. My own thoughts, and the feelings they triggered, were booby traps, unleashing ghosts intent on destroying everything I ever thought I'd known. Solution: stay out of my right mind.

The oversized *Starsky & Hutch* glasses had a dark-blue tint that masked my eyes completely. Undercover, the acid now blending with that last bong hit, I didn't think I could face the tube. Too claustrophobic for my state of mind. I caught the 36 bus instead. Had my sights on Brixton. Wanted to see if Scottie was okay and touch home base.

It was fairly early. Before work hours, the bus wasn't too packed and went quickly past empty stops. I took the limousine seat in the back. It had lots of leg space and was near the stairs. You could see everything. And it was harder to be seen.

At the front of the bus a video screen had been installed. Low-budget show reels featuring advertisements for the BBC programming and "Help the Police Stop Crime" trailers. Every once in a while it would show angles of the bus. People coming on, getting off, sitting on the top and bottom floors: proof we were "protected" from all angles. "We will use CCTV in the prosecution of criminals," another placard on the bus read. I recalled what Pieces had said the night before, nodding at the CCTV camera in the airport: *Be careful what you do in here, they're always watching*. Doing the undercover routine, I checked the angles. Where could the lenses of the camera reach? Where were its blind spots?

"Any more fares, please?"

The ticket collector went past me, giving me a chance to jump before he doubled back. But I'd gone farther than I'd intended to go. I found myself in front of the post office at New Cross Gate, watching the tail end of the number thirty-six. I asked the direction of the nearest tube and started walking. Straight ahead. Passed an antique flea-market stall, some of its wares organized in neat clutters on the pavement in front of the shop. A couple of kids' bicycles, an oakwood cabinet, ebony wooden table, and a frameless oval-shaped mirror. I caught a glimpse of myself. A self that I nearly didn't recognize. The bottoms of my jeans were crusty from stepping through beer and ash sludge. My dreads were longer, more uneven, my face leaner and the color of London skies. But it was more than a physical change. I slowly pulled up my sunglasses and looked into my own eyes. Vertigo. It wasn't me I was seeing. I saw eyes that looked like mine. But weren't mine. The snake amulet around my neck began to move. Then there was nothing around my neck.

"Can I help you with something?" the shop owner asked over my shoulder.

I came back. I shook my head no and moved on, thinking about what I'd just seen in that oval-shaped mirror. Wondered why I suddenly felt a lump in my throat. It was the necklace, something about the necklace. I'd actually felt it on my neck in that moment before it vanished. I struggled to swallow.

Continued toward the station only half-aware of the roadworks hitting a crescendo near New Cross Gate. It was difficult to cross the street. Nothing in London was a straight line, anyway. I knew that once I understood the nature of the roundabout, I would have caught on to an important part of British culture.

I walked onto the outdoor platform at New Cross Gate and sat on a bench. Watched people coming and going. Looked across the tracks at the junk heap on the other side. A storage space for unused city-construction parts. People walked past me in various uniforms. Some paint-splattered decorators mixed in with briefcase-carrying commuters. Over the intercom an electronic voice announced trains approaching and departing. I pulled out scraps of paper and wrote down the visuals I'd seen in the oval mirror, hoping to put together the pieces of the puzzle, Prof's voice still echoing in my head, in spite of myself. He made perfect sense, but I couldn't understand why.

After a while I gave up trying to figure it all out, stuffed the paper scraps back into my jacket pocket, constructed a rollie, and searched for a light. Pulled out a crude plectrum and an empty matchbox. I dug into the inside pocket of my jean jacket. Came across the pink Post-it note with a hastily scribbled address for Gennie Jah, the woman who owned the shop in West London. It was in Pieces's handwriting.

She was probably just waking up now, her first morning back in Amsterdam.

Had the blue metal bench to myself at New Cross Gate station. Lay back and watched clouds moving in the sky. Felt calmed. Imagined myself on each occasional plane I saw descending into London. Recalled that excitement of first arriving. Clutching worn copies of Kerouac and *Giovanni's Room*. I had to laugh at myself. I'd believed everything would just work out. Envisioned hanging out with Scottie and Pieces, doing stuff, traveling together, making things happen. For the first time in my life not feeling alone.

"Passengers are reminded there is no smoking on London transport platforms," a male voice broke through the breezy air.

I pulled the burnt-out cigarette from between my lips and eased myself up until I was facing a small dusty camera directly over a No Smoking sign. I flicked the dead fag across the tracks. The platform was fairly empty now. It was too easy to spot me. Time to move. I checked the tube map. Got lost in the linguini twist of directions, pondering which way to go and where, in fact, I was going. Adjusting my sunglasses, I decided I would take the Hammersmith line into West London and go check out Gennie Jah's. It was a sign that I'd found that pink Post-it. Pieces had given it to me as possible work contact, and though I knew I was in no shape for a job interview, it felt as if I were being *led* to her doorstep. On the train, in spite of the LSD, I nodded off, lullabied by the train's rhythm across the tracks. I dreamed in acid-print colors . . . *Pieces stands over me, pointing to tiny eyes surrounding my bed in the Trashed Palace. Unblinking eyes glance from side to side in unison. Then the routine begins: I am running. I fall, see the single eye of Sincara the serpent, it knocks my skull in* . . . Woke up searching for scraps of paper. Blues notes, a soundtrack in my head. I wrote down everything I could remember.

Out on the street again, I found Gennie's shop pretty easily. It looked like it had a new lick of paint. The base color was green. Red letters outlined in gold blinked out the words "Cultural Vibrations" over the doorway. Walking closer, I realized the shop was closed. I sat on the stoop in front, needing a break. I found a comfortable position and tried for invisibility. Directly across from me The Mangrove stood, a skeleton of what it once represented. Pieces told me that in the seventies and eighties it housed political meetings. Folks would discuss how to deal with racism and police violence. People were looking for solutions. Feeling empowered.

I continued staring ahead, concentrating on nothing, watching the road bend under the glaze of radiant beams that shot from the sky. It's impossible to know how long I stared, the street disappearing behind the still-rising pomegranate disk that seemed to open a gateway to somewhere else. Through this shimmering portal, a medium-boned ebony woman walked in slow motion like a vision. Her salt-and-pepper locs were tied up and glistened in the saintly sunlight. She approached me on the stairs.

"Can I help you with something?"

I looked up at her, glad for the sunglasses still hiding my eyes. Though her voice and presence had a sobering effect, I wasn't that sure my face could remain in place without the sunglasses. "Just waiting for Gennie . . . the woman who owns this shop." I felt uneasy adding "Jah" at the end, wasn't sure I would say it right, or if it was all right to say it.

"That's me." She eyed me suspiciously. "And you are?"

"A friend of Pieces, she . . ."

Gennie's face changed. She looked at me with amused curiosity.

"Are you Skye?" She extended her hand and helped me up. "Patricia told me you might be coming around."

"Yeah, Patricia," I said. "I know her as 'Pieces.'"

"Yeah, me, I prefer t' call her Patricia." Gennie opened the door and moved into the shop, flipping on the lights before organizing stacks of flyers for various events on the counter. "Pieces and Pieces . . ." she went on. "Why anyone would want to go and name themselves 'Pieces' is a mystery to me. Just inviting trouble . . . especially when she got a perfectly good and pretty name like Patricia."

The shop was crowded with everything: djembe drums; carved wooden canes; red-gold-and-green T-shirts; beaded bracelets, scarves, pins; posters of Bob Marley, Haile Selassie I, and Marcus Garvey, next to packets of Malcolm X air freshener—"fighting odor by any means necessary." One corner was dedicated to books on Black subject matters: Rasta, Black, and African history, poetry books by various diasporic Africans, even Black astrology. There were also a few tapes on sale: most homegrown mixes of reggae classics, swooners who covered R&B tracks, and toasters who talked you into letting your hips unwind. Behind the counter she had a stack of records and a small phonograph player hooked up to speakers hanging from opposite corners of the store. Gennie turned on her system, put the needle on a disc. Gregory Isaacs crooned over a bouncing bass line.

I stood at the counter trying really hard not to look as high as I was.

"You can take off them shades when you in my shop, ya know."

"Sun hurts my eyes."

"What? Are you a vampire now? No sun in 'ere." She took them off for me and had a good look before returning them to my face. "Mm-hmm," she said, satisfied. She walked purposefully over to the door and locked it.

"Come."

◎

Not sure how I got there but I found myself sitting on a couch in a room underneath the shop. There was a little lamp on an oversized wooden spool of a table, shaded with a translucent maroon cloth. The couch and the table were both on a large Indian throw rug in the middle of the room. Pushed against the surrounding walls were stacks of cardboard boxes filled with stock. Gennie came down the stairs behind and handed me a glass of fresh carrot juice. She eased herself down on a large black leather chair just opposite. A colorful scarf was draped over the back of the chair, making a royal backdrop to the locs crowning her head. In her left hand she held a staff. The top was adorned with what looked like a silver cobra's head. It began to move ever so slightly, twisting around her wrist before elegantly sliding up her arm. I looked from her arm to her face, which was a tunnel of light so bright I had to duck my head.

"You all right, daughter?"

I looked up at Gennie and blinked. There was no colorful scarf, no staff-turned-boa. Just Gennie watching me put the glass to my lips, like a nurse making sure her patient took her medicine.

"What 'ave you been taking?"

I let out a deep breath. Thought I might as well tell her everything. And so I did, the whole story from the squat party to Pieces leaving to me taking my second trip this morning—including all the strange hallucinations and dreams I'd been having. When I got to the part about seeing her with the snake staff, a slow smile spread faintly across her matter-of-fact face.

"Did it look like that?" She pointed at something behind me and got up to walk toward it. I turned to see her pick up a wooden walking stick leaning against the wall at the bottom of the staircase. She handed it to me. The handle was the chipped head of a snake, the rest of its body twisted down the length of the staff.

"Do you know about Damballa, daughter?" she asked, staring at me intently as she sat back down in her chair.

I shook my head no, unable to speak.

"They say those who are possessed with Damballa go mute. Have visions like Moses. Wisdom comes through in dreams." She paused for a few elastic seconds, holding my gaze. Then her expression changed. She looked away as if something else caught her eye. Pressing her index finger to her head, she said, "Before I forget, Patricia did tell me that if I saw you I should tell you to remember TAMT . . . TAMT."

I remembered the note I'd found creased in my pocket. The one I'd stuck onto the wall in the Trashed Palace: *The All Mighty They are watching*. Her words hammering my head like Foucault's pendulum. I grimaced. Told Gennie I needed some air.

I woke up on the stairs outside the Cultural Vibrations shop, the sun setting. Lying beside me was the staff Gennie had given me. Or I thought she'd given me, because at that moment I couldn't be sure whether I'd actually seen her or not. I couldn't be sure anymore if I was awake or in a dream, whether this was a trip or the real thing. I picked up my new walking stick and headed home.

When I got back to the palace, the door was open. The palace was empty and somewhat cleared up. Evidence Scottie had been around lay on the kitchen counter: broken guitar strings along with the residue of a spliff. I leaned my walking stick against the wall near the door, picked up the spliff, and cracked open a beer from the fridge.

I was tired. Why had Pieces left a message like that with Gennie? Was it even real? Or another hallucination? I needed to fill my head with other images. I flipped on all of the seven monitors stacked in a corner of the palace, all static except the one connected to an aerial. Sunk down onto the floor and flipped through the channels. The aerial needed fixing but I could just make out a shadow of an image, a man in a suit. Through the spitting white noise he said, "You could have your fifteen minutes . . ."

I clicked off the TVs and went to lie down, wondering if I could have a dream-free snooze. I was tired of this incessant mindfuck. Even tried counting eclectic sheep but it was no use. The last legs of the microdot twirled visual and sonic bites behind closed eyelids. Started hearing these sounds. Electric humming. The TVs were off. I switched off the main but still heard the electric humming. The moon was hanging half-cocked in the sky. For a moment, as a silver cloud passed by its surface, I glimpsed the iris, a reflection in the dead TV screens, looking back at me, until the sliver of cloud passed. Cool optics, but I'd had enough. Wanted to come down. Realized that I had finished the beer I'd started three hours ago when I began this marathon of staring: at walls, TV screens, the floor, out the window, at nothing. But then the sliver of silver cloud passed by the crooked moon again and I saw it once more; the iris moved for a flicker of a moment, a blinking glitch reflected in the dark screens of the TV sets. I closed my eyes. And still there was the electric humming.

I kept telling myself it was lack of sleep distorting visuals and sound effects. I closed my eyes and heard that man's voice coming from the TV: "fifteen minutes of fame." I opened my eyes with a moan. Hadn't I turned them all off? But there it stood, a dormant gray screen. The white noise would not stop, seemed to get broader and louder like waves lapping closer and closer to where I lay curled in a ball. I put my hands over my ears, reminding myself that I was coming down from a cocktail of drugs. Was prone to paranoia. It was all a hallucination. The noise would eventually fade, but each time I closed my eyes I'd hear the electronic buzz of a camera recording, zooming in and out, for a split second the lens shutter blinking through the electrostatics. I was being watched. By whom? The FBI? MI5? The CIA? My father? Sincara? And who the fuck was The All Mighty They, a.k.a. TAMT, anyway? This was mad thinking . . . Who was I fooling? Even Sincara was little more than the product of an overactive imagination, I told myself, not really believing it.

Snuggled down into my makeshift bed and closed my eyes, taking a deep breath. But again I'd get knee-deep into sleep only to have an electronic buzz wake me. I opened my eyes to a shuttering lens, a shadow behind the glass screen in the TV set. I snapped. Spotting the seven iron that Scottie had found leaning against the wall behind the stack of monitors, I threw off my duvet and grabbed it. Scottie said that it'd literally dropped right in front of him. He'd been convinced it was an act of God. Now I knew what divine purpose it would serve.

A passerby decided to stop somewhere outside my window, their portable radio broadcasting sports updates live to my screen. They were covering a golf tournament. No coincidences. I could still catch glimpses of a lens reflected on the TV, now flickering images, spots before my eyes, as if I had been looking at a light too long. Club in hand, I inspected each TV closely. I just wanted to sleep. I just wanted some fucking peace. Jumped on the stool and swung back my club just as the broadcaster noted Tiger Woods was preparing for a drive.

"Watch this!" I yelled, putting my full weight behind the swing. Boob tubes shatter nicely. As if they were made for it. A righteous rage energized me as I laid hard into each and every screen, one by one. I was an assassin gone mad. I bashed and bashed until there was nothing left but splintered cathodes and shards of glass. After creaming all of the monitors, I slid down against the wall, exhausted, and began staring at Pieces's multihued graffiti. Remembered her checking the walls and marking the less hollow points with dots. She'd said they were guides for shelves but in the end, she never put them up. I noticed little pinholes in the wall, making the dots look like pupils.

Stepping over the odd bottle missed in the cleaning blitz, I drew ovals with lashes around each, the pupil finishing the eye. After covering the length of the wall in eyes, I crawled into a corner, cradling the seven iron, and slept the sleep of the dead.

◉

I woke up to a cup of tea and Scottie's boots in front of my face. He had just put the hot, carefully stirred milky generic Earl Grey in front of my nose and was waiting for me to open my eyes. I looked up at him. He had a new guitar slung across his back. I wondered only briefly how he had replaced it so quickly—he had a knack for finding things.

"What. The. Fuck. Skye?" he said, jaw tightening.

I gradually came to, unsticking my eyelids, old battered club still in hand. The room seemed cloudy.

"What happened, Skye??? For Christ's sake!!!"

I looked around at the electronic carnage. A mosaic of tube innards, cracked circuit boards, and broken glass surrounded busted TVs in cubes of hard plastic and thin metal: hollowed-out boxes standing like tombstones in homage to what they'd once been.

I blinked. "I don't know, I just freaked out. Why did we keep all these TVs, anyway? They give me the creeps."

"You just 'freaked out'? The 'creeps'? It was *your* idea, remember? 'Multimedia rave,' you and Pieces called it. God, was I the only one at the jam, after all I've been through, first Pieces now—What the fu—" he stopped mid-run-on sentence. A doctor making sense of symptoms, he pulled the guitar off his back and walked away from me. He went over to the counter.

"That's it, innit? Pieces. She's gone and you freaked and took it out on the bloody . . ." His hands cut the air, an exclamation point, presenting me with the smashed TV sets. "I've been out trying to save the palace, Skye. Spent the night in the clink, haven't seen you since the jam . . . Left to clean this place up on my own, and now this?" He was getting himself worked up again. I heard a flow of "fucks" rumble under his breath as he paced around the kitchen. Plopping on a stool, he pulled out a square of black. I watched as he burned and crumbled the hash over the mound of tobacco.

I sighed. "Look, Scottie, I'm sorry. I can replace the TV sets."

He silently finished rolling the spliff, sparked it up, took a deep hit before passing it to me. We smoked for a while in silence. I lay back on my bedding and Scottie played with his cuticles. When he finally spoke his tone was softer, though still tense around the edges.

"Now spill it, what's going on with you?"

I shook my head. "I don't know."

I smoked without saying any more than that. Tried to make sense of everything. Decided it'd all been a bad trip. That's all. Said nothing, simply surveyed the mess I'd made, and began to feel calmer than I had in a long while. I knew what I needed to do. I had to go confront Pieces about the message she left me. I needed answers. I needed a change of scenery.

Amsterdam would do.

INT. TRASHED PALACE

Skye walks past Scottie, backpack snug on her shoulder, and picks up her walking stick near the door. Pauses before opening it and leaving. Scottie's face changes from sadness to anger. He walks into his room. He comes out with his golf club and, with a running start, swings at the wall over Skye's mat, making dents in the eyes painted there.

AMSTER-AMSTER-DAM-DAM-DAM. With my share of the money made from the Trashed Palace jam I purchased a ticket. Couldn't believe I was finally here. I used some of my remaining cash to rent a bicycle once I left Schiphol station. The sky was the color of milk. Splashes of blue began to seep through above me, and the rain slicking the pavement was slowly evaporating. I got on the bike, balancing my bag on my back; the staff sticking out made it slightly awkward but doable. I headed toward the Anne Frank House. Eddie told me Pieces was squatting in a boat on a canal not far from there. I wasn't sure I'd find her there, grabbed a tourist map just in case.

It was almost disconcertingly easy to ride a bike in Amsterdam. Every street had a path. There was very little risk of being hit by a car. The streets were busy, but the energy seemed lighter than in London, almost unreal. Natives trying to get where they were going mixed with tourists walking slowly and obliviously, teetering on rented bikes, or eating chips with peanut sauce from the street vendors. The locals seemed to put up with tourists the way one puts up with any necessity, no matter how annoying. They were a part of the landscape, at least in that part of town. One got the feeling that the real Amsterdam existed outside this bubble. I found the Anne Frank House easily enough. There were several boats moored nearby. Saw Pieces before I had a chance to look too hard. Felt her energy pull my attention. Blood rushed up from my gut, rouging my face as our eyes locked.

"Skye!" she called out, waving at me. I waved back, forgetting that I was on a bike. I could have been floating. I could have vomited.

"Watch it! The tracks!" Pieces yelled, pointing. I swerved just in time to prevent the tire wheel from getting stuck in the tram track groove. Pieces ran up to me as I stumbled off the bike. Grabbing my shoulders, she steadied me.

"You okay?" She looked at me and gave me a hug. "I didn't mean to startle you."

"I wanted to surprise *you*. Did Eddie tell you I was coming?" I asked. Pieces took my bike as I readjusted my bag.

"I just had a feeling you were headed this way soon," Pieces said, nonplussed. For a minute I thought I heard exasperation in her voice.

"Look, I should have let you know in advance, but it was a last-minute thing," I stammered. "I need a break from Scottie and . . . something about that place, the Trashed Palace post-jam, seems weird, something isn't right . . ."

Pieces turned to me and smiled, stopping my ramble dead in its tracks. "It's good to see you." Without saying another word, she grabbed my hand. I felt that she got what I'd been trying to say. That she understood. And I didn't want to ruin this fragile moment by saying something stupid. I stayed silent, still trying psychically to reach her. As Pieces walked me and my bike down to her humble abode, I felt that, though I could feel the pulse in her palm, her spirit was elsewhere.

We deposited my bags in the boat. It was a fishing boat, docked until the next season, left unattended. "The owners are on holiday," she explained as we climbed out of the hull onto the deck. "I've been dead lucky they haven't come back."

She left me for a moment by the canal to make a call from a nearby phone booth. Told me to wait there, she expected Eddie at any moment. And Eddie did arrive, on a light-green push bike, with a matching green jacket. We gave each other a big hug. We sat at the edge of the canal and caught up. She admitted that it had been a bad idea to dose like that before getting on an airplane, with no way out and no place to go. She'd ended up watching her face change in the toilet mirror for what seemed like ages.

"Good thing it was a short flight," she said. "Did you spend the rest of your trip in the airport?"

I told her the brief version. How in the end I'd freaked out a little. Wasn't used to having that many drugs in my body. Decided to come to Amsterdam to detox.

"'Amsterdam to detox'?" She laughed. "Okaaaay. Pieces was happy to see ya . . . ?" She strained to make the question into a statement.

I sucked my teeth. Pieces had *said* that she was glad to see me, but I still wasn't so sure. To deflect my insecurity, I joked, "Her first words to me were, 'Watch it! The tracks!'"

As if we'd summoned her, Pieces came back across a nearby bridge arching over the canal and came to sit with us.

"Well, women," she said, smiling, "what should we do? I suppose, Skye, you'd like to visit one of our fine coffee houses for refreshments."

We ended up in this place off the main strip. The guy at the counter wore a navy-blue alligator short-sleeved top, jeans, and a dark-blue baseball cap decorated with a marijuana leaf insignia. He recognized both Eddie and Pieces.

"Hello." His cheerful greeting tinged with what I guessed was a Dutch accent.

"Hey, Jo," Eddie said, softening the *j* into a *y* sound. Pieces left to go find us a table in the small, low-lit room just past Jo's counter stock of paraphernalia.

"This is Skye," Eddie said, presenting me. "It's her first time, so give her the beginner's shtick." As he went over the menu I half listened while scanning the room for Pieces. My heart skipped a beat when I didn't see her.

"So what would you like?" Jo brought me back.

"I don't know. I guess I'll take that one." I pointed to a random name on the list—"White Widow." Why not. Both Eddie and Jo whistled, as if to say *Are you sure?* I pretended to know what I was doing. Eddie ordered a couple of carbonated drinks, and we looked around the half-full space for Pieces. She was still nowhere to be found. I followed Eddie to an empty booth, trying to mask the disappointment I felt dripping off my face.

"She's probably in the toilet, innit?" Eddie said, passing me the slim joint full of pure weed. "I would take it easy on that stuff if I were you. It will put you in a coma." I stuck a straw in my can of sweet fizz, lit the joint, looked Eddie in the eye as I took a deep puff. Some of the smoke went down the wrong pipe and I began to cough.

"Three coughs and you're off!" Pieces said with a grin as she slid into the booth next to me. I laughed, spurting up the soda I had swallowed to soothe my throat, remembering our first meeting in New York. How awkward and stupid I had been. That was the first time I'd seen Sincara in her presence, and that armlet. I started to ask Pieces if I could see the tattoo hidden under her jean jacket, but she and Eddie were now in an animated conversation about some tourists that got completely off their faces in the coffee shop last week. Under the table, Pieces's fingers lightly touched mine for a brief spark of a second. I wanted to grab her hand

and was working up the courage when she moved hers to steal my soda.

◎

Tram tracks crisscrossed the street, stretching out before our bike tires as Pieces, Eddie, and I rode around Amsterdam. The three of us hung out the rest of the week. Most times Eddie would stay overnight in the boat with us. We would get lit around a small fire that, with a click of a rusting Zippo she'd found, Pieces conjured up in a tin bucket, a nightly ritual softening the cold dampness the evenings now sometimes brought.

I'd always end up in the middle of the two of them on the stitched-together sleeping bags, with Eddie spooning me. I snuggled in, enjoying her heat. I tried to cuddle Pieces but she protested. Said the reason she slept on this side of me was to get away from Eddie's roving hands, not to endure another's. My hurt feelings were eased as I felt Eddie squeeze me and whisper in my ear, "She's a grumpy ole git, isn't she?" which irritated Pieces even more. She yanked the covers over her head. "Can't a girl get any sleep around here?"

Eddie was fun and I liked her a lot, but I looked forward to some alone time with Pieces. I had a nagging feeling she was hiding something and I wanted to find out what it was. If she'd come back to Amsterdam for somebody, she kept it a secret. She didn't seem in love, though. If anything, she seemed distracted.

Finally the day came. We had some time, just she and I. Low on cash, we managed to liberate a bottle of tequila from a local chain.

"Hey, you wanna go to Anne Frank's house?" Pieces

asked. "I got a spot where I like to sit while I watch the sun go down."

"Yeah, sure!" I said coolly as I could, happy that at last she seemed to be on the same page. We needed time alone, to connect, to talk. "Did you ever read her diaries?"

Pieces smiled at me. "I read the book a few times when I was a teenager and fell in love with Anne Frank." She had that quirky look on her face that cued she was about to tell a story. "Her story made me try to make a go of it on my own instead of merely *surviving* my own personal hell." She opened the bottle of tequila as we walked and lit a cig. "Parts of me being murdered or hidden away, you know? Anyway, my Black dad left my white mom, and as the cliché goes, I thought it was my fault. Or for a long time I thought it was my fault 'cause he took my side." Pieces paused, sipped the bottle absentmindedly, then, as if suddenly remembering I existed, passed it to me. "My dad found out that my uncle, my mom's brother, had been sneaking into my room, giving me a little 'sex education.' My uncle said I'd seduced him, and my mom acted like nothing had happened, refused to talk about it, but my dad believed me. Wanted to kick the shit out of him but knew he'd end up in jail if he did. After all, it was my word against my uncle's—me, a young Black girl, against a white-collar white man. We know what those folks think about us, with a special, certain fetish toward your Dorothy Dandridge types." Pieces took one last drag of her cigarette before flicking it to the curb. "So my dad left town."

"Pieces . . ." I said, dumbstruck and at a loss for words.

Pieces grabbed the bottle back out of my hand and took a swig. "I feel like I've told you all this before." She looked at me, studying my face for a response.

"Hey, I think I blacked out most of our first night together, so it's possible," I answered, somewhat embarrassed. "I mean, I was a real lightweight then." I covered my awkwardness with a chuckle, stuffed my hands deep into my pockets as we continued walking. "Could you remind me?"

She gave me a somber smile. "It's all good, Skye. So, yeah, with my dad out of the picture my mother tried to make me into the white daughter she always dreamed about. I went along with it for a while, furious with my father for leaving me. Though my mother wouldn't discuss the 'issue' with me, my uncle thankfully wasn't welcomed around anymore. I mean, I eventually understood the shame my father must have felt, and I don't know, maybe it was already over between my mom and dad before the shit with my uncle happened. But it took a while for me to get there mentally, and I spent years trying to be what my mother wanted. But it was too much, hiding half of me away in the attic with Anne Frank." She lifted the bottle in the air, pointing at Anne's house-cum-museum.

"Well, Anne couldn't bust loose but I would," she continued. "I had to get free. I guess that's what attracted me to Scottie. He seemed to have figured out that 'free' part, and was comfortable with his own particular 'mulatto tragedy,' least that's what I thought. But he hasn't and isn't. He is 80 percent charade. He thinks the world owes him everything. The world owes us nothing, it's we who owe ourselves . . . What I'm trying to say is that I'm trying to deal with mine, my . . ." She looked away for a split second before turning back to face me. "My own shit, and I need to be able to be in a truly honest space with myself to do that. That's the main reason I had to get away."

We arrived at her spot, hopped up on the railing along the canal in front of Anne Frank House, and made a toast, pouring libation under dangling feet. We locked boots, swinging them in time with the movement of water streaming below us. I was still spinning from her story; a compote of emotions turned and knifed my chest, everything in me wanted to wail, but I swallowed it. I wanted to comfort Pieces but didn't know how. Looked at her and saw under dimming light the trace of a tear on her cheek. I wanted to kiss her. But checked myself on an exhale. I chuckled.

"What?" Pieces turned to look at me. Her lips were like magnets. I deflected.

"I wonder if Anne Frank was queer."

Pieces laughed. "Yeah, probably." She took another swig and lifted the bottle for another toast. "To the heartbreaker."

We created an oasis there in front of Anne's digs. I told Pieces about my microdot adventures and the trip's culmination: the TV smash episode. Pieces listened silently. As I spoke she seemed to retreat further and further into herself. But I couldn't stop talking.

"I just had this creepy feeling I couldn't escape being watched, you know what I mean? Like the CIA was after me or something, or my dad had sent out a private dick to track me down. Sounds like something he would do." I took a sip from the bottle and passed it to Pieces. "And all that stuff with Gennie and the staff, Sincara . . . It all seemed so real. Do you think I'm crazy? Losing my mind?"

She took two long swigs. "No."

"But come on, Pieces, why would anyone be watching me? It was probably a combination of drugs, lack of sleep, and a vivid imagination."

"Maybe."

"You ever feel like that?" I pressed, wanting to break through.

"Kinda." Pieces jumped off the railing and started

walking. I stared at her back, feeling like I was missing something, that she was holding back. She turned. "You comin' or what?"

Attempting a jump, I slipped off the railing and fell on my ass.

"On second thought, maybe you should just give me the bottle," Pieces said, laughing, and helped me up.

We walked arm in arm down the canal. Everything felt *almost* right, like that very first night we spent together in New York. The sun was setting and the occasional headlight tickled the surface of the water. Unlike London, things were peaceful here. Perhaps it was the water that moved through the city. London had the Thames, but most spots were backgrounded by heavy nearby traffic. Maybe it was the simple fact of being somewhere *else*. The stress of the London streets didn't seep in until I'd *lived* there for a while. Sometimes a change of scenery was enough. I could see why Pieces wanted to stay.

"You know, I was thinking of staying in Amsterdam for a while. Checking out the scene," I said, testing the waters.

Pieces tensed up. She was silent for a couple of beats before replying, "Yeah?" Her voice came to me from another time zone. I knew that I should just shut up but I couldn't. I wanted her to know I had a plan.

"Yeah . . . I was just thinking I could make my way back to the States eventually from here."

But it backfired. I'd had a feeling it would.

"You know what I think?" Her voice was a quiet knot.

"What?"

"Never mind. Do whatever the fuck you want to do." Pieces sighed.

"What . . . ?" I shifted uncomfortably, stunned, but at the same time not, by her sudden change in mood. *"What?!"*

"Damn it, Skye, weren't you listening to me earlier? I came here to get some honest-to-goddamn space!"

I pulled my arm away from hers, or maybe she pulled hers from mine. It was definitely mutual.

"Listen . . . I . . . *you're* the one always taking off when it—"

"With you right on my tail! My point exactly."

"—when it was *you* who invited me to London, and you never said I *couldn't* come to Amsterdam . . ." Everything I'd been holding down started floating to the surface, loosening my tongue. I'd been trying to reach her, but the barriers wouldn't budge. So I pushed harder. "And it's not like you're really *here* anyway," I spat.

Pieces stopped mid-step and looked hard at me. I wanted to stuff the words back in my mouth. All of them. But it was too late. I could feel this going south the way it had in front of the pub in London. Vertigo.

"Damnit, Skye, why did you have to come?" It wasn't really a question. "This can't work. Look, you just have to trust me on this. I can't pretend that—" She caught herself and walked faster ahead of me, toward the boat. "Fine, you want to stay? Then I'm going. Done and dusted. I am gonna leave in the morning."

I was shocked but not. The feeling was familiar now. At least she was consistent. I caught up to her.

"How is it that you just happen to have to leave whenever we get a chance to spend some time together?" I said angrily. "What's up with that, huh?"

"Come on, Skye. You must be over your little crush by now." Pieces stormed down to the boat and I went after her, mortified.

"Listen, fuck that. You and me . . . I mean, well . . ."

As she climbed down the ladder into the hull of the boat, Pieces interrupted my stuttering and spat, "There is a 'you' and there is a 'me' but there is no 'you and me.' Fuck, Skye. It was over before it began. Listen, do me a favor, go back to America, go back to school, write your lil Black Kerouacian adventures. After a while I'll become just another character in your story." She removed her boots and socks and started to build a small fire in the bucket.

I was fuming. I grabbed her boots and tacked them to the inside wall of the boat and wrote with a big nibbed marker I'd started carrying with me: SEE GIRL RUN.

And then it was my turn to storm out. To give her a chance to study my conceptual sculpture in solitude while I got some air. I felt like I was going to scream and tried not to cry. Took a few deep breaths and walked up the pier, sat down, kicked off my boots, aired my toes, tried to calm down. I was an idiot. What did I expect? That this was a forever story? She was right—there was no "she and I," and I needed to snap out of fantasyland, even if it was one fantasy I would never admit to. Still, there was something unfinished between us, and I knew she felt it . . . Why else would she keep taking off, going off? She was protecting herself from something; it was evident that that something was me.

"Who the fuck is running, Skye?" I turned and saw her bare feet first. Pieces was behind me, her face dark with anger. "Hey? Who was the little girl who ran away from daddy to discover the big bad world, hey? From her big bad daddy, who she thinks would send a private fucking detective to track her down. Yeah? Well at least you think your dad gives a fuck."

"Listen, Pieces, we established this a long time ago . . ." I stood up and tried to reason with her. "Both our families are fucked up. I mean, you and me—"

She sneered. "*You and me* are not alike, all right, Skye? I know I'm on my own, but *you* . . . Why is it that you're always running to me, hey? Do you know why? Maybe it's *you* that can't come to terms with things, as they *are*, hey? *You.* Classic textbook abandonment issues, don't I goddamn well know it. And I am tired of being that mirror!"

"Fuck YOU! What the fuck do you know?" I shot back. What she had said was a smack in the face. The truth in it stung.

"What I know you know already. Wake. The. Fuck. Up." Pieces had lost it. "You say you dream about being watched, you feel like you are being watched. Guess what? YOU *ARE* BEING WATCHED, SKYE. And this"—Pieces, raised both hands in the air—"aaalll of this? None of it's REAL!"

Her nose was two inches from mine. Pieces saw the look of confusion on my face and seemed to immediately regret her words. She muttered "Fuck it!" under her breath before continuing in a softer tone. "Unreal! You still really don't remember, do you?"

I could only stare back with mouth open. Pieces looked at me and shook her head before blazing off in a huff, carrying a boot in each hand.

Everything she said after "you *are* being watched" was an echo chamber of noise. I knew what she meant, I heard her, but I was working on unhearing her. Every cell in my body knew what she was saying to be true, and that truth was more profound than I was yet ready to accept. Something in my brain resisted. The same something that held at bay a stealthily mounting panic, now rising like acidic bile up my esophagus, dissolving my gray matter. The first "no" rested at the back of my throat, barely audible, but quickly crescendoed into a rapid machine gunfire, "no no NO NO NO NO!"

Then I smelled the smoke. I beat it back to the boat, jumped through the hatch and down the splintering ladder. Pieces, rushing back up the ladder, passed me. She had

been making a sculpture of her own with fire, an experiment in burning temperatures. Had chucked everything
she could find into the bucket, smoldering and spitting
flames. Pocketing the nearby Zippo, I rushed to put it out.
As I doused the fire I heard Pieces talking to a concerned
Dutch citizen. Knew it was time to jet. I was struggling to
put the boot on my left foot when Pieces came down and
stated the obvious.

"We gotta get outta here, quick."

But even "quick" was too late. The sound of fire-engine
sirens were in earshot. We stood outside the boats, facing
approaching Dutch cops, each of us with mismatched boots
on. She had on my left shoe. I had on hers. One of the officers said something in Dutch. We looked up at him blankly
so he switched to English.

"How did you get into the boat?" one of the cops asked
us. He didn't bother to ask us if the boat was ours. Evidently
it was impossible that of either of us could have a key; folks
like us didn't own boats, or even have friends with boats. No
matter what we said, in their minds we were clearly tres-
passing, and most likely up to some other illegal business.
Neither Pieces nor I uttered a word. They asked the question again. "How did you get into the boat?"

To me it was obvious—we got in the same way we got
out. But I guess overdoing it is a universal requirement of
all those who wear the uniform. Assumptions were made,
and they broke a window of the boat and scurried down,
in search of, I later found out, cocaine. They thought we
might be smuggling drugs.

"Are you a boy or a girl?" one of the officers asked me in a
thick accent foreign to my ears, trying to get to both of us, I
thought. I didn't answer. Pieces spat on the ground in reply.

Later, inside the Dutch cell, not sure what, if any, charges they were going to bring against us, I resigned myself to whatever. None of it mattered. The past months began to subtly take on a new hue. One that my mind was not ready to fully take on. I was bursting with questions. Most of which I wasn't sure I wanted answers to. But Pieces was right— it was all right there in front of me. She, who had left the biggest clue of all, was in the cell next to me.

"Pieces?" I whispered. "Who are TAMT? The All Mighty They. Who are they?"

"Good question, Skye. Who the fuck are they."

Her words, the way she said them, held a finality to them. Cemented the bricks in a wall thicker than the concrete between our cells. But then Pieces began the bluesy humming of a motherless child. I picked up the tune in call-and-response fashion. And I felt the barriers between us slowly start to disintegrate.

The next day Eddie met me in the Dutch-clink reception area. We hadn't been charged, but Pieces was nowhere to be found. She had been processed first. Apparently I'd been stone-cold out of it when they came to get us, and the officers decided to deal with her first.

"Where is she?" I asked.

"I think she said she was going to Spain," Eddie said, handing me my bag. "I don't know much else. You know how she is."

We went back to her place, a small studio at the top of a steep flight of stairs somewhere outside the center of Amsterdam. I was panting tequila fumes. Pieces and I had finished the bottle somewhere between Anne's house and the boat fire. I hadn't gotten much sleep in the clink; just as I was getting in deep, a guard was yelling at me to wake up. Suffering from a severe hangover, I crashed immediately on Eddie's sofa bed.

Out like a light, I dreamed dreams as vivid as the day streaming through Eddie's front-room windows.

Pieces is across from me, she holds the chain with the twisting one-eyed snake dangling from it. She puts it around my neck. I am sneaking past the guards in the dank dark dungeon. I undo the cuffs that shackle my mom's arms and feet to the queen's chair. She whispers, "They are watching." We sneak out and make it to my small canoe waiting outside on the canal. I will get her out of here. She begins humming an eerily similar bluesy riff. The canal leads to a swampy river, we can see nothing but darkness all around but can feel their eyes following after us. I paddle our raft as fast as I can without making too much noise. They are gaining.

I woke up at Eddie's, rays from a streetlamp swathing the gauzy curtains that hung over the window across from me.

"Hey, you all right? Hey?" Eddie's dark hair hung over her eyes as she looked down at me. "You looked pretty wrecked when I brought you back from the station. Pieces told me to make sure I gave you this journal." She handed me a new hardbound notebook.

"Go on, open it." Eddie watched me with a half smile on her face. I hesitated. It felt like a private moment on one hand, but on the other, I was glad she was there, terrified as I was of what I might find.

On the cover of the notebook, Pieces had used scraps of papers with different font letters to write *Skye Papers*. I opened it and read her slanted handwriting: *Sorry I had to be an ass. Hope you can use this to help write your story.*

My story. The one that I wanted to believe in was disintegrating. The dots resisted connecting. Pieces had cared enough to leave this for me. It meant something. The night before came back to me slowly. The argument, the fire, the necklace, the swamp. I felt around my neck for the snake pendant. But there was nothing there. *You* are *being watched*, she'd said. My brain shut down. I closed the journal, exhausted, unable to continue.

"Where is she?"

"She headed off. To Spain. Remember?"

I did remember, just didn't understand. Plopped my head down and said nothing.

"Don't tell me amnesia is contagious," Eddie teased as she pulled the curtains back, letting light from the street spill into her room fully. "When Pieces arrived here in Amsterdam, she was also a bit foggy. Are you hungry?"

Did Eddie know something? Her joke about amnesia was just the right amount of ironic. Whatever she might know, I was still struggling to grasp. And the person who had triggered it all was gone, again. I began to look for my shoes. I had to get back to London. Find Scottie. He would know *something*. I could get to the bottom of this thing that was beginning to feel like a sick joke.

"I think I'll go and try to see if I can change this return ticket. I don't want to be a burden." As I made to stand, I felt a throbbing pain brick my forehead. I sat back down.

Eddie smiled. "Take it easy. You need some food in your system, don't ya?"

"I'm okay, honest," I said, better for sitting.

"Just take it easy, now," she said, gently pushing me back down onto the pillow. "Anyway, Pieces told me to make sure I also gave you this." Eddie bent over and kissed me a little longer than she should have. "I like you," she said, her face still close to mine.

"Why?"

"Why not?" she said, kissing me again.

I kissed her back. Her lips were like something I had a taste for and needed more of, like a tune you have in your head that you can't quite hear but remember as you hum it. It was on the tip of her tongue, now kissing my neck. This felt familiar. The answer to the only question that was important in that moment. I folded into her. Eddie fucked me and I let her, releasing my will to her wild fingers flying through me. I did not hesitate. I needed this. My mind reeled, unblocking. Silver chords shone through her translucent eyes. I was the drum.

When I woke up the next morning Eddie had already left for work at the city-center café. Last night she'd told me that I was free to stay if I wanted. I wasn't sure what I wanted. Too many things left unanswered flooded my head. But maybe I would stay a day or two to clear it. I picked up the journal and reread Pieces's inscription. Though the lovemaking with Eddie softened the blow, it still stung. And what was worse, I couldn't find a real reason why I cared about Pieces so damn much. As stupidly cheesy as it sounds, it was as if we had taken an oath in a parallel life. My "little crush," she'd said. Fuck her. There was something undeniable that had passed between us; I couldn't shake that feeling, no matter how cold she was toward me every time I tried to get close. Seemed to me she thrived on not facing shit head-on. Thrived on speaking in vague-osities. *You are being watched!* she'd said. TAMT was the obvious answer. The note she'd left that had fallen from my jeans. The message sent through Gennie Jah. But who the fuck *were* TAMT? In the police station hadn't she, once again, given me a non-answer? Was she fucking with my mind on purpose? Or was it, as she insinuated, all in my mind?

I closed my eyes and willed myself back into dreamland. But my head was in too much of a swirl. I flipped through the journal carefully; all the other pages were empty. A familiar yellowed envelope dropped from its pages; I watched, in slow motion, as it feathered and floated to the floor. Pushing past panic, I leaned over the edge of the bed and picked it up. Holding it in my hand I took a deep breath and, ripping off the Band-Aid, I opened the letter on an exhale. I let the envelope slip back to the floor and read the neat cursive handwriting for the first time, all the way down to my mother's signature. And everything began unraveling. I took in every curve and nuance of her handwriting. Concentrated on the slant of her *t*'s and the roundness of her *a*'s and the way she looped her *o*'s. The letter was addressed to my dad.

Brandon. I am done. No more judges. No more drama. I don't want to drag this out and I don't want Skye to have to grow up under this mess. You are making it near impossible to stay close. It's obvious that you want me to disappear, whether it's by sending me into "treatment" or threatening me with a restraining order. I just ask myself, what are you going to tell her? Knowing you, you will probably make sure I barely even existed. I am sorry that you couldn't forgive me enough to share custody or even at least the right to see our child. What's best for Skye is more important to me than anything, even if it rips my heart to pieces. I hope you can find it in you to someday, when she's old enough, tell her the truth, that I fought for her, that I will continue fighting for her in my own fashion, and let her make her own decisions. Please take good care of my dear Skye.

Her signature was an illegible scrawl that reminded me of my own. *Kara.*

I found myself on an airplane headed to the UK. Everything was a blur from the moment I found my mom's letter in the journal up until that point, sitting in a window seat on a half-full plane. I reread the letter. Put it back in the envelope. It had our old St. Louis address on it, but the return address was scratched out. I stared out the airplane window. We were descending into Heathrow. I tried to contain the rising trepidation in my gut, with reason. Though the fact that Pieces had been holding on to this letter disturbed me, I batted it away into the same black hole I had been batting everything else into since I woke up in New York to find Pieces, and part of my memory, gone. Painful and repressed as they were, those were old questions, things I'd been struggling with in many ways, my whole life. I was trying to catch up to my present.

So I crash-landed, skint, in London on a Saturday. Relief. Decided to head for the Trashed Palace, find Scottie, and figure out where to next. Movement is my mantra. That is why they call me Skye. To be so high: this was the condition under which I believed I was conceived. To just move on. The sky thick with clouds forced me to believe in gravity. A conspiracy theory. There was no choice but to be grounded. Some people acquiesce easily to death. Some hold on to the vestiges of what they once were, for fear of losing balance. I was lingering in between, inside a kind of limbo, which made everything seem absurd. London's lateral ambience suited my mood. I had to keep it moving. That was what my dad had drummed into me. Somewhere along the line, movement became a metaphor for falling in love. Somewhere along the line, I lost faith. The one-and-a-half-hour tube journey from Heathrow to Brixton took me through the bowels of London.

The Way Out sign down the platform and the light smell of incense that the dreadlocked man burned accentuated some temporal reality. As I climbed the stairs to the exit, his familiar chant, "incense, incense," mellowed me. I used my last pound to buy a pack as a housewarming present for the squat. An older woman playing paper-and-comb in a nearby corner intensified his hymn. Her bright sequined paintings caught my eye as I stepped over the line into Brix-madness. Outside the tube, all that was solid melted into a mesh of watercolors, saturating my eyes like a Marinetti. It was late afternoon and just how I remembered it. People moved to and fro, carrying Shop and Save bags and unmarked plastic carriers bulging with market bargains. You could tell the locals from the rest as they weaved through the chaos of the crowds, not walking orderly on one side, but crisscrossing and maneuvering on autopilot. Foreigners, including Londoners from other parts of town, found themselves blocked at every which way—frustrated by the confusion, frustrated in collisions with high-turbaned African women who knew exactly where they were going. I took it slowly. No hurry. My backpack steadied me. My stick protected me. I knew where I was going, certain I couldn't be seen. My surroundings, with their workings and weavings, were a replica of just about any Black urban setting. Rounding the corner past Pizza Hut onto Coldharbour Lane, from the corner of my eye I spied the three-story McDonald's. Realizing that with my visa near the end I would have to eventually go back, I felt nauseous with paranoia—that AmeriKKKa was chasing me. These two establishments were monsters ready to devour; their colors did not blend in, but stood out awkwardly.

I retracted into my protective mental basket. Made my way down Coldharbour, past the Brixton mural: a skeleton wrapped in world-power flags dropping war planes out of one hand, his skull being attacked by peace signs on the other side. The peace signs evolved from doves, which one hand let go. Dr. Death raged through the London metropolis, amid nuclear rain clouds shadowed by horrified faces. Next door was the squat.

I was on the doorstep before I realized it was completely boarded up. Dropping my bag, I plopped down on the steps outside. So that was that. I'd run to London but had no place to go. Reaching for numbness, I lit a cig. Where the fuck was Scottie? I had the sinking feeling he was wasting away in a cell, done in for illegally squatting or resisting arrest or doing drugs or any combination of possibilities. But I could do nothing about it now. Maybe I would check Prof's flat later, but for now I was too worn-out to get on the tube again.

Felt like fall was kicking in early, damp cold air working its way to the marrow. Down to my last pack and dead broke in the middle of Brixton—fuck it. Not like I hadn't seen it all before. I eased out a stick of incense from its silver wrapping and burned it. The smoke rose and spread, creating a thin haze around me. I was determined to go it alone. I could go it alone. But I couldn't leave this place without grieving. I held the vision of someone who knew the world (as she knew it) would be ending tomorrow.

Exhausted, wet eyelashes weighing down already heavy lids, I drifted off. Brixton streets flickered in black-and-white still frames behind my closed eyes. Clicked off. My thoughts flowed to warmer times. To the last grind in the curtained-off space in the loft, around Eddie's sofa bed. The sweetness of a final lovemaking. The kisses lingering as I slipped on my knapsack. This cut at my gut, but I pushed the feelings down, determinedly aloof. Dreamed about the first day I met Pieces in the Lower East Side, all bright-eyed and wide-open to everything, because anything could happen, things that could change you forever. That was the high. Seeing her for the first time and experiencing everything that followed on that first night with her was that kind of rare surprise that makes you believe in "meant to be." Makes you believe that you are exactly where you are supposed to be. But I guess that was the point. All of this *was* make-believe.

None of this is real! I heard Pieces's voice on repeat, coloring every chaotic and trampling thought, demanding I *WAKE UP!*

I came to with a start in front of the squat, the strong smell of gas burning my nose. The incense I'd lit earlier was dust. I wiped the sleep from my eyes. A halo of orange haze hung way up, full and round, high in the night sky. I felt hollow. A rough tension, circling my shoulder blades and burning through the palms of my hands, begged for sacrifice. I pulled out the Swiss Army knife Scottie had given me when we were repairing my guitar. Beginning with the fattest dreadlock, which pulled at the back of my scalp, I sliced. After I'd finished cutting the last of my locs, my head felt light and lucid. I knew exactly where I would complete this ritual. I gathered my hair and pushed it inside my denim jacket, turning to stare at our empty squat. Where there was once life, love, creativity, now stood a chained corpse. It had represented our right to exist by any means possible. We studied time; her apprentices, we studied the art of eluding definition. But even in our fluidity we risked stagnation.

A heavy scent wafted through an opening the size of a child's fist in the now boarded-up kitchen window. I pulled the locs from inside my jacket and placed them on a flat surface near the hole. I almost added the letter from my mom as well, but decided at the last minute to save it, that it would be part of my future. I reached into my pocket and fired up Pieces's Zippo.

The smell of singeing hair hit me first, before the flames began to spark up and spread. I stood mesmerized. Sweating. Those locs had been so much of my identity. Now all of that past was rising up in smoke, flames catching so fast and ferociously, I barely had time to back away.

S oaked in a harsh sea of flashing blue lights, I came to my senses. Blue uniforms framing doughy Mr. Men faces spitting questions in rapid-fire British accents:

"Do you know anything about the explosion?"

"Did you see who did this?"

"Can you tell us anything about the squat?"

I stared back at them blankly. A blur of whizzing lights and sound around me; nostrils were filled with smoke. I retched.

A white coat pushed them away. I was lifted into the back of an ambulance. The white coat held my hand and, in a calmer voice, asked scripted questions:

"Do you know your name?"

"Do you know where you are?"

"Can you tell me where you are from?"

"What is your name?"

I had memory of nothing. It was hard to keep my eyes open. The white coat tried to keep me awake, but it was too late. I'd already drifted into my own mindscape.

Inside this sphere, abstract flashbacks floated past my inside eye, in patches of turquoise, aqua, and dark blue; they all drifted across a crimson canvas.

I woke up in a private room in King's College Hospital, to Prof's face staring down at me. The last thing I remembered was a swirl of lights and faces asking me my personal information. Disturbingly, my Social Security number was one of the first things that came to mind before I was out of it again.

Disconcerted, I tried to sit up but Prof put a gentle hand on my shoulder.

"Easy, now," he said. "You have been through an ordeal." His forehead seemed to crinkle a bit more than usual. His eyes told me that he knew everything I needed to know. I looked around the sterile room. A rectangular window looked out onto a parking lot. On the small table next to my bed was a bowl of fruit and flowers and a card marked *TAMT*.

I looked up at Prof. "What the fuuuck . . ."

"I know it must be a lot to take in." Prof held my hand. "But you're safe."

Safe? That was funny. Safe! A panic-tinged anger was rising. Prof saw it too, didn't flinch when I snatched my hand from his.

"What the fuck is going on?!" I didn't scream, but the intensity was there in my raspy, smoke-rusted voice.

"What do you remember?"

The memory domino effect that had started in Amsterdam continued now, in staccato snapshots falling, pushing against one another in random sequence:

Pieces gives me a note with the words The All Mighty They are watching. *She takes the snake armlet off . . . We are in an office of some sort. We're here to sign a contract . . . On the table in Pieces's New York loft is a package from London . . . Pieces's and Scottie's signatures are on the contract. The TAMT logo is blazoned across the top of the document . . . A cop tells us the package came from Scottie.*

I blinked, swore under my breath. Scottie! I had come to London to find Scottie. But then I somehow blew up the Trashed Palace, cameras and all, and . . .

"How did I get here?" I said, slowly pushing myself up. Prof adjusted the pillow behind my back. "And where is Scottie?"

"Scottie is no longer in the country, Skye." He cleared his throat and looked at me, forcing eye contact. "Skye, I've been working for TAMT, and as soon as the doctors clear you, they're going to send you back home to Crickledown to begin your reassimilation sessions with Dr. Thomison."

I panicked, then snapped. "Wait a fuckin' minute! Is this a joke! Who *are* you? What is TAMT? How do you know where I'm from? Fuck this! There is no way I am going back to that hell—whoever the fuck you *really* are, you can't force me to do anything!" I searched the room for my clothes, my bag. I was just about to jump out of the bed when I spotted the man I'd come to call Bug Eye just outside the door. He entered the room like he'd been waiting for his cue.

"I am afraid in this matter you have no choice," he said. "We'll need to restore your memory, Skye, and the best place for you to be is where some of your earliest memories were formed. It will ensure that the process is safe and expedient."

I struggled to form a response. "Wait a second, I—"

"You need to rest. It's a lot for the psyche to take in all at once," Dr. Thomison said in what I guessed he thought was a soothing voice, but it grated. As I made to get out of bed, a nurse appeared and stuck me with a needle. I heard Prof's voice as I descended into oblivion say, "And that's a wrap."

After London, Crickledown was the last place I wanted to be, fought it as hard as I could, but Bug Eye insisted it was best that I "reassimilated" in my hometown. I was told that once I successfully completed the sessions, I could go back to New York. So I decided I'd pretend to make an effort, with my sights secretly set on leaving. Being in the middle of nowhere was bad enough, not to mention I wasn't exactly looking forward to seeing my father again.

He picked me up from the Lambert–St. Louis International Airport and we drove home to Crickledown in silence. I stared out the window, endless fields, all the same, endless nothing. Dad pulled up in the driveway of our house, and I waited outside. He said he wanted to grab something before taking me out for a bite to eat.

I used the opportunity alone in the car to search for some raucous music on the radio and smoke a fag. I was searching for a lighter inside my old blue-jean jacket when I found my mom's letter tucked away in the denim. I hadn't worn the jacket since the accident in London. Remembered how I'd almost destroyed the letter in the fire. Recognized it the way a war veteran recognizes the sound of land mines erupting. Two clicks later Dad got in the car holding a small black box. He handed it to me but I didn't move to take it, so he set it on the dashboard. I looked out straight ahead, ready to burst. Just holding the seams together. I barely managed to ask, "Why?"

"I'd been wanting to give it to you, but I never found the right time."

"No, I mean, *why*?" I said, shaking the letter in his face.

There was a long pause. Dad turned the music down to an uneasy murmur before continuing.

"What she did was against God."

"What did she do that was so bad that—"

"Skye, she was having an affair."

"And so you became god of our lives and sentenced her and me to a life not knowing each other . . . That is so fucking Christian of you, Dad, I mean, wow—"

"With a woman," he interrupted me.

He turned the radio dial from the hard rock back to his jazz station. The air between us filled with a DJ's voice. "That was Miles Davis's *Kind of Blue*, and before that *A Love Supreme* by John Coltrane, and before that, we—" Dad switched off the radio.

It didn't make sense. But it all made sense. Even his frequent comments about me becoming more and more like my mother. Well, wait until he found out along with the rest of the world that, like my mother, I had a thing for women too.

"Let's talk about this over food." He glanced at me again, trying to read my face.

"Cut the crap, Dad, you never . . . Nobody ever told me the truth about my own mother. You made me believe she was *dead*." I was incredulous that he seemed to not get how horribly wrong all of this was. I gently put the letter back into its envelope. It irritated me that he thought just because my mom had an affair with a woman that I would suddenly understand his choices. I didn't understand his choices, and I didn't understand why my mom hadn't fought harder to be in my life, regardless of what she'd said in the letter. Perhaps she would've understood those things about me that perplexed my father. I didn't know "normal" was ever something I wanted to be, but maybe I would have felt more normal, less alone, more confident with whoever the fuck I was, whoever I was becoming, if she'd been there. It began to rain. Little drops at first, like someone blowing a peashooter at the car window . . . *tat-tat* . . . *ti-ti-tat-tat*. Dad exhaled hard.

"I suppose I should have told you." He started up the engine and slowly began to back down the driveway. "Maybe by leaving her letter in the sock drawer, I subconsciously wanted you to find it, wanted you to know the truth."

"How did you know I would look there?"

"I knew you were taking money."

I stared at the dashboard.

"Open it." Dad nodded toward the black felt cube perched there, as innocent as Pandora's box.

I was stone.

"I'll open it for you, then." He stopped the car at the end of the driveway. From the box he pulled out a thick silver chain. On it hung an uncoiling cobra. A topaz oval the shape of an eye decorated the back of its head. He told me the necklace had been passed down from my grandmother to my mom. That my mom used to sing me a lullaby while I played with the necklace, always on her neck. He sang a bit of it to me, that bluesy hum that I had been re-remembering in my dreams.

First worn by great-grandma Juanita, passing it to my daughter Bonita sings Juanita, then on to the neck of her charmer daughter Kara sings grandma Bonita, then on to my daughter, oh, Skye of mine sings Kara sings Kara . . . Then on to my daughter oh Skye of mine sings Kara.

Kara was my mother's name. Dad chuckled softly. "You would always say before bedtime, 'Singkara singkara.'"

Sincara.

A couple weeks later Dr. Thomison carefully folded my mother's letter and took off his glasses. The aged envelope was sitting in his lap. It was my last session.

At this point I was as "reassimilated" as I was ever going to be. All my missing memory bytes were more or less back in place. We'd spent weeks talking through my experiences in New York and in London, all of which I'd learned were just an experiment, a setup—sometimes literally a set!

"I'm sincerely sorry, Skye, for everything you've been through," he said, rubbing the bridge of his nose before putting on his glasses again. "But I'm glad to say that you've demonstrated a full recovery."

I nodded. "I'm just glad to be headed back to New York so I can think and write about all this. That's where everything started, anyway."

"Of course. And I'll see you there for the screening." Dr. Thomison shook my hand a little longer than usual, making sure our eyes locked. "In spite of your reticence, I believe the reality show will be a huge success for all involved."

PART III

Missing Pieces

INT. PIECES'S NYC APARTMENT - AFTERNOON
Sunlight falls through the window near the
adjacent kitchen. Skye is on the sofa, one
leg dangling off, an ashtray full of cigarette
butts on the floor near her head.

The truth is, when I woke up in the studio in New York to Pieces's farewell letter, a couple of weeks had gone by, not just a few hours. That first night, I'd passed out on the couch after two more forty ounces following the one we'd shared during our first walk through the city together. And the next day, Pieces hadn't left. Instead she'd woken me up by pushing a paper cup of coffee under my nose. She'd bought it from a downstairs deli, along with some bagels.

"I ran outta coffee," she said. "So this will have to do . . ."

I peeled myself off the sofa and sat up, bleary-eyed. I was still in the clothes I'd arrived in; my boots stood near the couch, spicing up the aroma of hot java. I held the doubled-up blue paper cup between my palms, slowly coming out of a fog and assessing the situation the best I could. My head was pounding. I was in the Big Apple. Had only a little cash on me. No definite place to stay. No definite plans as to what to do next. I should have been panicking, but the overriding feeling was one of exhilaration, which my pounding head only somewhat dulled. While Pieces was in the shower I pulled out my journal and wrote about the night before: the paper sculpture, three coughs and you're off, Sincara, and sucking roses.

"Shower's yours if you want . . . Laid out a clean towel for you."

Pieces had a towel wrapped around her body. Her brown,

honey-hued skin seemed even darker against the tan lines where her bra straps would normally be.

Pieces tied up her wet locs in another towel, grabbed a bagel from the kitchen, went over to her paper sculpture, and stood transfixed, mumbling to herself.

"Shower sounds like a good idea," I said, more to myself, as Pieces was obviously in her own world. As I headed to the bathroom the doorbell rang.

"Who the hell could that be?" Pieces snapped, visibly irked at having her morning meditation interrupted. It was just after noon. Still, for us it was morning. The buzzer rang again, this time rattling my skull. A shower would help. Stripped naked, I turned the taps to hot and let the room steam up as I brushed my teeth.

In the shower I broke into my own rendition of "Wanderer" and contemplated my next moves. Would ask if I could stay here while I looked for work. Maybe Pieces would be into letting me take Scottie's old room, pay some rent. I could find a job at a café or something. Maybe even investigate schools here. There was no way I was going back to Crickledown, and definitely couldn't go back to Chicago.

Chicago.

I grimaced. The wound still hadn't quite healed. I turned off the water, dried myself off, and put on fresh clothes. I let my short locs dry in the open air as I walked through the kitchen toward the makeshift living room. There, standing over Pieces, who was sitting on the couch with an open box in her lap, were two police officers. One had a crew cut, an older-looking ex-army dude. The other was a young dark-haired rookie out to prove himself. He glanced at me. "Come on over here and sit next to your friend, please."

I shot a questioning glance at Pieces.

"So you are trying to tell us that you don't know anything about this?" said the GI Joe veteran. Inside the box was a nice-sized bag of cannabis along with a note. He pulled it out while staring at Pieces and gave it to baby robo-cop to read.

"'For you, P, and your friends, imaginary or real. It's better than the last batch.'"

Met with Pieces's silence, they took us both in, me just because I was there. They didn't cuff us, but still folks in the neighborhood took notice of us being prodded into the police car. They checked the situation, then got back to minding their own business. After we spent some hours waiting in a holding cell, they brought us both into what was too poorly lit to be an interrogation room. It didn't look like what I'd seen in the movies. The table and the chairs looked like something found at an eighties flea market.

We were ushered in by the police but they left, and in came two new characters. One had a cheap, well-worn suit with a too-wide tie. He was the detective assigned to our case, I assumed. The other wore a sleek-looking suit and smiled as soon as he saw us. He sat down in a chair, just beaming. The guy in the too-wide tie and tired suit with a face to match started in on us.

"Look. Your boyfriend, or whatever he is to you, sent you these drugs. We know for a fact that it isn't the first package he's sent. We've been keeping track. Now, both of you are looking at some time. These days, we are cracking down on possession as well as trafficking, which means you could be looking at up to ten years without parole." The detective spoke as if he were reciting scripted, often-repeated phrases. "We already talked to Scottie and he is gonna take the deal. I advise you do the same."

"What deal?" Pieces shot.

"That's where I come in," Slick said, and his smile seemed to beam even brighter, if that was possible. He gave us his business card. It read, *Trevor Williams, Producer for Terrestrial Association of Media Transmissions.* "I work for TAMT. We're partnering with some tobacco companies on a groundbreaking project to help us better understand memory. As you might know, tobacco companies are under public pressure right now, and medical marijuana will be legal on the West Coast in a few short years. The future is green, in more ways than one." He winked at us. Detective Wide Tie coughed, but otherwise looked as if he'd heard nothing out of the ordinary.

Pieces and I traded glances and said nothing. Ambassador TAMT continued, "We're also interested in data collection, and as a way of securing such data, you'll all be filmed and documented. We'll eventually turn the footage into a TV show." He paused to gauge our reactions. Both Pieces and I held blank expressions. He tried again, "If you agreed to participate in this project, you would get your records wiped clean, *and* if things go as planned, you could be comfortably set up for years to come."

Pieces scowled, looked from one man to the other. "How do we know you're not lying? 'Cause this feels like a setup."

An office pig in blue was summoned. He brought what looked like a fax. "Here you go, sir," he said, handing the long sheet to his boss, Detective Wide Tie.

The exhausted Dick handed the paper to Pieces, pointing to a signature. "It's all there in black and white." Pieces looked down at the paper and pushed it back across the table. The detective took off his jacket, revealing moist spots under his pits.

"Are you about to do good cop, bad cop on us now?" Pieces snickered under her breath.

"I'm not a cop," Trevor protested, but the detective interrupted.

"Look, smart-ass, it's a no-brainer." He got up out of his chair and slung his jacket over his shoulder. "Up to ten years in jail or a few months helping out science, your country, or whatever. Either way it's up to you. Me, I'm going out for a smoke." He stopped in the doorway before exiting and added, "If it were my call, you would still be sitting in that cell awaiting a bail hearing." With that he left us in the room with Trevor.

"Patricia, Skye," he said, smiling too wide, "this is the deal of a lifetime for the both of you . . ." He let that sink in before continuing. "And the best part is you won't remember that you're being filmed!"

He stood up and started pacing the room as he spoke. "You may be angry with Scottie now, but he did you a favor, Patricia. This is clearly better than rotting away in the prison system." Ambassador TAMT caught his breath, shifting back to that made-for-TV voice of his. "Think of the benefits. Not only are we prepared to pay a handsome commission for your participation, but after the filming we will help you with travel expenses anywhere you want to go for a year, plus studio space in your chosen destination. Possibly even help promote a show of your work." Trevor switched his attention to me, letting Pieces mull over the information.

"And Skye, for you it would mean an opportunity to publish. We want you, as part of the deal, to write a book about what happens over the next few months. When this airs on TV, you'll have a ready-made audience. You will receive a handsome advance that will keep you financially stable for a while. Living in New York, no problemo. Travel across Europe, no problemo—"

"Hold on. *Problemo* here," Pieces broke in. "What. Are.

You. On. About!" She was losing her patience. "What is this experiment *really* about? How will we not remember being filmed?"

"That's where Dr. Thomison comes in." He opened the door separating us from freedom and waved someone in. And that's when I really met ole Bug Eye for the first time.

"We will be using a mixture of hypnotherapy and a serum that, once in your bloodstream, makes you more vulnerable to suggestion. We have done our research, and there is a very low risk of . . . Let's just say that with proper supervision, it's safe and effective."

"'Safe and effective,'" Pieces echoed. "This isn't exactly aspirin you're selling us here." Ambassador TAMT went on to explain that there would be a doctor and psychologist monitoring us, and that after the experiment, or when the serum and/or hypnotherapy had worn off, there would be mandatory counseling to help ease us out of the partial memory loss. We had a week to tie up loose ends. They would book Pieces's ticket and I would join them later in London.

He smiled. "The three of you are perfect: you'll look good on-screen, know one another, get on well, are representative of now—you know, the multiculti bohemian tribe"—he was trying hard to sound cool—"you guys encapsulate this century and the next. Very *current*. Couldn't be more perfect."

And I couldn't believe my ears.

"How do you figure we're perfect?" Pieces asked, her face looking pale.

Slick flashed us his retouched and cropped smile.

It was a win-win-win for TAMT. They could test out and improve their surveillance technology but also collect data, which they would sell to the tobacco companies, international science labs, and finally to a broadcast TV network for considerable profit. Surveillance tech was the platinum-plated future.

I sat uneasy in my chair. Stole a glance at Pieces. Was she *hearing* all of this?

"First of all," Pieces said to them, "Skye has absolutely nothing to do with this."

"Well, if she doesn't sign, the deal's off. We need all of you," Slick said.

"At least give us a chance to speak with Scottie about all this."

Slick put both hands on the table and leaned in close. "Look, I'm sure you can understand that time is of the essence. If you want to think it over, you can think it over right here. New York's finest would be happy to keep you overnight. But you know, I'm concerned that they may change their minds—war-on-drugs crusade and all—so if I were you I would make the obvious choice ASAP."

"This is fucked up and wrong—we should at least have time to think it over," Pieces pushed back.

Then Detective Wide Tie came in with another officer, muttering something about not having *time* for this and needing the room for another matter. We were put back into our separate cages, no phone calls. If we called in lawyers, the deal was off; if we told anybody about this, the deal was off. In the end, we opted to sign just to avoid another night in the holding cell.

The next morning, Pieces and I walked back to her flat in silence, in a state of shock. We'd just signed a contract that was null and void if we talked to anyone about it. We risked ending up in prison if we broke the contract at any point during our lifetimes. The ink was barely dry when they informed us that cameras had already been installed, and in fact had been unofficially installed for some time. Our signatures acknowledged this and gave them the permission they needed to monitor us until the project reached completion. We barely shared two words on the walk back from the cop shop. I entered the loft first, cautiously, wondering where the cameras were located. We'd been told that they were disabled for the time being, but . . .

Pieces stopped at the open door for a stretched second or two. She seemed to be thinking the same thing I was, surveying her apartment with a slow, sweeping glance. Then, shaking her head, she walked across the threshold and into the kitchen.

"I am fucking parched. I think there is juice in the fridge." Pieces grabbed the carton, slammed the fridge door. "Want some?"

"That would be cool," I said, happy to avoid the unspoken point. I really didn't know *what* to say. Pieces was still furious, and I was terrified of being caught up in something that was in no way my fault, something I still didn't really understand.

"Listen, I gotta be at work in a couple of hours, so make yourself at home while I get myself sorted . . ." She poured herself a glass of juice. "Why don't you meet me at work, and we can talk this shit out after my shift."

"Okay, sure," I said, wanting to talk about it now. I mean, we had just agreed to something that was going to change things drastically for us, and not necessarily for the better. And on top of it all, I wasn't even sure if she'd let me stay the night.

Pieces went off to get dressed as I sat uneasily in the front room. We left the apartment together, her walking off toward the bar with purpose, leaving me on the street with my thoughts.

The few hours I had to kill before meeting up with her passed by quickly. Hung around the Lower East Side for an hour, sampling pizza slices and people watching. Took in the lush, decaying, graffiti-soaked walls and the menagerie of brown, beige, pink, red, and white faces watching over their front yards, their community's streets, which included the perspiring vendors selling knickknacks, their wares spread on the sidewalks: everything from old shoes, outdated magazines, litter boxes, antennae attached to nothing. I blinked and the images seemed to dissolve as I walked past. The air felt rich with struggle between what had been there for generations, ignored, forgotten, and a newer, foreign invading force. Next to derelict buildings, bright, new, trendy, mostly empty cafés stood out, misplaced among the worn-out and disused.

I was checking everything out with new eyes after learning that Pieces and Scottie and I had been, unwittingly, under surveillance. Like criminals in those old spy movies, or those documentaries that revealed that folks like the Black Panthers and the so-called commies were being subjected to FBI wiretapping. I began looking for hidden cameras in my surroundings. I found that some commercial spots, including local bodegas, now had private cameras installed to survey their customers. Folks in more affluent residential areas had cameras installed so that they could see who was at the door when they rang. It wasn't nearly as pervasive in public spaces as I would later see in London; in fact it was easy to miss. Perhaps the infiltration was stealthier. There were eyes everywhere. It was the same technology that brought modern-day police brutality into the living rooms of the masses as they watched the cops shamelessly beat the crap out of Rodney King.

Later I made my way down through a bustle of office workers and delivery bikers to Broadway and into Fusion Lit, a warehouse full of new and secondhand books. I found an old copy of *On the Road* and bought it. It seemed an (un)likely companion to the copy of *Giovanni's Room* I had bought in Chi-Town, but at the time I didn't see why. When I emerged from that small slice of heaven, it was time to hook up with Pieces.

She invited me for a drink at the bar while I waited for her to finish up. Above the bar, a wide screen showed an *Absolutely Fabulous* rerun. Later, when I started working there, I would find out it was a favorite among New York queers. "You don't love me enough, darling" was the line of the moment and dropped often.

I half watched the stream of bland advertisements during the commercial break: Coke Is It, summer-clearance sales, "Where's the Beef" eat American meat campaigns, previews for various daytime TV soaps and talk shows, a young man calling in for auditions and seeking talent for a new, real-life TV drama. The young man's dark, crisp suit accentuated his blond hair. He twisted a ring on his finger while he spoke. "Have your fifteen minutes . . ." I recognized his voice. I'd heard it over the radio the night before. It had prompted Pieces to switch it off and pull out her vinyl. I looked around for her. She headed over with her boss Toney in tow and did the introductions.

"Oooh, she's cute." Toney shot a nod at me and then arched an eyebrow at Pieces. She ignored him and ordered two margaritas from the bartender. They were delicious. Apparently some of the best in New York.

"So, what do you wanna do tonight?" Pieces asked as she licked the salt off her glass and took a big gulp.

"I'm easy," I said.

"Let's go down to the pier." She looked at the clock hanging over the bar. "One more margarita first; might as well, they are on the house," she decided. We finished the second round and split. It was a nice walk. Roller skaters, in-liners, and hanger-outers congregated around the concrete slab watching the Atlantic, some with music, many just chilling by the water, as night began to slowly descend. Pieces and I joined them and sat for a while, staring out at the route our ancestors took to get here, one way or another.

"I'll be crossing these waters any minute now," Pieces said after a bit.

"I don't think it's a good idea to swim from here," I joked.

"Yeah, right." Pieces laughed. "But seriously, what do you make of all of this?"

I shrugged, unsure of where to start.

"I mean, I'm sorry we got you into this mess." She kicked a rock in front of her. "It's really Scottie's fault, the stupid ass. I told him it wasn't a good idea." She went on to explain that he'd tried to convince her that this was the future, the cannabis trade was already international, and the boys in blue were in on it too. He said that the Reagan war-on-drugs era was a dead duck no matter the lip service Nancy's one-woman campaign gave it. "It won't be long before they 'legalize it,'" she sang, mimicking what I guessed was Scottie's version of the Peter Tosh tune.

"And though he seems to be right, it is the future," she said. "I still can't decide if he was genius or a fucking dumbass, but I'm leaning toward fucking dumbass!"

I, too, was confounded as to how he thought he would not get caught eventually.

"This might sound crazy, but I am a little excited about the prospect of traveling, even if this memory-manipulation business is, well . . ." I let out an exhale.

"No. Shit."

"I mean, anything could go wrong!"

"What's worse, it all might go exactly as planned." Pieces lit a cigarette.

"What do you mean?"

"Well, how do you think you're going to feel after however many months, suddenly remembering that you agreed to be filmed, all this time knowing that those images would be made public! And that you *gave* your consent!"

I really had no way of knowing how I'd feel. The thought of possibly going to jail trumped every other thought, the fear of that, every other feeling.

"I mean, what the literal fuck!" Pieces lifted her hands in exasperation. "Consent or not, it's exploitation! Money made off watching us, *studying us*! It's one thing when they do it and you don't know, another when you do know. I just don't know if I could ever forgive myself for letting that happen." Pieces took a drag; then, echoing my overriding sentiment, she said, "But hey, I don't know if I'd be able to live with myself in jail either."

We sat in silence, sharing the cigarette and trying to come

to terms with everything, watching the angry waves beat up against the shore.

"After I go," Pieces said, "you can stay in my apartment if you want, maybe find a job, keep up the rent—could take over my job, even." The thought of it all began to overwhelm me. In our short time together we had gotten closer, a deeper kind of intimacy than I ever remembered sharing with anyone else. And now I was suddenly faced with having to make my way on my own, in a city I less-than-barely knew, without her.

I tried to crack a smile. "Can't you just pack me in your suitcase?"

She put her arm around me, pulled me in close. We watched the lights reflect off the indigo waters.

R esistant to the whole experiment from the outset, Pieces wrote her goodbye letter in front me, deciding to test a hypothesis. "Their so-called methods can work on the conscious mind, but what about the subconscious, Skye?" She also wrote bits of my poetry in inconspicuous places on the walls. All week she did this, sometimes in places I didn't catch. Her plan was to throw a monkey wrench in the works.

Pieces also gave me a tiny piece of paper that she told me to keep in my pocket. On it she'd written *TAMT = The All Mighty They are watching.* She said that between the note and the poetry on the wall, something in my memory had to be triggered, even subtly. In case that didn't work, she was also sending her armlet to Eddie. The sooner we could remember what happened to us, the better. The game would be up, and it was written in our contracts that even if the drug didn't stick as long as they intended, we got the same deal: no jail time, with the other perks dependent on how successful the TV show turned out. Pieces asked me if I had anything I'd like to send to Eddie. I gave her my mom's letter.

We went through a series of sessions that laid the ground-work for the moment we would wake up with some of our memories missing. These intensive counseling sessions happened daily, were meant to help us make the descent into partial amnesia as smooth as possible. The produc-ers reviewed some of their tapes and discussed with us at length how Pieces and I met, what happened, where we went. Afterward they decided it would be perfect if Pieces and I woke thinking we'd just met the day before. Pieces would wake up with the memory only that she had a plane to catch, that she'd purchased her ticket the same day she met me. In the final session, hypnotized and under the influence of whatever drug they dosed us with, they said those magic words that would make us forget what they wanted us to forget upon waking the next day.

◎

After that last session, we decided to celebrate, or at least give our memories a good send-off. We were both due to lose the past couple weeks.

"How was your meeting with the rapist?" Pieces meant "therapist" but found separating the word after the *e* more accurate. "Was it good for you? It was good for me. He made sure I was good and fucked."

"How do you know?" I asked.

"Just felt worn out afterward, didn't you?"

I did, but it wasn't just the sessions—it was the whole thing. The whole time, we both waded through the murky waters of what-ifs: What if we came to damaged? What if that shit they claimed they'd tested affected other facets of our memories? What if we never woke up or went mad? Not to mention the possibility of media attention afterward— if not right away, eventually. In a short period of time we could go from nobodies to television personalities, the subjects of office conversation, and the butts of pub jokes. What if the public took a real distaste to us, didn't like what they saw? What if we did something while we were under that was so inexcusably wicked, or worse, irredeemably embarrassing? In any case we were rats in an experiment that would line a lot of pockets.

The fear factor motivated us to share deep shit with each other that last night. We decided to down a bottle of tequila and were in the kitchen preparing the shots. With the bind we were in, we had to trust each other. That's when I told her about my mom. A story I never intended to tell anyone.

"My dad told me she died not long after giving birth to me," I said, letting out a sigh. "But I found out before I left Crickledown that he lied. That letter I gave you to mail, I found it in his room. I still haven't read it, but she wrote it. Her name was on the back of the envelope. Which means she didn't die, and as far as I know, she has been alive all this time."

"Damn, Skye, that's heavy," Pieces said. "You don't have any idea why she left?" Pieces tilted her head, shooting me a side-glance sharp enough to cut through bullshit. I ducked. Shook my head no, slicing a lime to accompany our drinks, slowly, careful to miss my finger, thinking about all that time with my dad, how I'd felt like something was wrong with me, wrong *about* me.

"Damn, that sucks," Pieces said, locking eyes long enough so that I knew she fucking meant it. "But whatever happened, it wasn't your fault, Skye. You know that, don't you?"

"Knowing or not knowing, hey . . . doesn't make a damn difference. I grew up feeling guilty without really knowing why," I said. "Bcsides, every time my dad looked at me he saw her. You know the script, I have her genes, look just like her . . . Anyway, I had to get out of there."

"He's a bastard. Fuckin' 'ell Skye, I get why you jetted." Pieces poured us two shots. "I was fifteen when I left home. Just went off one day and stuck my thumb out. Had nothing but the shirt on my back and fifty bucks I stole from my mom's purse."

After telling me the story she would tell me again in front of Anne Frank's house some months later, Pieces went quiet for a while. At length I raised my glass. Toasting our visit to the doctors and impending selective amnesia, we slung down tequila slammers on into the night. Wanted to stay awake as long as possible, because when we woke we wouldn't remember any of it.

"Here's to coming from nowhere and everywhere." We clinked our glasses and slammed down the last of the bottle.

"You wanna eat the worm?" Pieces dared. I laughed as she struggled to get it out of the bottle. We split it.

"It can't be any worse than that shit they sent through our veins," Pieces said, gulping her half down. I held my nose and did the same. The look on my face had Pieces cracking up. She crunched up into a belly giggle on the floor.

"What are you laughing at . . ."

She grabbed and pulled me down with her. "You."

Her face was inches from mine, and then there was no distance at all. It was far from an almost kiss. Her hands all over me, taking off my shirt. "Is this okay?" Pieces asked, desire in her eyes reflecting my own. I'd never done anything like this before, but there was nothing I wanted to do more. I nodded and caught my breath as her lips found my neck, then nipples.

She grabbed me around the waist and pulled me in, her fingers now lightly stroking my back. I arched into her and we kissed deeply again. Rolling on top of her, I helped take off her shirt, her bra, releasing the full curve of her breasts. A hunger took over as I held first the left then the right one hostage under my hands, my lips and tongue unearthing breathy moans from her that exhilarated me in ways I hadn't dreamed possible. I kissed her as if she were a discovered treasure, exploring salty flesh from the center of her chest down past her navel, my head all fire and pulse. Pieces grabbed my hair playfully and pulled me up. Kissed me long and gentle before flipping me on my back, and with a snarky, sexy smile, she slid off my jeans, my nakedness now trembling under the direction of her sure hands.

We devoured each other with mouth, fingers, and intention, bringing each other to the brink over and over and over again until we both finally arrived. Our release reverberated in the air around us, accenting the sweet, intimate smells impregnating the space we shared. A mess of entangled limbs, our glistening brown bodies intertwined. I don't know if I'd ever felt so safe, so at home. Later, I would collapse into a deeper sleep than I'd ever known.

Remembering this now, the closeness I'd felt to Pieces all this time made so much sense. Those dreams I had of her licking jam off my fingers when I first arrived made sense. In London she'd also felt the chemistry between us but had forgotten as I had, and when she did remember, she couldn't handle being around me. But that night in New York, as we moved inside each other, I let out a sigh and settled in. We both were every ounce of *there* for each other, for every moment passing, with the knowledge that the time we shared, after that night, could be lost forever.

After my reassimilation sessions with Bug Eye in Crickledown were finished, I came back to face the music in New York. I decided to bite the inevitable bullet and show up for the "show" at Pieces's flat. I was hardly looking forward to it, couldn't take watching myself reflected back to me in moving images. It wasn't the same as looking in a mirror. In the mirror I could always reconnect with something that was real, something that centered me. What part of my soul would be lost in that footage? And this was just the beginning. There would be another, more public screening after the final edit. There would also be interviews with us after that. They wanted to get a fresh reaction from us about what we saw and how we experienced it. One of the many conditions of our contracts with TAMT.

I knew Scottie wouldn't be there. Since everything had come to the surface, he had been playing ghost under the pretense of working on an album. I wasn't surprised. If I were in his shoes I wouldn't be in a hurry to face me or Pieces. He'd gone under before Pieces and I, but it didn't stick for long. By the time Pieces arrived, the gig was up for Scottie, but he opted to continue the charade, desperate for his fifteen minutes of fame, I guess. I imagined that Pieces wouldn't have wanted him having that kind of power. Having knowledge of something that he could manipulate in his favor. Him knowing something she didn't know. I certainly knew how that felt. Once you realize it, you feel like a huge asshole. A fool. Joke's on you.

But . . . Pieces. I hadn't seen her or even heard from her since Amsterdam. To say I was excited to see her was an understatement, despite how we'd left things.

It was strange retracing the steps I had taken less than a year ago when I first climbed up the subway stairs out into Alphabet City. Familiar characters were a part of the scenery on my route to Pieces's old place on Avenue B. But there was something different in the air. Was I seeing things or did there seem to be a new breed of trendy trustafarians now roaming the streets? Maybe I was just noticing them this time around, but the air smelled different. Smelled of something that was dying, sprayed over by a cool, antiseptic pine aerosol.

TAMT had bought the building in which Pieces rented her studio. I didn't know it at the time, but they had taken over the building during my brief stay there. Her neighbor Alex was a kind of caretaker the company hired to keep an eye on things and make sure all aspects of the production were running smoothly. He was on his way in when I arrived. He looked at me as if he was unsure whether or not I recognized him; he was probably a little nervous about what my response to all this would be.

"Hey, Skye," he said, backtracking to light a cig I'd just pulled from a soft, battered pack. "You remember me?"

I nodded, breathing in the smoke. "Alex," I said, exhaling the smoke into his face.

"You got it," he said, backing away. Smiling a pleased-with-himself smile. He *had* made an impression. "See you in there," he said, but his statement held a question mark at its core.

I turned and puffed on my cigarette, leaning against a

wall. I could see ole Bug Eye coming up in the distance. Wanted to move but couldn't. I would rather wait until after the screening had started, enter anonymously into the private cinema that had once been Pieces's flat. I bet they thought it was a clever joke doing it that way. A good way to amp up a false authenticity in this whole manufactured story.

"Hello, Skye." Dr. Thomison smiled, extending an earnest hand.

"Hey," I said, shaking his hand briefly. I smoked my cigarette, looking down at the pavement.

"So how are your nerves?" he asked.

"Well, I'm here, aren't I?" I said, flipping the cig into the street. "Came all this way, might as well stick it out. I want to see what parts of my life millions of people might see. But maybe it won't make a difference."

"What won't make a difference?" he asked, in the way he did when he found something potentially intriguing.

"Knowing," I said. "Knowing what they will see doesn't necessarily mean I will really know *what* they see, will it?"

"Yes." He looked down momentarily. A brief look of sadness and slight irritation passed across his typically blasé face as he looked back at me. "In some ways I suppose it's no longer your story." He took a deep breath. "Honestly I don't blame you if this doesn't mean a damn thing coming out of my mouth." Hearing him cuss was enough to bring my attention back. He never swore. "I find this whole thing disgusting, exploitative, and beside the point." For a second he looked like he was truly sorry. "The truth is, well, science needs funding, what can I say." He threw up his hands. Truth. I was pondering the unreliability of this slippery word when I heard the mellow-yellow voice—

"Hey, Skye, the doc isn't still trying to get into your head, is he?" It was Prof interrupting our conversation. He looked like he could have come out of thin air. I believed he had. "How are you doing?" He shook Bug Eye's hand. During our sessions, I'd found out that they used to work together on the same project. Prof had dropped out of it once certain investors got involved. But Scottie's unfortunate fiasco with the law got him back into it.

I moved slightly away from the doc and Prof, who were catching up.

"Give us a fag, mate," said a voice with that familiar sarcastic smile behind it. Pieces, finally. I recognized her even though she no longer carried an assortment of thick and uneven demi-locs. In fact she had almost no hair, as if she'd shaved it bald a week or so ago. She gave me a hug straightaway. I waited for my knees to turn to putty, but I was concentrated on swallowing the heart in my throat. She nodded in the direction of Prof and the doctor, who continued their conversation while pretending not to watch us. I didn't get the feeling that Pieces's misgivings about Prof had changed. She seemed neither happy nor sad to see him. Understandably. Prof had lost his mystery; like the Wizard of Oz at the end of the eponymous movie, he wore the robes of the hippie-generation nostalgia turned sham.

"See you ladies in there! Save you a seat?" Prof proffered as he pushed gently at the doctor's shoulder, guiding him into the building.

"Thanks," I said, then turned to face Pieces.

We smiled at each other for a moment, smoking our cigarettes.

"So," I said, ashing on the pavement, just missing my well-worn jungle boots. "You ready for this?" I nodded in the direction of the building. "And welcome home, by the way," I offered with a wry smile.

Pieces chuckled. "Yeah, right." She put her arm around my shoulder. "I only came to get you." At those words, a certain weight I hadn't known I was carrying disappeared. What appeared was the first genuine smile I had had in eons.

"Let's get the fuck outta here." We walked in the direction of Margaritaville, covering old ground.

Strolling away from the screening toward Margaritaville with Pieces, I felt anxiety garroting my belly. Was thinking about how sooner or later we'd have to face what we were walking away from. It was true I'd signed the contract, but I still felt tricked, lied to, manipulated. And though I had gotten the "all okay" from Dr. Thomison, I still had real trust issues with everything and everyone around me, issues that were magnified under the lens of this whole so-called experiment.

"You okay?" Pieces moved closer, playfully bumping into me as we walked. Startled a slight smile out of my pensive expression.

"Honestly? I don't know how I feel."

Pieces grabbed my hand as we continued our traipse. She squeezed it. It felt like something real, something I could almost trust.

I turned my attention to Pieces, who seemed to be enjoying our silent promenade through the clamorous Manhattan streets. Streets that I had so hungered for while still in Crickledown. As my anger cooled while back in the 'burbs, I realized that I missed Pieces most of all, even as I came to understand that I'd fallen in love with an ideal of her. Pieces or Patricia, I knew her better than some people I had known for most of my life, yet simultaneously, I was chasing someone that never existed, except for in the conjurings of my mind. She became that "something" I felt lost without, and that something would be replaced again by another something, until I finally understood that "something" simply does not exist. Still separating the "real" from the "fantasy," I kept sneaking furtive glances in her direction, as if to confirm her presence, until we finally arrived at the restaurant.

Though Pieces and I looked nothing alike we must have given off the energy of being related. None of the usual suspects were there because it was the early shift, but the guy who seated us asked if we were sisters. Pieces and I looked each other up and down and laughed, both of us presenting slightly differently from the last time we'd seen each other. My Afro was beginning to grow. Pieces's nearly bald scalp was dark from the Spanish sun. She looked like a monk. We sat by the window watching the eclectic New Yorkers' frenetic passings: on the way to work, on the way out of the office to grab a quick cuppa. Students, briefcases, artists, homeless people. Workers dug up the street in front of us, intermittently drilling. When the drilling stopped it was replaced by another kind of city noise—the voice of the mad. A crazy, natty-headed woman walked past us, hitting two pieces of metal piping, singing about her rhythm stick. She seemed resolute, like she was on a mission to spread the beat throughout New York. As she passed, Pieces and I looked at each other and smiled.

"Get that beat, girrrl, hit it, get it!" Pieces made a response to her call, causing the other customers to turn and stare. Briefly. This was New York. It took a lot to catch people's attention, and even more to hold it. And the rhythm-stick woman was kind of a regular in these parts. Didn't stop me from cracking up though. Pieces was on form. She seemed happy and alert. Her mind more present. It didn't take her long to comment on the snake necklace around my neck.

"It was my mom's," I told her, my hand absentmind-edly playing with the silver chain. The argent around the topaz eye on the cobra's head would intermittently catch and reflect the light coming through the window next to where we sat.

Pieces smiled to herself but didn't say anything. Instead she pulled her sleeve up to her shoulder to reveal the armlet circling over her tattoo.

"Eddie sent this back to me, said something about how it didn't suit her." She took it off and gave it to me. "Why don't you take it? It's a good match." I studied the silver serpent coiled in my hands before hailing the bartender.

"Thanks," I said, catching her eye for an instant before shyly glancing away. Her stare was intense. That armlet brought back sensations, an internal soundtrack of resur-faced memories, and the poignancy of this moment was not lost on me. The waiter came over, and we both ordered a margarita.

I put the armlet on the table between us and poured myself a glass of water. I wanted to tell Pieces that I got it. I mean, I did get it, but I was still processing everything. I got what mattered though. My mom's pendant, the chain around my neck, seemed to move of its own accord, as if it were sparked by electrostatic shock. I put the water down.

Pieces looked over at the armlet briefly, then up and out the window. She exhaled and faced me.

"I am really sorry, Skye, how things went down. Look, I don't have any excuse." She shifted in her chair. "I told myself I was looking after you. But I guess it was more about control. All of it. Aaaaall of it. The TAMT note I left you, the poetry I scribbled on the walls, even sending you to Gennie was all about control. But it was also about protecting you— at least that was what I told myself."

She reached out across the table and grabbed my hand.

"You mean a lot to me, Skye." Pieces followed my eyes with hers, forcing me to make direct contact. "I am so sorry." I knew in my gut she was being honest. Her frustration with me in Amsterdam and the subsequent outburst were proof of it. The journal that she had passed on to Eddie to give me was proof of it. She held my eyes, made sure that I saw that she was being for real, before a small mischievous twinkle brightened her pupils.

"According to Dr. Thomison, by telling you the truth about being watched that night before I tried to burn the boat down in the 'Dam, I could have triggered a psychotic episode in you."

"'A psychotic episode'?" Sounded absurd the way she said it.

"A psychotic episode."

Still looking each other in the eye, we both burst out laughing. As we caught our breath again, she reached for and examined the pendant around my neck, and it felt more like a form of intimacy than a simple interest in the necklace. I watched her thoughtful face transform into a dawning smile. We were in concert, that one moment was an eternity in itself. She looked up at me grinning, my face a mirror image of hers.

"It's good to see you," I said, nodding. I slowly pulled my hands away from hers and wrapped them around the half-full water glass. It was beyond good, but the wounds were still open. At least I was having the chance to face her and tell her how I felt. And Scottie's absence was as loud as the signature guitar strum he made at entrances and exits.

"So have you heard from bloody—"

"Scottie?" Pieces read my mind, rolling her eyes as if he were an irritating afterthought. "He's *resting* in Berlin, his city of choice for post-reassimilation." I looked at her as if to say, *What?* She shook her head. "Don't ask me, evidently he's in the process of writing more songs for his album."

"Yeah, I'd heard . . . Cool for him," I said, not meaning it. He was the one who'd gotten us into this mess to begin with. And all that "power of three" rubbish, to boot. "Fuck, man, all this is his fault!"

Our margaritas finally arrived.

Silence.

"Pieces, I don't know if during your reassimilation therapy they showed you some of the tapes." I recounted some of the images I saw. Told her how I felt that even if I had agreed to this somehow, I was being violated. And the footage picked up by their surveillance cameras didn't seem to show the whole picture.

"I mean, it's there, it happened like that, but it *didn't* happen like that."

"Of course not. They can't get into our heads really, can they?"

"Apparently they can," I said, still feeling more than a little foolish. "I honestly thought I got to England on my own sweat."

"You did get there on your own sweat." Pieces took my hand again, but this time I pulled it away. "You still angry with me?" It was more of a statement than a question.

I wasn't, really. I just didn't trust myself. She, after all, tried to tell me the truth in the end. It was Scottie who had kept up the charade, knowing the potential cost it had for all of us yet still making the decision for us, just as my dad had for me and my mom, getting to be the same selfish pricks most men get to be. At the bottom of it, I was more hurt than angry. It was as if a huge curtain of disillusionment had fallen, and all that was left was complicity.

"Listen. None of us acted like angels," Pieces said. "Anyway, we'll all see each other soon enough, you know, to preview the final cut. Everyone's presence is *mandatory*." She made a rude gesture.

"Looking forward to it." The words were dry out of my mouth.

Still, it *was* good to see her. Part of me wished that she would just take me in her arms again as she'd done before she left for London. All of me knew it wasn't about to happen.

"Pieces, I missed you, you know," I said, looking down at my reflection in the margarita.

"Yeah." Her fingers lightly traced my hand for a breeze of a moment. "I missed you too, kiddo."

We sat for a while, no words needed. I waited for my heart to swell, but it didn't. It kept on pumping at its normal rate.

"When exactly did you begin to suspect?" I asked.

"You know, I knew something was weird as soon as I got to London. Scottie seemed to be more rambunctious than usual—you know, always *on*. And of course the whole thing with"—she gestured toward the silver serpent coiled on the table—"but I only understood why, really, just before I left for Amsterdam. That night you slept in Dan's squat I went back to the flat and found it open and some blue jumpsuit changing cameras placed in various inconspicuous places around the flat."

"So you weren't really mad at Scottie because of the keys."

"Yes and no." Pieces paused and sipped her margarita. "It was all linked. He kept the keys so that the techie could go in and sort out the cameras. But more than that, he had broken an agreement we had . . . He knew we were being filmed the whole time you and I were in London, Skye . . ."

She waited to catch my expression. It was blank because I knew the story, but she thought I wasn't convinced.

"So you see I *had* to get out of there, had to detach myself," she continued. "I knew I'd blow it for you and everybody else . . . I was fucking furious."

"So when I arrived in Amsterdam you knew everything . . ."

"And I didn't want to tell you because I was afraid I'd fuck with your head, but then we started fighting . . ." She put her glass down and reached for my hand. "I was really mean to you, I'm sorry, but I was mental at the time . . ."

"You seriously made me feel like shit," I said. "But it's done."

"You were so . . . intense, and I was confused," Pieces confessed. "Before you, I never opened up to anyone about my past . . . and I was so angry with myself for doing that. Hell, I never told *anyone* about my family story until I met you. I had a code: I was from nowhere and everywhere, right? But I broke that with you. And when I realized what was going on, I felt as if the legs had been pulled out from under me. I took it out on you because you reminded me of my, uh"—she had a hard time getting the next word out—"vulnerability. I couldn't forgive myself for actually *going along* with something I thought was rubbish. Reality TV, talk shows, and soaps are all part of the same dung heap . . . all for suckers."

"Beats being a sucker in prison I guess," I said before taking another long sip of my drink. Pieces gave me a look that put a period at the end of that forbidden subject. We continued to discuss what the next chapters of our lives might look like. Pieces decided she was going to start hers in Spain.

"Can't think of anyplace else at the moment. The light

is good, I can get a lot of work done." She pulled out a cig. "Speaking of which, how is the book coming?"

I picked up my Dictaphone and dropped it back on the table.

"I haven't really started; I gotta get going. Up against a deadline. Under the crunch." I put the Dictaphone back in my bag and said in a TV presenter voice, "Contracted to be released in the spring next year, just in time for the start of the series."

Pieces chuckled. "Are you ready for that?"

"Hell no! But hey, I guess we make for some good television."

"True, but you, Skye," she took a drag, "you took the cake with your last trick."

"Oh, how I accidentally on purpose torched the Trashed Palace?" We both laughed.

Pieces pulled out the light-blue lighter that Scottie had given me what felt like years ago and fired up for effect. In my memories of the past few months, the material and dream world mixed effortlessly. All of the visions were mirrors of reality. And reality was nothing more than a vision.

"I kinda miss my Zippo though," she said, smiling.

"One hell of a psychotic episode," I said. I picked up the serpent armlet, raised up the sleeve of my jean jacket so that I could slide it up my arm, with Pieces's help. We decided to continue the night in Washington Square Park with a bottle of tequila for old times' sake.

In the wee hours of the morning I walked Pieces to the subway. Classic Pieces, she was catching a plane from JFK back to Spain later that night. Said I was welcome to come visit her in Barcelona. I said maybe, knowing that I wouldn't. Not right away, anyway. As Pieces ducked down into the subway station I waited for that sledgehammer to crush me, as it did every time she left. But it stood suspended in midair. And I found a way to walk out from under it.

On the way back to the park, I picked up a forty and sat at the same spot we had been sitting at all night. Best way to waylay the destined hangover. I kicked the empty tequila bottle under the bench. Tried to hold back the urge to escape before the AmeriKKKan dream consumed me and spat me out again. The urge to travel moved through me like lightning. But first I had no choice but to finish that fucking bastard of a book. Afterward I would go back to Europe. Maybe France. Maybe Germany. Maybe Italy. Who knew, maybe I would try to find my mom. For now though, I would settle in here. I had missed being in New York more than I knew. But in my heart, London had become another home.

Wherever I will end up, I can no longer swallow it . . . the subtly seductive lie, this drug forever infecting imagination until your original dreams look nothing like what you first desired, but are an exact replica of everything on television. It is clear to me now that we are all complicit, even if unwittingly, in maintaining the reproduction of our lived lives as fodder for the machine. To be free of this is perhaps costlier than most of us could fathom or believe we could handle. To see things as they are, and live your truth in spite of it; to have the courage to embrace where your own pulse might lead, even and especially when everything around you presses you to acquiesce to the script, to what has "always been"; and ultimately to have the courage to face yourself as you *are—this*, I suspect, is the price of the ticket, the path to wherever freedom lives. So, regardless of any contracts I might have signed, regardless of how The All Mighty They might frame this book to fit their agenda, it is important that I tell my story, *our* story, as close to the truth of this moment as I can get. The tape that is circling through this recorder as I speak bears witness to that. Finally I am getting the stomach to uncrumple the ink-stained pages of the prose-poetry I wrote, most of it while in London. But a lot of it started here in New York. I'll try to decipher the jerky tube writing and clarify as far as memory allows. What I can't figure out is, will this be a book based on a movie or a movie based on a book? Here in Washington Square Park, I can hear the low clicking hum of a Super 8 camera. What I assume to be film students working on a film, making me part of the scenery. Smiling in spite of myself, I lean back, close my heavy lids and . . . fade to black.

ACKNOWLEDGMENTS

I would like to thank all those who over the years along the long road of writing *Skye Papers* supported and encouraged me, including: Yinx, Walter, and Kulture, long-time fam in spirit, who never stopped saying, "I will be glad when you finish that book, Jamika"; Fork, who *overstood* at exactly the moment I needed it most; Georgia (BookBlast), who was there for the first drafts; and Stephanie for connecting the dots to Amethyst Editions. I also want to thank Michelle Tea for *getting it*, and lastly, but not at all least, to Lauren Rosemary Hook and the crew at Feminist Press for helping me get this book into shape, and ready for the whole wide whirl/world.

Amethyst Editions
at the Feminist Press

Amethyst Editions is a modern, queer
imprint founded by Michelle Tea

**Against Memoir: Complaints,
Confessions & Criticisms**
by Michelle Tea

Black Wave by Michelle Tea

Fiebre Tropical by Juliana Delgado Lopera

The Not Wives by Carley Moore

**Original Plumbing: The Best of Ten Years
of Trans Male Culture**
edited by Amos Mac and Rocco Kayiatos

Since I Laid My Burden Down by Brontez Purnell

The Summer of Dead Birds by Ali Liebegott

Tabitha and Magoo Dress Up Too by Michelle Tea,
illustrated by Ellis van der Does

We Were Witches by Ariel Gore

amethyst editions

The Feminist Press publishes books that
ignite movements and social transformation.
Celebrating our legacy, we lift up insurgent
and marginalized voices from around the
world to build a more just future.

See our complete list of books at
feministpress.org

THE FEMINIST PRESS
AT THE CITY UNIVERSITY OF NEW YORK
FEMINISTPRESS.ORG